CONT

Contents

ACKNOWLEDGMENTS

Thank you to the many experts and all the people who talked to me during the writing of this book. Names and details have been changed to preserve identity but I am truly grateful to the insight they gave me.

Thank you to my agent, Michael Alcock, for his encouragement and friendship. Thank you to Cathy Fischgrund for her support.

Thank you to Gill & Macmillan for giving me the opportunity to write about such a universally frustrating subject.

Thank you to Dr Priscilla Stuckey for her fine developmental editing work.

Thank you to my brother Terry and his partner Robin. And finally thank you to my husband Ray, and my two beautiful children Robert and Ruth for their patience, support, love and enthusiasm while I went into exile to complete this project.

BIOGRAPHICAL NOTE

Theresa Francis-Cheung (B.A. King's College Cambridge, M.A. King's College, London) is a freelance writer. Her books include: *Androgen Disorders in Women: The Most Neglected Hormone Problem* (Hunter House, 1999); *Pregnancy Weight Management* (Adams Media, 2000); *Cope with the Biological Clock: How to Make the Right Decisions about Motherhood* (Hodder and Stoughton, 2001); *A Woman's Guide to Healthy Living Through the Thirties* (Adams Media, 2001); *Help Yourself Manage Your Weight and Fitness Through Childbirth* (Hodder and Stoughton, 2001) and *Men and Depression: Helping Him Help You* (Thorsons, 2002).

A health consultant and teacher before writing full-time, Theresa lives in Windsor with husband, Ray, and their two children, Robert and Ruth.

INTRODUCTION

Pain, suffering and injustice are inherent in life. We feel fear. We worry. To a greater or lesser extent worry affects us all. The worry-free life doesn't exist. Everyone, even the most calm, confident and enlightened among us, worries.

Worry can be good. It can be all we have to warn us that we are in danger. It can create positive change and remind us of what is meaningful in our lives. More often than not, though, worry is harmful. It holds us back by putting the brakes on change.

Worry often prevents us meeting and solving the problems that give our life meaning. Instead of taking action, we get trapped in fear and indecision. Worry can sabotage relationships and careers, cause self-destructive patterns and hold us back from achieving our full potential.

This book suggests that worrying about problems rather than confronting them is the basis of all unhappiness; the root of all evil.

Worry: The Root of All Evil doesn't just discuss the nature of worry, it will also share with readers the self-help techniques that doctors, scientists, writers, experts and even computers use to control and manage worry. Being a seasoned worrier herself, the author writes from an insider's perspective. She shows how the principles that the book advocates can really work for everyone who wants to turn their worry and fear into contentment and confidence.

We can't banish worry completely — worry is a universal and some might say natural and spontaneous human function — but clearly we need to understand how worry can turn our lives sour. We need to know how to turn worry into a helpful force in our lives.

Those who can turn worry into a positive force generally have successful lives. Worry can be the root of all good, as well as the root of all evil. If we can learn to manage worry we should gain confidence in our abilities and fulfilment in our lives. It sounds like positive thinking. It really is about positive doing — positive living. That skill can't move mountains, but it can change our lives for the better.

PART 1
EXPLORING WORRY

Strangulation or choking is the first definition of worry in *Webster's Ninth New Collegiate Dictionary*, which details its roots in German, French and English with that meaning. Worry can immobilise or choke the worrier and/or worriee (the person about whom one worries).

Betsy Martin

CHAPTER 1

WHAT IS WORRY?

Worry is something all humans do, like eating and sleeping; it is something we all do rather well. Our brains are uniquely adapted to worry because they can reason, feel, remember, reflect and imagine at the same time. But, what exactly is worry?

The term 'worry' comes from the old Friesian word *wergia*, meaning to kill. In the seventeenth century to worry a person or an animal was to strangle them; to seize them by the throat with your teeth, to tear and lacerate them and to shake the life out of them. As time went on the word only applied to dogs 'worrying', usually sheep, while we progressed to figurative worrying by repeating hostile and threatening words for prolonged periods.

The common theme here is sustained attack. Victims of worry are pestered by repeated demands and defeated by repeated attacks. Gradually we began to speak in terms of worrying about problems, coming at these problems over and over again. And by so doing we can spend our days and nights worrying and being beset by worry.

Most of us can relate to the theme of dogged persistence. Once gripped by worry we find it hard to struggle free. Let's take the example of Paula, whose fifteen-year-old daughter, Laura, had promised to be home by eight o'clock.

At ten past eight Paula noticed the time. She ate a bag of crisps without enjoyment. At quarter past eight Paula looked at her watch again and picked up a book. At eight twenty-five she put the book down unable to remember anything she had read. She felt slightly nauseous.

Paula was getting concerned. She wondered why Laura

was late. Surely she would call if there were a problem. She tried calling Laura's mobile, but it wasn't switched on. Paula started to tidy the living room, but made little progress. The thoughts started again. There must be something wrong. Is she all right? What if there has been an accident? What if she needs me? Only the other week she had read in the paper about the disappearance of a girl the same age as Laura. My God, what if Laura had been kidnapped by some lunatic? At that moment the phone rang. Paula felt panicky. What if it was the police? It was Paula's friend, Susan, calling for a chat. Paula didn't want to stay on the line, in case Laura called, and hastily finished the phone call. At eight forty Paula sighed with relief as Laura walked through the door cursing the train for being late, and apologising for not calling her Mum.

Throughout the scenario Paula couldn't concentrate. Her attention was constantly being interrupted by thoughts about her daughter and these thoughts tended to be anxiety creating ones. If Paula could have turned her attention to something else she might have been able to enjoy half an hour of peaceful reading or chatting on the phone with a friend. However, her thoughts went from bad to worse.

Put simply, worry is thinking about things that scare you. You can't control repetitive, bad thoughts. You feel anxious that something worrisome will happen to you or to others. You imagine all sorts of negative outcomes, 'what ifs' and catastrophes. Ordinary problems are blown up out of all proportion and a sense of perspective is lost. Welcome to the world of worry....

I worry all the time. I lie awake at night worrying. I don't seem to be able to switch off. Sometimes I feel really tired and am sure that I will fall asleep but the minute I get into bed my brain starts up again. Thinking about everything and everyone. I've tried the doctors; I take sleeping pills but nothing helps. I can't get to sleep. I can't stop thinking. I can't stop worrying. Can anyone help me? I'm desperate.

What is Worry?

It's getting to the stage when I'm afraid to go out of the house. I want to love and trust other people but I can't. I'm worried they will hurt me or let me down. Advice and suggestions please. Life frightens me.

My days are filled with worry. I worry about my job. I worry that I am not good enough. I worry that I won't meet anyone who will care about me. I worry all the time. Nobody knows how anxious I feel. On the surface everything looks good — I mean I have a job and my family cares about me — but why am I so unsettled and sad? What's wrong with me? Why can't I stop worrying and start living?

(Messages posted on various anxiety/depression/insomnia message boards by internet users in November 2000.)

CHAPTER 2

WORRY THAT HEALS —
WORRY THAT HARMS

Y ou live in a twilight world of peace and warmth. All your needs are met. Then suddenly you can't breathe. To survive you must wrestle towards the bright light. Out you come. You are bruised and bewildered by the change. Anxiety floods your system. What is this place?

The human condition is an anxious one. Freud believed that this anxiety goes right back to the absolute beginning of life.

> Birth is in fact the first of all dangers to life, as well as the prototype of all the later ones we fear; and this experience has probably left behind it that expression of emotion which we call anxiety.

Whether you agree with Freud or not, at birth you have more brain cells functioning than at any other time in your life. You are intelligent and super sensitive. When you scream you express anxiety at its most complete and primitive.

Worry has been described as the mental counterpart of anxiety. Anxiety is what you feel. Worry is what you think. As soon as you are developmentally ready fearful thoughts start to accompany or precede anxious feelings. You start to worry.

Your ability to lead a healthy, happy life now depends on how well you can manage worry. If you can learn to worry well, at the right time and to the right degree, fear and confusion can be replaced with contentment, peace and calm. Even death, the ultimate fear, won't be a terrible and terrifying void, but a peaceful and natural passing away. If, on the other hand you can't control worry — disappointment, unhappiness and frustration will constantly present themselves to you. Seen in this light, coping with worry is the greatest developmental challenge you face as a human being.

WISE WORRY

Essential to managing worry is understanding when it is helpful and when it is dangerous. You need to learn to distinguish between wise worry, which alerts you to real danger, and toxic worry, which serves no useful purpose and destroys the quality of your life. Worry is unpleasant, but it is also unavoidable, and at times helpful.

> Paul was worried that his ex-wife might be drinking too much. He was becoming increasingly apprehensive when he left their two-year-old son, Leo, in her care from Monday to Friday. Initially Paul tried to dismiss the idea. Whatever their differences his wife was a good mother and would never do anything to harm the child. However, he soon began to feel more and more distressed, thinking ...
>
> What if she drinks and drives and Leo is in the car? What if she neglects Leo? What if Leo sees her drinking? No she wouldn't, she's a good mother and loves Leo. If I accuse her of being an alcoholic, she's bound to take offence, but I can't stand by and do nothing at all.

Eventually the increasing intensity of his worry forced Paul to take action. He made an unexpected visit to the house and found his ex-wife in a drunken stupor. Leo was wandering alone in the garden. While his ex-wife sorts out her drinking problem Paul is taking care of his son on a full-time basis.

Worry can be a useful internal alarm system that alerts you to potential danger. It can also help prepare you for a situation that you fear.

Mary was very worried about her driving test. She imagined

First imagine the worst
→ it will reduce fear

every conceivable disaster occurring in the test; she drove on the wrong side of the road; she drove with the brake on; she went through a red light; she ran over an old age pensioner! She also imagined how disappointed she would feel if she failed. On her actual test day Mary wasn't half as nervous as she thought she would be. She had already imagined the worst and this had somehow reduced her fear. She passed her test, with only a few minor driving errors.

Effective planning must anticipate danger. If thoughts and images keeping coming into your mind, this may help you deal with an uncertain situation when it actually happens. Repeated rehearsals of a coming event may make you feel less apprehensive and better able to cope.

A certain amount of worry can be helpful. In fact, worrying too little, or avoiding worry through alcohol, drugs or other distractions, can be more harmful than worrying too much.

Richard, age 73, had noticed severe pain in his chest for several months and friends had urged him to see a doctor, but he had shrugged off their advice. He had been fit all his life and couldn't face the idea of slowing down. One afternoon, while still recovering from a heavy bout of flu, Richard played a game of tennis. He collapsed and died of a heart attack.

It isn't healthy not to worry at all. Everybody worries about something. The world can often seem a dangerous place, and it is natural to be concerned about your life, your health and the people you care about. The person, who claims to be an oasis of calm, with no worries at all, isn't being honest with him or herself. Like eating, drinking and sleeping, worry is something humans need to do, but like everything else we need to do it in moderation. Worrying too much isn't good for us.

TOXIC WORRY

Too much worry can make you sad, mad or sick and it usually doesn't help. There are several kinds of toxic worry as the following examples will show.

You may worry about a particular problem and not know what to do.

> I'm worried about security. I've had an alarm system installed but I'm worried that the police won't be able to respond in time if there is a break in. It's nerve wracking when I leave the house for work because I worry all day about the house being empty. It's nerve wracking when I'm at home because I worry that an intruder might break in and rape me or something. I'd like to take in a lodger for security, but then I'd worry that we might fall out. I do like my privacy. Sometimes all the worrying is too much to take.
>
> *Peter, age 50*

Sandra worries constantly about the appropriate choice of day care for her one–year-old twins while she works. When she drops them off at nursery, she feels horribly guilty. She imagines all sorts of terrible things happening to them while she is away. Her worry is so great that it often affects her ability to work. Even the constant reassurances of the nursery staff and the smiling faces of her children when she picks them up, doesn't stop her worrying.

Worry, as the research of psychologists Elizabeth Roemer and Thomas Borkovec from Pennsylvania State University, has shown, is in one sense a useful response gone awry — an overly zealous mental preparation for an anticipated threat. But such mental rehearsal becomes disastrous when it becomes trapped in endless repetition that captures your full attention and all your attempts to focus on anything else.

This kind of worry seems inescapable, and it destroys your

peace of mind. It is hard to complete tasks. Concentration is poor and enjoyment of anything else is virtually impossible. Your mind keeps returning to a particular problem. Worry doesn't just torment by day; it increases in intensity by night where there is less opportunity for distraction. Sleep can be restless and fitful. Worry can also trigger a descent into depression.

> Samantha has sustained several losses over the last year. She divorced and her mother died. Samantha worried about her declining productivity at work. She wondered why she wasn't on target anymore and why she seemed unequal to even the most simple of tasks. She started to question her competence.

Samantha's ruminations — those internal questionings of her ability and self-worth — seemed to divert her attention from the emotional pain in other areas of her life. The worry got more intense, and at night she tossed and turned, agonising about whether she would be fired or not and what her colleagues were thinking about her. She lost her appetite, and her concentration continued to wane. Worry edged her feelings of low self-esteem, loss and sadness into full depression.

One of the main determinants of whether or not a depressed mood will persist or lift is the degree to which you worry. When appropriate emotional responses are avoided, or frozen by worry, it becomes dangerous and can push you perilously close to depression.

Worry can be an understandable reaction to some kind of injustice or uncertainty.

> Lucy discovered in one of her pre-natal check ups that her baby-to-be had Down's Syndrome. After a great deal of agonising Lucy decided to have an abortion, but to this day she is haunted by worries and regrets.

Sometimes life inflicts unbearable worry upon us through some

10

tragedy, dilemma or trauma. There is every reason to feel anxious, but if a solution to the dilemma isn't found, or you aren't able to come to terms with it in some way, worry can become toxic and totally destroy peace of mind.

Worry could simply become a way of life. You may worry constantly no matter what. Others may think you are worrying about things that sound trivial, but to you the suffering is just as intense. You may spend time worrying about things you can't do anything about. You may worry about what may not happen or you may worry about what might happen. Sometimes you may not even know what you are worried about. You may feel that you are a born worrier — genetically programmed to worry yourself sick.

Part of the problem when worry becomes toxic is that many of us think we haven't got any control over the way we think and act. You may know that you are worrying too much, but you don't know how to stop.

Of course, some of us worry more than others, and as pointed out previously the human condition is an anxious one, but you DO have a choice in the matter. This doesn't mean that you obliterate worry — worry has some real advantages — it just means, as you will discover later in the book, that you find ways to manage worry when it becomes dangerous and unhelpful.

CHAPTER 3

LIVING WITH WORRY

The world of worry is a harsh, unforgiving and gloomy place. Living with worry means:

- Settling for nothing less than perfection.
- Never making mistakes.
- Frequently reflecting on your inadequacies, failings and past mistakes.
- Avoiding holidays and any form of relaxation.
- Losing the ability to concentrate.
- Sleeping less.
- Always imagining the worst possible outcome of events.
- Constantly thinking unwanted, bad thoughts.
- Never making decisions unless you are absolutely sure you are right.
- Reminding yourself that there is no end to your worries, they will go on forever.
- Increasing your risk of illness, high blood pressure and heart disease.

It's a mystery why anyone would want to live in a world like that, but many of us do. If you are a worrier there may be some comfort in knowing that you have millions of other people to keep you company. According to recent research one in ten of us is pathologically worried to the extent that it hinders work and personal life or both. The rest of us don't let worry affect us to that degree, but worry can still make us feel miserable. One in four of us is suffering from worry that is debilitating.

Take John, Jill and Susan, for example. All three admit to spending most of their life in a state of acute anxiety. John, age 42, is typical — he worries about anything and everything.

> If I didn't have anything to worry about, I'd worry about why things were going so smoothly. I worry about everything in my life — the children, the house, my job, and my seventy-year-old mum who lives with us.

Although John has a busy life, John worries that he's not doing enough and this plays on his mind.

> Perhaps it's because my job is quite stressful that I keep mulling things over in my mind. When I go to bed thoughts whizz around in my brain and I can't get to sleep. I bite my nails constantly.

In fact, John does have some genuine concerns. His son, Luke, is diabetic and he's worried about his health. Also he and his wife, Julia, agonised for two years over which schools they should send their children to. But like many worriers John gets too anxious about other parts of his life that he should be enjoying.

> If we are going on holiday, I'll fret so much about whether it is the right holiday that I spoil the excitement and anticipation that should make it fun. Also when I do organise a treat for the family I try so hard to make it wonderful that I'm always disappointed with what I achieve, even though everyone seems to be having fun. I'm a perfectionist. It's just impossible for me to sit back and enjoy the good things, and I'm always anticipating what might go wrong.

Although John admits he's always been a worrier, things have deteriorated over the last three years.

> My father died, I've got new responsibilities at work, and both children started new schools. I eat when I worry, which

means I'm overweight and unfit. I've also lost a lot of confidence. I wish I could be content with my family, job and home, but it's all such a headache.

Jill, like John, also finds it impossible to stop worrying. Jill is 24, with a successful career in advertising and her whole life ahead of her. Many would envy her situation, but Jill isn't happy with her life. In fact, she spends most of her time worrying that she can never live up to her sister.

The more I realise how brilliant my sister is at running a home, bringing up a family and managing her own internet business, the more I worry that I will never be able to do the same. I find it difficult enough just looking after myself and doing my job.

Although she has worked hard to build her career Jill would still like to get married and have children one day.

I think it would be fulfilling, but there's so much pressure on women these days to be superwoman and hold down a successful career as well as having a family. I don't think I'm up to that. I need to find out what I want to aim for in life.

Jill worries that she has put her career above the development of her personal life.

I've never had a relationship with a man that lasted more than six months. The longer it goes on, the harder it gets. I'm shy around men and don't know what they expect of me. Traditional female and male roles seem to be changing so fast and, frankly, I'm confused.

To help her cope with her bewildering thoughts Jill buys self-help books and tapes.

I'm always quoting bits to my friends and they find it amusing, but the books do help me when I'm feeling very confused and worried about my life.

Some people find it easier to project their anxieties on to something they can control — like their weight or cleanliness — which can sometimes lead to obsessive behaviour. Worries and fears can sometimes develop into compulsive behaviour.

Susan is divorced and works part-time. She has two teenage daughters and has recently become obsessed with cleanliness.

If I see a speck of dirt in my kitchen I think the whole kitchen must be dirty. I think there are germs everywhere and am obsessed with killing them. I never buy foods with chemicals and additives — it's just not natural and I would worry about the harm they might do to my body.

Susan's fear of not having control also affects the way she brings up her children. All mothers worry about their children's safety, but Susan spends most of her time fretting about things that will probably never happen.

I'm always thinking. What if the boys get mugged, kidnapped or run over? What if my car breaks down or I lose my job? I know that worrying has made me over protective and my children complain about it.

If you can't retain a sense of proportion about the risks you face it might be time to ask your doctor for some advice. There is sometimes an overlap between worry, anxiety and depression. If you are reading this, and you feel depressed most of the time, you should seek help.

Living with worry doesn't just affect you; it affects those around you too. You can pass on anxious habits to others. Children are especially impressionable. If they see you worrying all the time they may want to copy you. Worrying can be contagious. Have

15

you noticed how the atmosphere in a room can change if one person appears anxious? But it's not just those around you that may be adversely affected by your own worrying. Your own health and well being are also being compromised.

> Three years ago I suffered a heart attack and I think my condition could have been made worse by my worrying. I often feel sorry for myself as I've had a hard life. But I still have this constant worry that nothing is ever going to go right in my life.
>
> *Rachel, age 66*

Technically you can't be killed by worry, but worry can trigger a descent into poor health. Seen in this light the old saying, 'worrying yourself to death', isn't really a wild exaggeration. Worrying too much can shorten your life span. Let's explain why.

WHAT HAPPENS WHEN YOU WORRY?

Your body reacts to worry the same way it reacts to physical danger, such as a car approaching. You worry that it might hit you; you fear for your life, and you experience anxiety. This is known as the stress response. Certain chemicals, like adrenaline and cortical, are released into your bloodstream, and these cause certain physical changes to take place. Your heart rate increases, breathing is heavier, you may perspire and blood may move away from some areas of the body — for example from the skin to the muscles — so that you may look slightly pale.

> In a matter of seconds the body is transformed to prepare for exertion; blood pressure and heart rate rocket; the liver pours out glucose and calls up fat reserves to be processed for energy; the circulatory system diverts blood from non-essential functions, such as digestion, to the brain and muscles. This is precisely what you need if your goal is to survive the next ten minutes.
>
> Description of flight or fight syndrome, *Time/Life*

Generally the physical changes that occur equip your muscles for action. If the threat is physical you are better prepared to fight or run away. Fear and worry alter your body to improve your chances of survival, but psychological changes also occur. Stress changes the way you think and feel, which again helps you cope better.

When you are faced with danger, your thinking becomes more focused and there can be an improvement in concentration and decision making. This is an ideal state of mind for anyone facing a serious challenge — a parent catching a child before it falls off a chair; a policewoman chasing a thief. Without the stress response your reactions would be too slow.

The problem is that many of the things we worry about today can't be attacked or run away from. The threats to our survival aren't wild animals or tribal disputes anymore, but financial pressures, work stresses, relationship problems and so on, when the flight or fight response isn't appropriate. Our bodies, however, still react primitively when we are worried or frightened.

If you can't do anything about the worry, or if you don't even know you are worried, then your mind and body remain mobilised for action. Your heart may slow down and your muscles may relax a little, but you are still tense. Chemicals circulate in your body where they can have a toxic effect on circulation, glands, the nervous system and the heart.

The changes brought about by the stress response are helpful if the stress is short-term because they prepare your body for action and focus your mind, but if the stress is long-term and the stress response is not switched off then stress becomes chronic. This tension is hard on your body. Compare it to revving a car engine for hours on end. It drains you mentally and physically. It saps your vitality and makes it hard to get on with your life.

> I used to feel happy about my life, but I've lost all my energy since my divorce. Now I really have to push myself to do routine things because I feel so disappointed, tired and alone. Even if I do get things done I feel no sense of achievement.

Everything is a chore. I worry at home. I worry at work. I can't stop thinking about what went wrong with my marriage. I don't even try to be sociable anymore. I feel unwell and I haven't slept properly in months.

Matthew, age 39

When stress and worry becomes excessive the bodily changes, so important for flight or fight, can damage your health. In Part 2 you'll see how they can increase the likelihood of fatigue, illness, high blood pressure and a heart attack. But worry doesn't just affect physical health. When intrusive, unpleasant thoughts and images won't go away, peace of mind is destroyed too. Given all this, it's hardly surprising that worry can be the starting point for depression, and is central in many problems such as low self-esteem, relationship difficulties, pessimism, timidity, underachievement and inability to make decisions.

As worry invades your thoughts it diminishes your enjoyment of your life, family and achievements, because you live in constant fear that something may go wrong. Your ability to eat, sleep, dream, love, play and work will all be undermined. It will be hard for you to concentrate on anything and you won't be able to relax. In short, worry can make you ill and unhappy.

WHY DO WE WORRY?

If worrying too much makes us feel unhappy, the big question is why do we do it?

Many of us worry because we believe that if we worry enough this can determine the outcome of events. Worrying is an attempt to control the future, or events and other people when we feel we have lost control. Worry is an act of despair. We can't do anything, so we worry instead.

When an exasperated mother tells her child she is worried about her, worry does seem to take on a mysterious power, but the painful truth is that worry has absolutely no power to determine the outcome of events. This is because worry never

Worry is an attempt to control
the future

deals with reality. Worry is always about something that hasn't happened or may or may not happen. Worry is always about things that don't actually exist.

Webster's Medical Dictionary defines worry as 'mental distress or agitation resulting from concern, usually for something impending or anticipated.' We worry about things we fear may happen in the future or that are happening now, but somewhere else. Worry, put simply is the process of becoming distressed about the non-existent. Or in the words of Hal Roach, 'Interest paid on trouble before it is due....' When you worry you are literally worrying about nothing — because the events are in your mind, not in your physical environment.

Unless worry prompts us into some kind of action, or into finding some kind of solution, there is nothing powerful about worry. Worrying doesn't save lives or solve problems. Worry by itself achieves absolutely nothing. It doesn't even make us feel better. Yet still we continue to worry — why?

Excessive worry could be a sign that we are not giving ourselves all that we need to feel happy and fulfilled. And what do we all need?

We need to feel loved and valued by those close to us; by the community we live in and those we work with. Whether or not we believe in God, we also need to have some kind of faith in a higher power. And most important of all we need to love and value ourselves.

If any of these needs aren't met we are likely to feel restless, unhappy and anxious. We may conclude that we are worrying because we are not getting what we want in life or that something isn't going our way, but most of the time this isn't the case. Outer success is rarely as fulfilling as inner happiness. The great majority of the time worry sets in because we don't feel happy and confident inside. Our needs aren't being met. There is something essential missing from our lives. The worry management skills in Parts 3 and 4 of this book are all designed to help you find the contentment that may be missing from your life.

WHAT WE WORRY ABOUT

You worry about what is important to you: your health, how you appear to others, your family, your relationships, your work and your finances. Yet you also worry about what seems important at the time but isn't really: the clothes you are wearing, missing a train and so on. It's quite possible to worry about anything.

Below are some common worries, but bear in mind, that if you have a tendency to worry too much, you are likely to worry about anything and everything, however trivial it may appear. You may even worry about having nothing to worry about. This is known as Paradise Syndrome.

I worry that …

- I won't be loved.
- I won't have any friends.
- I look unattractive.
- I won't be able to express my opinion.
- I won't have confidence.
- I might look stupid.
- I'll never achieve my ambitions.
- I may have an accident.
- I will lose some one important to me.
- I will be late for an appointment.
- I won't get all my work done.
- I don't work hard enough.
- I will make mistakes at work.
- I won't be able to afford holidays.
- I can't pay my bills.

Whatever the worry trigger, the key to persistent problems and unhappiness in your life is maintaining cycles of worry and this will be explored further in Part 2. Individual circumstances may affect what you worry about — a speeding fine for a millionaire won't be as upsetting as it would for someone who is hard up —

nonetheless personal, social and financial circumstances don't have as great an impact as you may think.

If you have a tendency to worry, you will worry. As the next chapter will show, it doesn't matter how successful or unsuccessful you appear to be, worriers will worry whatever the circumstances of their lives. Money, talent, good looks, good genes, and even good luck, do not guarantee a worry free life.

CHAPTER 4

FAMOUS WORRIERS

In this chapter we'll pause a little to think about a few famous people who were plagued by worry throughout their lives. Each of them found different ways to cope. Some coped better than others did, and some didn't cope at all, but hopefully reading about their struggles will comfort, intrigue, surprise, warn and inspire.

Before we turn to real-life examples, let's begin with two fictional characters who seem poles apart, but whose characters are defined by worry, hesitation and uncertainty. Helen Fielding's Bridget Jones and, arguably the most famous character in English literature, Hamlet.

Bridget Jones' Diary exploded on the literary scene in 1996 to massive critical and popular acclaim. The diary rings with the unmistakable tone of something that is true to the marrow. Bridget is a thirty-something, single career girl who spends her life hesitating. She is wracked with doubt and uncertainty about her looks, her ability to attract a partner and her life in general. She seems incapable of making decisions without consulting self-help books or her misguided but well-intentioned friends for advice.

Bridget doesn't just worry occasionally; worry is her life. The appeal of her character may lie in the fact that everyone can identify with her, because everyone has from time to time felt as uncertain and as baffled by the world as she does. When we laugh at Bridget we laugh at the insecurities within ourselves. We all have Bridget like moments when life is chaotic and everything seems to be going from bad to worse.

Bridget's dilemmas seem desperately important to her, but much of the comedy in the book resides in the fact that Bridget's worries are often creations of her own mind, with little substance. The worries of Hamlet, however, are anything but melodramatic exaggerations. While Bridget worries about her weight, and not having a boyfriend, Hamlet's conflicts are a matter of life and death.

Hamlet, the Prince of Denmark, is the central figure in Shakespeare's tragedy, and much of the dramatic impact of the play derives from the complex nature of his character. His famous hesitation is a central element in the play and has long fascinated directors, critics, readers and audiences.

When we first meet Hamlet he is worried, downcast and disillusioned. His father has died and his mother has married his uncle within two months of his father's death. When Hamlet learns that his father has been murdered by his uncle, instead of taking action he broods and hesitates.

Hamlet is an intriguing character. His natural inclination is to worry. The reasoned arguments of his soliloquies show a man wrestling with a dilemma and the appropriate course of action to take. He seems unable to act or find a solution. Instead he debates the issues over and over in his mind, constantly requiring further evidence, to make a decision. The result is that he doesn't make any decision at all. Like many worriers Hamlet is deeply disturbed by the evil and injustice around him, and this makes him unduly pessimistic and negative. His faith in people has been undermined to the extent that he doubts everyone and everything.

> How weary, stale, flat and unprofitable
> Seem to me all the Uses of the world.
>
> *Hamlet*, 1.2.133–4

Eventually inactivity and indecision frustrate and depress Hamlet so much that he lashes out with impulsive recklessness. His sudden mood swings from dithering to rashness make him one of the most tragic and perennially interesting characters in literature. His famous dithering gives us a timeless example of chronic worry gradually paralysing and poisoning a man's life.

Hamlet seems only capable of imagining the worst and the worst is what he gets.

In many of his plays, Shakespeare seems to be interested in dealing with human weaknesses. Hamlet, therefore, seems to represent a type as well as a unique individual. He can be seen as a young man unable to cope with the harsh realities of life and paralysed by worry. Worry causes indecisiveness, confusion, loss of perspective and despair. Hamlet is a warning to us all, but Hamlet is, at the end of the day, a fictional character. Let's turn our attention to real life.

REAL-LIFE WORRIERS

The apostle Paul made it his lifelong mission to dispel any doubts and worries anyone might have about Christ. He succeeded, but he succeeded because he understood worry. He understood the need of the worrying mind to dispel any kind of doubt.

There was no aspect of the appearance of Christ into which Paul's restlessly inquiring mind did not penetrate. His thirteen epistles, when arranged in chronological order, show that his mind was constantly getting deeper and deeper into the subject. It was not enough for him to know that Christ was the Son of God; he had to unfold this statement into its elements and understand precisely what it meant. It was not enough for him to believe that Christ died for sin; he had to go further and inquire why it was necessary that he should do so and why his death took sin away.

Paul was a great thinker; his mind was of majestic breadth and force. It was a relentlessly busy mind, never able to leave any subject with which it had to deal, until it had pursued it back to its remotest cause and forward into all its consequences. The process of this thinking was determined partly by the various forms of error that he had encountered, but it is possible that he also wrote out of his own experience and struggle with worry. To understand worry so well, Paul must have struggled with it himself.

In retrospect, it is astonishing how Paul viewed himself. He never felt that he was doing enough; and yet here we have a man whose life was a frenzy of productivity, writing and missionary zeal. From the moment of his conversion he worked tirelessly and unselfishly for the Christian cause. Physical danger and hardship never frightened him; his greatest fear was uncertainty, which he often described as weakness.

What is so moving, and I think helpful, to all those who struggle with worry, is the fact that worry didn't destroy or weaken Paul, it actually strengthened him. The need to dispel worries and fears, both in himself and others, drove Paul to call forth the clearest statement of doctrine, which didn't leave any room for doubt. In his final epistle to Timothy, Paul writes, 'I have fought a good fight, I have finished my course. I have kept my faith.' At the end of his life physical and mental suffering was no longer a weakness; it lead to an unshakeable conviction. It was his greatest source of strength.

The apostle Paul had an awe-inspiring ability to transcend worry. The circumstances are less incredible, but the following well-known literary figures also managed to rise above worry to achieve greatness.

Jane Austen began writing before she was twelve years old. Her first attempts to get a work published, however, were unsuccessful, and she was thirty-five years old when *Sense and Sensibility* appeared in 1811. Thereafter she published *Pride and Prejudice* (1813), *Mansfield Park* (1814) and *Emma* (1816). She died at the age of forty-two, leaving to be published posthumously *Northhanger Abbey* and *Persuasion*.

Human nature, as manifested in an ordinary English setting, is Austen's subject matter as a novelist. Few novelists have had her economy and mastery of tone, nor her sense of structure in a novel. A Jane Austen novel surprises the reader by the perfect way topics are illuminated from different points of view.

Jane Austen did have a tendency to worry. In her late twenties negative thinking struck so greatly at the core of her being that her writing came to a halt. But this tendency also had a positive effect on her writing. Not only did it provide insight and depth to her novels — her account of Marianne willing herself into

se and Sensibility, shows how well she understood
it also directly contributed to the perfection of her

...ike many people who worry, Austen set high standards for
herself. In her writing Austen would settle for nothing less than
perfection, and in the opinion of many today perfection is what
she achieved. Unfortunately, during her lifetime her novels didn't
receive significant acclaim, but this didn't make her lower her
standards or stop believing in her work. Each of her novels was
tirelessly reworked and revised many times. And in the clarity,
beauty, precision and thoughtfulness of her writing, we see the
worrier's need to 'get it right' transformed into genius.

Samuel Johnson (1709–84) was a man who endlessly struggled
with worry, which he described as 'a desponding anticipation of
misfortune, (that) fixes the mind upon scenes of gloom and
melancholy, and makes fear predominate in the imagination.'
Throughout his life Johnson was tortured by worry; uncertainty
terrified him. He never found a cure for worry, but the secret of
his genius may lie in the ways he tried to manage it.

Johnson found ways to distract himself from worry. He was
always on the lookout for new insights and information. His
curiosity and love of learning were phenomenal. He loved
meeting and talking to people. He also worked incredibly hard. It
was difficult for him to write, because he always felt that what he
produced was inadequate, but he doggedly persisted. He never
gave up, no matter how worthless and anxious he felt. He also
found that regular exercise and a sense of humour would ease his
troubled mind. But perhaps the most effective way Johnson dealt
with worry was a method often employed by creative minds to
combat worry — he found work that used his imagination
constructively.

When a person worries their imagination continually
rehearses visions of bad outcomes. But if the creative imagination
can be turned onto a project, such as an essay or a poem, this can
engage the overactive mind more constructively.

Samuel Taylor Coleridge, Mozart, Dostoyevsky, van Gogh,

Melville and Tchaikovsky all found relief from worry, anxiety and depression through creativity. But even though worry can be transformed into inspiration, it's important to bear in mind that extreme worry can also drive a person to despair. Coleridge was addicted to opium. Mozart died in poverty and depravity. Nijinski went mad. Chronic worriers such as Rudyard Kipling, Robert Louis Stevenson and Edgar Allan Poe, to name but a few, were rarely happy. Others like Sylvia Plath took their own life. Marilyn Monroe and Elvis Presley worried themselves into an early grave.

Creativity, it seems, can only temporarily relieve the anxiety of worry. There are endless examples among gifted, remarkable people of worry leading to neurosis, depression and unhappiness, but few illustrate this better than, poet and writer, Edgar Allan Poe.

Poe was born in 1809 and died in 1849. He is the most often read of all his contemporaries today; this is no accident, for this neurotic and chronic worrier is strangely modern, oddly in keeping with our neurotic and unhappy age. He knew what the death wish was long before Freud defined it. He was in love with violence half a century before Hemingway was born; he knew how to create suspense before the psycho-thriller was born; he used the theme of the 'double self' before the term split personality was invented. But most important of all, he was endlessly concerned with a major theme of present-day literature — inner conflict; the endless worries that whirl around in a person's mind and create utter despair.

Poe's life was a nightmare, more horrible even than his stories and letters indicate. His writings are a reflection of the inner turmoil that was destroying him and the fact that pain, cruelty, premature burial and the corruption of the grave were an obsession with him. He was an alcoholic, and drink probably killed him, but towards the end of his life he said,

I have absolutely no pleasure in the stimulants in which I sometimes so madly indulge. It has not been in pursuit of pleasure that I have periled life and reputation and reason. It has been in the desperate attempt to escape the torturing memories, from a sense of insupportable loneliness, and a dread of some strange impending doom.

In Poe we have an extreme example of how worry, the 'dread of some strange impending doom', can slowly devour a person's mind until the very act of living becomes unbearable. His poem *The Raven* written in 1845 is a brilliant analysis of the dreadful power of worry over a man's mind. The innocent tapping of a raven at a window is transformed by the poet's mind into a series of nightmare scenarios culminating in oblivion. But in Poe's work we also have an example of how worry and frustration can foster fantasy. Out of his misery came the stuff of dreams and the materials for his poems and stories. He enriched posterity, but it was at the cost of his personal happiness and eventually his sanity and his life. Worry drove him to create, but it also drove him mad.

Poe's life and work show how worry can drive a person to unparalleled heights and incredible lows. But Poe is a figure from the past. Let's finish this chapter on a contemporary note and take a look at the life of a woman we all know and whose battle with worry and insecurity was also a dance of inspiration and despair.

Princess Diana died in a car accident in 1997 at the premature age of thirty-six. She is destined to become an icon forever surrounded in controversy. Diana's was an action-packed existence, cramming into those thirty-six years events that would normally comprise several lifetimes. It was a life of the most fantastic highs and miserable lows, of pride and embarrassment, achievement and loss, happiness and tragedy, brilliant hope and constant worry. Often thwarted in her attempts to find true love in a one-to-one relationship, she was nonetheless adored by millions.

Throughout her short life, Diana gave us a spellbinding display of a life of worry, anxiety and pain; a life of beauty, grace, charm and love; a life that encompassed the good and the bad; and a life of sharing with us the truth about it all. She was a woman of notable contradictions who made her fair share of bad decisions. Her desire to maintain a high profile while craving privacy comes to mind. But it was her shortcomings, her emotional fragility and the openness with which she displayed her worries and anxieties that made her all the more human in the eyes of the public.

There have been many explanations for the incredible and unprecedented outpouring of grief when she died, but a lot of it was because we could all identify with her. We watched her play out her insecurities and worries in public. In her we recognised ourselves, our joys and our sorrows, our hopes and our worries. We lost a companion in worry. With her early death she will always remain anxious in the eyes of the world. Many of us grieved when she died because she didn't give us the happy ending, the victory over worry and insecurity, we all long for.

Hopefully this section has made it clear that worry is a double-edged sword. It can drive you to unparalleled heights of creativity, but it can also drive you to the depths of despair. It is at one and the same time the driving force, the inspiration, the comforter, and if ways can't be found to manage it, the destroyer.

A tendency to worry doesn't determine how happy or unhappy you are, what is significant is the way you react to worry. Successful management of worry, not worry itself, is what makes the difference between a fulfilling, healthy life, and a life full of struggle and heartache.

NB

CHAPTER 5

WHY SOME PEOPLE WORRY MORE THAN OTHERS

> I've always been a born worrier. I always imagine the worst.
> I don't think anything can go right for me. I don't suppose
> it helps that I have a stressful job. I cope by doing much less
> than I would like because I worry so much. This means my
> life is rather dull. I don't have many friends and this makes
> me feel down.
>
> *Linda, age 33*

If you worry a lot you may well ask 'why me?' It's positive that
you are asking yourself this. Understanding why you worry so
much can indicate where changes need to be made in your
thought processes, lifestyle and attitudes. Managing worry
depends on understanding the aspects of your life that make you
more prone to worry. It seems that there are several factors.

WHY ME?

Your vulnerability to worry may be determined by many things.
If you want to answer the 'why me' question you need to look at
the three aspects listed below. Looking at these three aspects of
your life together may make it easier to see why you can't stop
worrying.

- Personal risk factors: family history and coping skills.
- Social stress factors: stressful life events.
- The current problem you are worrying about.

PERSONALITY TYPE

Everybody is different. Two people may be worrying about the same thing, and they may seem to have similar reactions, but their thoughts will not be the same. A certain situation may worry one person, but not another.

Worriers have a tendency to 'catastrophise' everyday concerns. Ordinary problems, such as late trains, lost car keys, a heavy cold, are blown up into potential disasters. Small problems become big ones in the worrier's mind. Why some of us do this more than others is not certain, but much centres on the inability to keep a sense of perspective under crisis. Take Michael and John, for instance:

> Michael and John were travelling together to an important conference in the States. Traffic problems were delaying them on the way to the airport.
>
> Michael worried that they would miss the flight, the following flight would be overbooked, they wouldn't make their meeting on time, and this would reflect badly on both of them. Michael couldn't afford to lose his job. He had a family to support.
>
> John, however, was hopeful that they would get to the airport in time. He would be annoyed if they missed their flight but was sure they would be able to get on another one, and even if they were late for the conference their colleagues in the States would be understanding about the unpredictability of long distance travel.

Clearly Michael has a more negative view than John does in this scenario. Michael saw nothing but problems and confusions. He even thought it might affect his job and family. John, on the other hand, remained optimistic that things would sort themselves out, and even if they didn't it wouldn't be the end of the world.

A term often used for people who worry excessively is neurotic. This label emerged in the 1960s to describe the type of person most likely to be overcome by worries and fears. The trouble with labels such as 'neurotic' or 'born worrier' or 'worrying type' is that they don't suggest the possibility of change, when in fact many studies show that everyone is capable of changing their outlook and the way they feel about themselves.

If you are the kind of person who tends towards anxiety and negative thinking you can change.

DECISION MAKING

Worry reminds you that a problem needs to be solved. Worriers tend to be good at identifying their problems but bad at taking action to solve them.

Sarah and Rebecca are both caring for their elderly mothers with dementia. Both are finding it hard to cope and keep their own lives on track. Both are considering putting their mothers into care.

> Sarah fears that her mother will be unhappy in an old people's home, but at the same time she acknowledges that her family and her work are suffering with the responsibility and she can't cope. Unable to make a decision she continues to take care of her mother. She worries continuously.
>
> Rebecca on other hand recognises that it will be traumatic for her mother to be cared for outside the family, but she also realises that she has to be realistic and put her own and her children's needs first. She decides early on that when her mother needs twenty-four hour care a nursing home will be appropriate. Because she has made the decision there is less dilemma and worry.

Making a decision reduces levels of uncertainty and helps reduce worry, but worriers tend to delay decision making. Why?

It's possible that worriers were brought up with high expectations and an intolerance of mistakes by their parents or caregivers. By the time adulthood is reached a child will have learnt to be cautious and when faced with decisions will have problems making them, urgently looking for signs that the right decision has been made. But, although early upbringing may have something to do with the tendency to worry, it's impossible to generalise. You can have the most tolerant, supportive and loving upbringing and still be a worrier.

Whatever the reason, worriers tend to need a lot of evidence before they make a decision. They want to be absolutely sure that they are making the right decision. They don't like making mistakes. As such they set themselves up for unhappiness and insecurity. There is no such thing as the risk-free decision. No one can see into the future. There often isn't enough proof available to confirm that your decision is the best one. Worriers find this hard to accept. They want to be sure they are doing the right thing. But you can never be completely sure you are doing the right thing. It is only by making mistakes that you learn and grow.

COPING SKILLS

Whether you know it or not you may already have found ways to cope with worry. Unfortunately, the ways you choose may not support good mental and physical health.

Worriers have a tendency to choose negative coping skills when overwhelmed by worry. This can make the situation even worse. You may sometimes use unhelpful coping techniques, perhaps because unhelpful strategies, like overeating or drinking too much, seem the easiest option at the time. Overworking, overspending, emotional outbursts, excessive behaviour, compulsive behaviour, dieting or watching too much television, may all be negative or destructive coping patterns you have developed in response to worry. You may have turned to coffee, cigarettes, alcohol or drugs to find calm. In reality these coping patterns make you feel even more anxious. Let's take chemical dependency for example. The relaxation induced by caffeine or nicotine is short-lived and ultimately adds more stress to the system.

Worry can be significantly reduced if you avoid negative coping skills. This isn't to say you can't indulge now and again.

Nobody is perfect. It just means that you learn to distinguish between pleasurable activities and avoidance habits that don't leave you feeling comforted.

If you want to turn worry into a positive force you need to learn to replace negative coping skills with positive coping skills. Part 3 will suggest ways you can do this. Drugs, smoking, alcohol or food dependencies are all attempts to create positive, happy feelings in you. What is so often neglected is the fact that within you lie all the chemicals you will ever need to feel powerful and positive. You can achieve a natural high yourself without developing negative coping patterns and this natural high will help you cope with worry. As we shall see later you can condition your mind to experience more pleasurable, less anxious thoughts.

LIFE STRESSES

Since the 1970s stressful life events have been linked with the development of anxiety and emotional problems. These life events don't always have to be unpleasant, like death, divorce or debt. Adjusting to any new situation can cause stress: a new job, a wedding or the birth of a child. To estimate the risk of worry and stress you need to calculate not the event but the degree of adjustment you need to make to deal with that event.

Painful experiences in the past, which you haven't come to terms with, can also have a habit of re-emerging when current situations become tense or stressful. Understanding the impact of stressful life events in your past can help put things in perspective.

For instance, a mother of a two-week-old baby who is beset by worry for that child's health would not be reacting inappropriately if one realised that her firstborn died at three months. Sometimes though anxiety may be less easy to explain. For instance, you may not connect constant worry about your appearance to the trauma you experienced as a child when you were bullied at school.

FAMILY HISTORY

Why some of us seem more anxious and pessimistic than others is hard to explain. Some believe that the way you were brought up has a strong influence.

Children are born copycats. The influences around us teach us about the world. If your parents or carers always imagined the worst, and always responded to setbacks with worry, pessimism and gloom, you are more likely to pick up on the habit. If your schoolteachers, or other important mentors, were unfairly negative about life, you may have unconsciously imitated their responses.

Your early upbringing is one of many factors that may shape your personality. Other factors to be taken into account include physical, sexual or psychological abuse, hardships, distressing events or circumstances or continual bad luck. If life keeps presenting you with pain and suffering it will be difficult for you to expect anything less.

But however negative the circumstances, or unstable the upbringing, some people still manage to emerge optimistic while others flounder in pessimism. Why is this? Perhaps it all goes back to genetics. We know that risk increases for certain illnesses and anxiety disorders if there is a family history. It's possible that some of us are just born with a greater tendency to worry.

There's nothing wrong with that. Don't be mislead into thinking that only the vulnerable, serious, sensitive and artistic types worry, or that worry only affects the weak-willed, non-achiever. Worry can be a feature of the lives of the most dogmatic, charismatic and strong willed of individuals. Winston Churchill, for instance, contended with worry his entire life. Search long enough and you will find notable examples of scientists, doctors, lawyers, and even comics, such as John Cleese, who have worried too much. In fact it's often the case that the 'life and soul of the party' type or the 'confident, I'm in control' type, worries just as much or more than anyone else.

A tendency to worry can give you incredible courage, strength, determination and insight. It helps you cope with the great divide between how things ought to be and how they actually are. Difficulties only occur when the tendency to worry gets out of hand and you can't stop worrying. Poor coping skills and ongoing stresses just continue the vicious cycle. Worry isn't helpful anymore; it becomes a problem.

CHAPTER 6

ARE YOU WORRYING TOO MUCH?

Worry is a problem for us all. But we don't really discuss worry as a problem perhaps because worry, like the common cold, has become so commonplace that we don't even realise we have developed an epidemic. We have become so used to living with worry that sometimes it can be hard to know if you are worried.

Worry has a tendency to creep up on you. It starts quietly in the background, like a radio broadcast you aren't really listening to, because you are busy with something else; then suddenly you hear something that grabs your attention and you start to listen more intently. You don't decide to start worrying. Worry just happens, and once worry begins it can be hard to stop. A few unpleasant thoughts may go through your mind, and before you know it an imagined catastrophe is pending and you are totally preoccupied with worrying thoughts.

Because worry often appears without any warning it's important that you recognise it early on. There are good reasons for this. It's easy to become upset by worry without really knowing what is happening. When something is going on in the back of your mind it may change the way you think, feel and behave. You may get upset but not know why and when this happens you may start to misinterpret things. You may blame other people or things for making you tense, even when they are not the cause.

Sometimes worry hides in your emotions and your body. You might feel angry, sad, confused or sick, but not know why. You don't understand that it may be because you are worried about something or someone. Sometimes you are worried when:

- You overreact to situations that normally don't upset you.
- You have trouble sleeping or you have nightmares.
- You constantly think about things that scare you.
- You get a headache or stomachache for no reason.
- You feel like whatever you do will be wrong.
- You can't concentrate or sit still.
- You are always tired and have little energy.
- You eat too much or too little.
- You feel sad or angry for no reason.
- You start to become obsessive about work, diet or exercise.

These things don't always mean you are worried, but when they happen it's a good idea to ask yourself if something is worrying you. Remember that the way you respond to worry won't be the same as someone else. Feeling tense is often a sign of worry but it may not effect you that way. You may feel despondent or defeated instead. Everybody is different, so you need to start paying attention to early warning signs.

You may find that you worry differently depending on the situation. A social function may make you feel tense, whereas a job interview may make you feel negative. The sooner you start paying attention to your feelings the easier it is for you to recognise the early warning signs of worry so that you don't get overwhelmed.

If you can't recognise that you are worried you can't start to deal with it. Another important reason to recognise worry early on is that worry, as Part 2 warns, often tends to get worse. If you can catch worry early it is possible to stop the feeling of being overwhelmed.

When worry totally preoccupies you it can be even harder to deal with your problems constructively. It's important to turn worry around at the earliest possible stage. But how do you know if you are worrying too much? How do you know when it is time to seek help? How do you know when worry has become a problem?

The answer is simple — if your worry seems to be getting you nowhere, you are worrying too much. Unnecessary worry is a stress you could well do without and you might also want to consider the effect this is having on your health. If you can answer 'yes' to most of the following questions you are worrying too much.

- Are you unable to make decisions and take action?
- Are you getting ill more often than usual?
- Are unwanted thoughts making it hard for you to go to sleep?
- Do you always expect the worst?
- Do you need to deal with an outstanding problem?
- Is worry leading to more worry?

It's crucial now that you start to take a closer look at those unwanted thoughts that are tormenting you day and night. Perhaps they are trying to tell you something. Do you need to deal with an outstanding problem?

Worrying about problems rather than confronting them is the basis of all unhappiness. Worry that isn't dealt with appropriately leads to stress, anxiety, poor health and despair. It isn't the useful alarm system it was designed to be anymore, it has transformed into something with the potential to make you unwell and unhappy.

THE ROOT OF ALL EVIL

Worry is the perfect starting point for the creation of a vicious cycle. It can effect you physically and mentally. Worried thoughts, whether conscious or repressed, create tension in your body. Physical tension makes it hard to think clearly and you worry more. Worry leads to anxiety, stress, confusion and more worry. The cycle perpetuates itself.

> Once I start to worry, I don't seem to be able to stop. Something gets into my head and takes over. It upsets me

when this happens and then I get upset that it's not healthy to be so tense all the time. This leads to more worry and then I'm scared I might be going mad. I try to avoid situations that cause worry, but then I get concerned that I am getting too withdrawn. There doesn't seem to be any escape.

Rachel, age 49

Mentally, all of us are capable of creating potentially painful experiences. Since we are all unique the fears will differ with each of us. For one person, the ultimate horror may be the loss of a loved one; for another the loss of health may be a terrible scenario; for another the thought of losing a job may create anxiety; another's nightmare may be gaining weight. When taken to the extreme, such fears can totally take over your life.

Worry can paralyse its victims. It can destroy your self-esteem, your relationships and even your health. It is the starting point from which all forms of unhappiness springs. As we shall see in Part 2, worry is the root of all evil.

THE ROOT OF ALL EVIL

The love of worry is the root of all evil.

Worry is a thin stream of fear trickling through the mind. It encourages and cuts a channel into which all other thoughts are drained.

Arthur Somers Roche

CHAPTER 7

THE ROOT OF ALL EVIL

The first step towards breaking out of the pattern of worry is awareness of your fears. Understanding your worries holds the key to managing them. In this section we will explore how worry is at the root of most problems and can trigger a negative downward spiral into frustration and despair. The intention isn't to terrify you whenever you worry. The intention is to:

- warn you of the dangers of worrying too much
- to make it clear that worrying is never a solution to problems it simply creates more
- to stress how important it is to learn how to deal with worry quickly and effectively before it gets the opportunity to spoil your happiness
- to remind you that the longer you let worry last the harder it is to escape.

The second step towards worry management is changing the mindset that conditions you to worry. As you read the following chapters pay attention to how you are feeling. More often than not when you don't express what you really feel this leads to worry and the problems worry causes. Ask yourself if there is anything you think you need to know, or do know, about the information you are reading. Part 3 will help you with this process.

The basis for all forms of unhappiness is worry. Worry grows into insecurity and the resultant feelings of helplessness then feed on themselves. Helplessness is characterised by a negative mindset. Emotionally there is anxiety and stress as you try to regain control, then unhappiness and giving up when the situation seems out of control.

INSECURITY

When you obsess about something or someone your energy is tied up in worry. The price you pay is a state of chronic tension, which can show up physically in headaches, nausea, insomnia and psychologically in feelings of insecurity.

> Nothing I do ever seems to go right. There must be something wrong with me.

> I'd like to apply for that job, but there isn't much point. I'm not good enough for it.

Insecurity begins with worry; worry that you simply haven't got what it takes. That little voice inside you that keeps questioning, doubting, condemning and telling you that you aren't good enough. Listen to it often enough and your self-esteem will erode into nothing.

LOW SELF-ESTEEM

Sooner or later constant worry eats away at your confidence. You start to doubt yourself and self-doubt is the starting point for low self-esteem. Worry too much and your self-esteem will suffer. If you don't let worry overwhelm you your sense of self-esteem is high. You believe you are an OK human being. You feel attractive and vital. You have confidence, energy and optimism. You trust the world and the people around you. You take positive action to meet your needs and wants. You feel a sense of pride, satisfaction and happiness in your life. You see problems as challenges and opportunities. You believe that you can be happy and successful whatever you choose to do.

If you worry all the time life is doubt. You doubt yourself and those around you. Self-esteem is low. Instead of taking action you worry. You feel uncertain about what your needs and wants are. You see problems as obstacles. You feel isolated and anxious. You don't have much confidence in yourself or your abilities.

People who don't let worry destroy their sense of self-worth are calm and relaxed; self-esteem is high. They exude a sense of well being and take care of themselves and their appearance. They are full of life, both mentally and physically and have a clear sense of direction, most of the time. They are open and expressive and communicate in a direct and straightforward manner. They can be spontaneous if they want to, but they are in charge of their emotions. They are usually positive and optimistic. They are capable of acting independently and autonomously, but are also friendly and trusting towards other people from any creed or culture. Although they have a high degree of self-worth they can also be self-reflective and are happy to acknowledge their imperfections and mistakes, as well as their strengths and achievements, because they are always looking for ways to improve and learn.

Don't be daunted by this idealised description. It's rare to find someone who displays all these characteristics all of the time. It's just a way of being that we can aspire to, even though we know it's impossible to be that calm and centred all of the time. Everyone, no matter how confident, has worries and insecurities. Self-esteem can be dented by any number of common experiences, such as losing a job, gaining weight, being taken for granted, ignored or criticised, making a mistake or having your needs disregarded.

Many experiences have the potential to hurt your self-esteem, but the extent of the damage caused will depend on the nature of the crisis, as well as the current state of your basic, inner sense of self-worth. If constant worry has weakened your sense of self-worth and your ability to fight back you may doubt your ability to cope. You may feel that life is staring to spin out of your control.

LOSING CONTROL

Worry is at the root of feelings of helplessness and loss of control. People who worry too much don't feel in control of their lives. They are insecure and worry about how bad things might get; this type of person is represented by the emotionally frail, male characters in Woody Allen films. On the other hand people who feel in control of life can withstand change and confront problems as challenges. They still worry, but worry does not make them lose a sense of perspective. The truly cool, in-control type of person was often played by Clint Eastwood in his films.

'Most of us eventually feel that life is out of control in some way' writes inspirational writer, Joan Borysenko. 'Whether we see this as a temporary situation whose resolution will add to our store of knowledge and experience or as one more threat demonstrating life's dangers is the most crucial question both for the quality of our loves and our physical health.'

In other words, your ability to create a fulfilling life depends on having some control over events in life — both those you orchestrate and those that come unbidden. If you let worry destroy your belief that you have some kind of control you start to feel vulnerable, indecisive and helpless.

INDECISION

One of the defining characteristics of the person who feels in control of their life is the ability to make decisions and embrace change. People who don't feel in control often have problems making decisions. Their lives get stuck in worry and indecision.

I worry long and hard about what is the right thing to do. Should I leave him and make a fresh start with my life, or should I stay and make the best of a bad decision.

I'm so worried about my career. It keeps me awake at night. I'm in a job I hate and my boss criticises me constantly, but the money and the perks are great. I don't know what to do.

When we worry, even if the worry is about what action to take, our lives stand still. Instead of taking action or finding a solution we worry. Many of us don't want to accept that life can be difficult. But, however optimistic and lucky we are life will not always be easy. This isn't being pessimistic; it is simply being realistic. Suffering, pain and injustice are inherent in life, but life finds its meaning in confronting and solving problems, not worrying about them. When we avoid problems and don't take action, we avoid the growth that life demands of us. We stop growing, learning and living.

INACTION

'I'm really worried and I don't know what to do.' Worry is often used as an excuse for inaction. Worrying about something can make you feel like you are doing something, but the truth is worry can be the easy option to take when you don't know how to deal with a situation. Instead of facing up to the situation and finding a way to deal with it, you worry about it.

The same applies when you tell someone you are worried about him or her. The worry is intended to express your concern, but you are choosing to express that concern in a passive way. Worrying about a person may make you feel good about yourself, but it won't help the other person. It can even put unwelcome pressure on them. Telling a person you are concerned about them and that they have your understanding and support, should they need it, is far more positive and encouraging.

Sometimes it can be good not to take action, to postpone and keep your distance, but the problem with worrying about things, rather than doing something about them, is that you live in a constant state of division. Sitting on the fence, trying to maintain the status quo is stressful. The state of indecision takes its toll. When no resolution is found you may experience emotional exhaustion and lack of direction.

> I don't know if I want to have a baby or not. I worry that it will ruin my career, my figure and my life. But I also worry that if I don't have one I will always regret it. I can't make any decisions about work because I don't know if I'll have a

baby in the next year or two. Until I sort this out in my mind my life is on hold.

Carolyn, age 34

Uncertainty and indecision, and the chronic worry that nurtures them, can lead to paralysing feelings of impotency and helplessness.

HELPLESSNESS

It's my fault he left me. I must have done something wrong. I'm just no good at relationships. There's no point going out and trying to meet people. I'm going to end up alone.

Amy, age 40

Martin Seligman, a research psychologist at the University of Pennsylvania, has performed many experiments that demonstrate how most human beings when placed in a situation over which they feel they have no control are permeated with a sense of helplessness. Seligman paid close attention to his subjects' thoughts about unpleasant experiences, and he found that those who became helpless tended to worry constantly, to blame themselves for problems, and to have a negative mindset. Helplessness is characterised, according to Seligman, by decreased motivation to do anything about life's difficulties because you don't believe you can make a difference.

If you feel that you have no control over your life, if worry and fear stop you making decisions, there may be a decrease in motivation to do anything at all. If your actions and ideas don't seem to make any impact, motivation to act may wither completely. Why bother? You may ask; nothing I can do or say will change anything. A mood of despondency sets in.

DESPONDENCY

The dictionary defines despondency as feeling dejected and in low spirits. When we feel despondent we believe that nothing we, or anyone else, can do or say will make us feel better.

> I may as well face it. Things are never going to get better. If we can't sort things our after three children and ten years of marriage we never will. Perhaps this just isn't working.
>
> *Wayne, age 53*

When worry makes you doubt your ability to cope; when worry makes you feel that even if you do your best things won't change; when worry makes you want to give up, despondency has taken hold. You may try to seek temporary escape: a drink, a cigarette, a chocolate cake, anything to keep your worries at bay.

Sometimes it is hard to change the outward circumstances of our lives. Sometimes things are out of our control and there is nothing we can do. Sometimes we have to admit defeat. If this is the case the only way we can find relief is to change our attitude towards a certain situation, but when despondency strikes even this is hard to do.

When you feel despondent it is hard to find meaning in anything. Worrying has become so intense that life isn't black and white anymore, it's just black. The only possible outcome in your mind is a negative one.

NEGATIVE MINDSET

We don't want to live like Pollyanna and believe that happiness is to be found in everything, but neither do we want to be like a prophet of doom nervously dreading the worst outcome to everything, beginning each day convinced that nothing will work out.

'You can if you believe you can,' and 'life is what you make it,' have become modern day mantras, but those with a tendency to worry lack confidence in their abilities and find it hard to believe that anything can go right. 'What ifs' crowd their mind.

What if ...

- I lose my job?
- I can't make any friends?
- I can't pay the bills?
- I can't find a partner?
- I go bankrupt?
- No one likes my work?
- I can never find the right career?
- He or she leaves me?
- I am late?
- My parents get ill and I have to take care of them?
- I lose my children in an accident?
- My partner dies?
- My car breaks down?
- I am attacked?
- I get burgled?
- I put on weight?
- I get ill?
- Some one else steals my ideas?
- I don't understand?
- I die a slow and painful death?
- I fail?

'What if?' 'What if?' 'What if?' When the 'what ifs' begin there can be no end to them, for life can offer up an endless stream. Take any given situation and you can imagine it branching in a hundred different ways, then each branch itself branching and so on until the design becomes unbearably complex.

According to author and worry expert Edward Hallowell, worries are fed by our very powerful fear system. Nature wants us to think of 'what ifs' so that we keep ourselves out of danger.

> The price we all pay for having a cerebral cortex on top of our animal-like brainstem is, in part, this ability to use our imaginations to worry — to torture ourselves, to ask

over and over again, 'What if ... this is the price we pay for having imaginations': we worry.

As if pulled by a magnet, our thoughts can be drawn relentlessly to negative possibilities. Witness the slow traffic passing the scene of an accident or the gathering crowd of passers-by. We don't want to look, but something makes us want to examine what terrifies us. There is something ghoulishly fascinating about horror, disaster and the grotesque.

As much as we dread our fears they also hold us spellbound. 'That's just terrible' we say, and we want to hear more. 'I can't bear to look' we whisper as we take a step closer. We don't like hearing about death, debt and divorce, but we want all the details.

The worrier will take this bizarre fascination with disaster one stage further. He or she will turn all the negative outcomes upon him or herself and agonise about what can go wrong for him or her. The possibilities are endless. There are many ways a person can make a mistake, lose money, get fired from a job, have an accident, get ill, die, lose a loved one and so on. The worrier's tendency to dwell on imagined negative outcomes could completely defeat him or her. Fear of what might be, may actually create problems that wouldn't otherwise exist.

Peter wondered if he had some unconscious desire to be alone because every time he started a new relationship his mind went crazy looking for fault in his partner or reasons to be jealous. 'What is it with me?' he asked. 'Do I want to drive everyone away?' Peter didn't want to be single, and many reasons could be offered for his faultfinding and jealously. Perhaps he had a traumatic childhood; perhaps the fact that his first wife left him for his best friend led to a lack of trust; perhaps he didn't want to give up his freedom; perhaps he lacked confidence. All this could have held him back, but it's also possible that excessive worry was holding Peter back.

Every time Peter met someone new worry stopped his relationships flourishing. He worried about the high divorce rates; he worried that if he got too involved he would get hurt; he worried that he wouldn't have so much time for his other friends or his work if he devoted himself to one person; he worried that his parents wouldn't like his partner; he worried that his partner might get bored with him and so on.

Peter needed to learn to worry less and trust people more. He needed to learn to like himself more. He needed to learn to take a risk.

Once again the answer lies in taking action. You can be cautious and consider all your options but the only way to escape the 'what if' nightmare is to take action. You have to leave the world of your imagination behind and move into the world of action. If you can't take action, you risk getting so tangled up in the forest of fears and negative possibilities that you lose all sense of perspective.

LOSS OF PERSPECTIVE

Worry begins with the possibilities of your imagination; your secret fears. The same mind that allows you to dream of success and happiness also allows you to worry about the possibility of failure and unhappiness. Original worries tend to branch spontaneously into other worries. Worries go wild on contact with your brain, like an anthill that has been disturbed. In the blink of an eye they multiply, so that in seconds you are fighting a vast net of dangerous, intricate detail, all stemming from that one original worry. It's amazing how fast this happens. How you can leap from a 'what if' to fighting a tangled web of worries. A single worry can kindle a whole bonfire of anxiety.

My car horn isn't working. What if there is something seriously wrong with the car? I can't afford the expense? How would I get to work? I'd have to take out a bank loan, but I was reserving that for a rainy day. What if something happens and I've spent all the money on a new car? What if I have an accident? What would happen to the children?

When 'what ifs' crowd your mind, when you are constantly drawn to the negative, minor problems can turn into potential disasters. When everyday concerns are pumped up into possible catastrophes you inflict great harm upon yourself.

The imagination works both ways. You can create beautiful images, but you can also create all sorts of terrible and miserable images. Everyone has control over what they think about, but if you have a tendency to worry you don't feel that you have any control. You feel as if you have to experience whatever thoughts your mind brings to you.

BLAME

Another unhappy outcome of the negative worrying mindset is the tendency to look for fault in oneself or in others.

'Should' is a very powerful word in our society today. All of us hold beliefs about what a person should and should not do. You shouldn't kill, steal or lie. In everyday life, however, we use 'should' to express displeasure whenever we don't get what we want.

Mark is unhappy because he feels he should have got a pay rise. What he doesn't realise is that even though he didn't get a pay increase he can still be happy, but he doesn't allow himself to admit this possibility. He tells himself that unless he gets a pay rise and life meets certain conditions he won't be happy.

When you hurl the accusation of 'should' at someone you can inflict more suffering. You imply that you are perfect and the other person has made the mistake. Insistence on being right nurtures anger and blame and limits choices. If you won't listen to another's point of view, communication stops and relationships suffer. You may, on the other hand, turn the blame on yourself.

> I should have known better than to expect a pay rise. I mean there are plenty of other people who would be willing to work in my place. I should be grateful for what I have.
>
> *Charles, age 30*

When problems won't go away it is easy to feel inadequate. But when you label yourself inadequate in some way, you don't allow any opportunity for change. Worrying how you think you should be stops you thinking about why or how you behave. It dismisses your power to change the situation. You feel helpless. 'Shoulds' only serve to make you feel worse about yourself and when you feel bad about yourself the resultant feelings often spill over into anxiety, which we'll explore in the next chapter.

Worry can create feelings of insecurity. It can make you doubt your ability to act. It can lead to a negative mindset that makes it hard for you to believe that anything can go right.

Worry can stop you making progress with your life. Life rewards action, but worry can stop you taking action. Instead of doing something about your problems you worry about them. Life doesn't move forward, it stands still.

Worry, if it isn't checked in time, can make you feel helpless, despondent, frustrated, unhappy and anxious.

CHAPTER 8

THE HEART OF ALL ANXIETY

Worry is the heart of all anxiety. Chronic, repetitive worry that seems uncontrollable, and recycles on and on, never getting any nearer a positive solution creates feelings of anxiety.

WHAT IS ANXIETY?

Anxiety is an unpleasant emotional state ranging from mild unease to intense fear. It is the emotion we experience when we feel threatened. It could be described as the emotional counterpart to worry. Worry is what you think. Anxiety is what you feel. The intensity, frequency and urgency of a worrying thought can push you towards anxiety.

Anxiety is part of the human condition. It is something we have to learn to deal with. The triggers of anxiety may vary from person to person, but anxiety has always been part of the fabric of daily life. The caveman feared attack from wild animals; kings, queens, emperors and conquerors were anxious to retain their power; today's stockbrokers bite their nails every time the market crashes, and you live with plenty of anxiety — your health, your job, your relationships and so on. Although the things we get anxious about change as our style of living changes, the emotional tension remains the same.

Anxiety is closely linked to fear. When the cause of the emotion is readily apparent or obvious we tend to call the emotion fear. The word fear comes from an old English word meaning sudden calamity or danger. Somebody who is facing an oncoming vehicle may be frightened for his or her life.

Anxiety, on the other hand, comes from a Latin word meaning troubled in mind about some uncertain event. The cause of anxiety is either imagined or uncertain; it hasn't happened yet. But even though the threat isn't necessarily apparent, the physical and emotional responses produced are the same as if the fear was real.

Physically the most common reactions are difficulty falling asleep, waking in the night, awareness of a more forceful or faster heartbeat, throbbing or stabbing pains in the chest, a feeling of tightness and inability to take in enough air, and a tendency to sigh or hyperventilate. Tension in the muscles of the back and neck often leads to headaches, back pains and muscle spasms. Other symptoms can include pale skin, sweating, hair standing on end, dilation of pupils, trembling, tightness in the throat, sinking feeling in the stomach, nausea, a sensation of faintness and falling, dryness of the mouth, dizziness, digestive disturbances, and the constant need to urinate or defecate.

Severe anxiety can produce feelings of intense fear and dread, perhaps leading to emotional confusion and panic attacks. If the anxiety goes on for too long, even healthy people become tired, depressed, restless and lose their appetite for food, sleep and social interaction. When the fear becomes very intense we call it terror.

THE SPECTRUM OF ANXIETY

To avoid misunderstandings let's define anxiety and some of its related terms.

- Anxiety is the unpleasant emotion associated with a feeling of impending danger that may not be obvious to the observer. It is the emotional counterpart to worry.
- Worry is mental distress or agitation associated with a feeling of impending danger. It is the mental counterpart to anxiety.
- Fear is a similar feeling that arises as a normal response to a realistic danger or threat.
- Panic denotes a sudden surge of intense anxiety or fear called terror.
- Phobic anxiety is the anxiety that occurs only in contact with a particular situation or object.

The Heart of All Anxiety

WHEN ANXIETY IS HELPFUL AND WHEN IT IS NOT

Although anxiety is generally thought of as unpleasant, we don't always try to avoid it. On the contrary, some of us seek anxiety and get great pleasure from mastering difficult situations: dangerous sports, driving fast and so on. The game of peekaboo played with young children, when parents disappear for a few moments and then reappear, usually elicits a squeal of joy.

Mild anxiety can be quite useful. It leads to rapid action in the face of threat and helps you keep alert; a father pulls his child to safety when he sees an oncoming vehicle. While a little fear can help you deal with problem situations too much fear is not beneficial and can be destructive. When there is a threat to your welfare and you don't feel able to handle the situation, anxiety may make you restrict opportunities by playing safe and avoiding new experiences and those that have been hurtful in the past.

> Jill had been hurt several times in her relationships. She has divorced twice and has vowed never to marry again. When she met Dave she started to fall in love with him as they were very well matched and he returned her feelings. As soon as Dave mentioned marriage though Jill ended the relationship.

Anxiety can make you brood and endlessly ruminate about a threat or concern. This can become a way of avoiding the challenge of facing it. And when you start to avoid challenge and change unhappiness creeps in.

I CAN'T COPE

Our anxieties don't usually have a realistic cause. They tend to be about inner states of mind rather than exterior situations. We fear loneliness, rejection, failure, success, disease, dying and so on. And at the bottom of it all is the ultimate anxiety that terrifies us most — not being able to cope.

- I couldn't cope without him.
- I couldn't cope without her.
- I can't handle illness.
- If I lost my job I would go to pieces.

The majority of anxieties centre on our ability to cope with challenging situations and lack of faith in ourselves. Coming from this place of low self-esteem, whatever the nature of the fear, it will spill over into other areas of our lives. If you fear loneliness, for instance, this won't just affect your relationships but your work and your health too. Loneliness is loneliness wherever it is found.

The most common response to anxiety is avoidance, or running away from the situation or object that triggers anxiety. You convince yourself that you can't cope. However, when you don't deal with problems the relief provided by avoidance is only temporary and leads to loss of self-confidence so that the situation seems even more difficult to face.

Anxieties that aren't dealt with become barriers to success and happiness. Life is all about meeting and facing challenges but anxiety makes you avoid challenges. You convince yourself that you don't have control. When life seems out of control you feel emotionally vulnerable. Worry and anxiety often bring about feelings of anger, apathy, guilt, shame, envy, jealously and confusion. Let's explore them in turn.

ANGER

Everyone gets angry sometimes, whether it is a threat to our well being, or that of someone or something we care about. How you respond to frustration depends on the level of frustration experienced and your anger threshold.

If constant anxiety and worry seem inescapable, this may cause frustration and pent-up physical tension. Anger is a natural emotional response that helps us cope with frustration. Different names are used to describe the various degrees of anger, ranging from frustration and irritability through to fury and rage.

Depression can be caused by anger turned in on oneself. Apathy is often the result of denied chronic anger.

Many of us fear anger. We know about or have experience of blind rage when someone totally loses control, but it's important to remember that anger does have a positive function. It is a form of self-protection, and it is a way of helping the immune system switch back into a normal, relaxed functioning state. This is what is commonly known as the calm after the storm. If constructive ways can be found to release tension from our bodies, anger won't harm us; indeed, it can help us cope with the trials and frustrations of life. But chronic sustained anger can lead to habitual patterns of behaviour that are self-sabotaging or hurtful to others. You may find yourself bursting out in rage or irritability at inappropriate times and places, or to the wrong people or things.

> I just saw red. I snapped at the children for no real reason.

> When the traffic lights turned red I was furious. I put my foot down and sped through the lights narrowly missing another vehicle.

You may direct your anger inwards, rendering yourself speechless, depressed or sick.

> I always put a brave face on things but underneath I was seething.

> I didn't tell anyone I was being bullied; I just binged and vomited in secret.

Or you could find that anger reduces you to tears.

> I was so angry I started crying. Now they think I can't cope with anything.

I didn't know the answer. When my friends made fun of me I couldn't defend myself and got really upset.

More and more of us these days are having trouble controlling our frustration and dealing with the frustrations of others. We expect to be treated with respect, and we expect to have the freedom to express our feelings. But the trouble is that very few of us have had the opportunity to learn, either through role models or through practice, how to manage our anger.

Anger is an emotion we have grown up feeling uncomfortable with; it is seen as destructive and bad. But there is no such thing as a bad emotion. From time to time it's important to stand up for your rights. Anger, jealously, guilt, sadness and shame exist in order to alert us to areas of discomfort in our lives. When these emotions are not felt and acknowledged, they cause even greater stress.

REVENGE

Sometimes all we have left is our feelings of anger. We feel so betrayed and let down that the driving force in our life becomes revenge.

The wish for revenge is the ultimate form of worry. For a time it is all you can think about. If you have been wronged you may want to turn your anger into a desire for retribution; you may start to fantasise about how you will take revenge, or take your fury out on whoever hurt you.

In trivial ways this happens all the time. Someone cancels a lunch date at the last minute, and you spend the rest of the day imagining how you can punish him or her. Or someone cuts across you in the traffic and you imagine yourself yelling at that person. Gradually this role-playing helps your anger subside and the incident is forgotten.

It is when the hurt is deeper that the wish for vengeance can become an abiding worry. It will preoccupy you like no other worry. It will keep you awake at night. You can't let go of the desire for revenge. It becomes your only focus until vengeance is taken. Unless you can bring the desire for revenge under control, you could end up doing something you regret.

APATHY

If worry stops you making decisions, if worry makes it hard for you to believe that anything you do can go right, it is easy to become apathetic.

> I can't be bothered.
> What's the point.
> I don't know what I am doing with my life.

Underlying apathy, you will often find frustration, helplessness, indecision and negativity, all of which have their root in worry. When apathy strikes it's likely that you:

- Don't bother to seek out opportunities to achieve.
- You continue mindlessly with a way of living that clearly doesn't interest you.
- You are unreasonably negative about the future.
- You allow others to take the lead and guide you in a direction that you don't need or want to go.

Like a slow poison, apathy creeps up gradually. You may not even notice its presence, but it slowly eats away at you until it becomes ingrained. You progress from being someone who is having a bad day, to someone who doesn't care anymore. Gradually you start to drift into an easy, low-key lifestyle that doesn't challenge or stimulate. Bored with life, you become boring.

As apathy is one of the evils of the twenty-first century, it is easy to feel that you are normal. You may regard those who get off their backsides and challenge themselves, as eccentric. You may also start to believe that you are a victim of external forces, which have made you the way you are. You find reasons to explain your inertia — your partner is ill, your job isn't stimulating, the stock market is disappointing, and it might rain. When apathy strikes life is a series of 'yes, buts'.

Apathy is a difficult attitude to shift; but it can be useful at times. We all need periods of rest and recuperation when we rebuild our strength, but apathy should never be anything more than a temporary form of self-protection. If it becomes a way of life you run the risk of becoming depressed and lonely. Nobody wants to be around someone who is despondent all the time.

GUILT AND SHAME
Guilt and shame are often experienced together, even though they are slightly different emotions.

Guilt is feeling that you have let yourself or someone else down. Shame is when your self-esteem and well being are too dependent on what others think. Embarrassment, inferiority, shyness and loneliness are often by-products of guilt and shame.

You feel guilty when you worry obsessively that you should have achieved more, regardless of how successful or hard working you are. In our changing and fast developing world where the moral climate is uncertain, a certain level of guilt is understandable. We all feel pressure to do more, be more, and achieve more; to sacrifice ourselves completely to a cause or to others. But too much guilt can drive you into self-destructive habits, such as excessive dieting, or alcohol and drug abuse. Guilt can sabotage every waking moment by making your thoughts continually return to what you haven't achieved.

Shame punishes you too. Shame makes you hide who you really are. When you feel ashamed you try to be someone you are not, so that you can please others or go unnoticed. Shame can also make you shy and relentlessly ego-centred. The world revolves around you. You enter a room and feel that everyone is looking at you, or thinking about you.

The root cause of shame is worry that you aren't good enough. Unlike guilt, you don't necessarily have to do or think anything wrong before you have that feeling. You have it just by being the person you are. You can feel ashamed of your family, culture, gender, weight and so on.

Guilt and shame can help societies become stronger because they reinforce shared values (about what constitutes success, beauty, morality and so on). They can humble the arrogant and make the insensitive more aware. But, more often than not, shame and guilt are uncomfortable, frightening and isolating emotions that contaminate every chance of happiness. They strip you of your confidence to be the person you want to be.

JEALOUSY AND ENVY

When you feel jealous you worry about getting the love and attention of another person. When you feel envy you worry about something you do not have.

Jealously is almost always accompanied with anxiety and may lead to anger, which turns outwards rather than inwards. Jealousy is linked with envy, but it is not quite the same as envy. Jealousy is the great saboteur of relationships. If one person is constantly trying to gain reassurance about their commitment to their relationship, or overly demanding of another person's time or energy, or takes action to make the other person jealous, the relationship doesn't usually stand much chance of survival.

Jealously is the green-eyed monster. It can wreck relationships and lives; because it is such a poisonous emotion it is often associated with shame and feelings of low self-esteem. Jealously isn't always bad; in fact, at one time it was considered a noble emotion. The knight defending his lady was applauded a hero. It is a natural, self-protective response and in moderation can make a relationship more exciting, but when jealousy gets out of hand it can be dangerous, painful and destroy confidence in yourself and others.

Envy is usually accompanied by feelings of powerlessness, apathy and shame. When we are filled with resentment that we don't have what we think we should have, or when we try too hard to copy the qualities, skills and lifestyle of others, we under use our own potential. We can't enjoy our own achievements because we are too busy comparing them to others, and in our bitterness we may even start to criticise the people we envy.

Envy can motivate you to achieve; I want to be like that or I want that. But over dependence on the power of envy can make you vulnerable and easily dependent. You also lose sight of what you actually want and need in life.

LOVING TOO MUCH

Another emotion that worry can contaminate and make you lose sight of what you want from life — is love, not love in the harmonious, giving sense, but love that is misguided. Even positive emotions like love, when mingled with worry, can wreak havoc with your life. Loving people are admired for their kindness, generosity, devotion and selflessness. But when love undermines self-confidence and sabotages all chance of leading a happy, successful life, we aren't talking about love anymore; we are talking about a misguided understanding of what love means.

If you spend too much of your emotional and physical energy on someone, or a group of people, at the expense of your own welfare, if you can't let go of a relationship that has ended, you are loving too much. Caring for others more than you care for yourself can endanger relationships, or the growth of another person, by smothering them with unnecessary and inappropriate displays of love.

Overwhelming feelings of love can be an exciting form of escapism, but to let so much of your self-esteem ride on the shoulders of someone else is risky. Love is worshipped in our society as a source of inspiration, happiness and self-renewal. Most of us would argue that the amount we love is beyond our control, but these kinds of myths make it hard for us to take responsibility for our feelings, and the actions we take, as a result of our feelings. Love can be the most healing and wonderful of emotions, but only if it is based on a firm sense of self-esteem. Love of others without love of self isn't love — it is need.

Like any other emotion, love needs to be harnessed and taken responsibility for. But when anxiety mingles with our emotions we lose that control. Emotions control us; and when emotions control us we start to get confused.

CONFUSION

When emotions take the lead and you can't think logically, it can be hard to know what you are feeling.

Sometimes your inability to handle a certain emotion interferes with the expression of another, or you get your emotions confused. You may be angry when you feel fear, or be too frightened to show your anger. When worry creates emotional confusion and you don't know what you feel anymore, you can completely lose track of what you are worried about. You feel permanently anxious but don't know why. You may find yourself frozen in terror in the face of some minor setback or imaginary threat, or you may take a ridiculously hurtful risk and later wonder what possessed you.

When you reach this stage of permanent alert it is very hard to keep control of your life. The danger now is drifting into panic or depression.

PANIC

In extreme cases the anxiety worry creates can produce what are known as 'panic attacks' — intense feelings of fear.

Panic attacks are associated with high levels of lactate in the blood and may occur independently of anxiety, but are most often associated with generalised anxiety or agoraphobia. It is estimated that panic attacks are much more common than previously thought. Results from recent surveys suggest that up to three percent of adults aged between twenty-five and fifty-five experience panic attacks.

It strikes without warning usually in the most public of places, like a supermarket queue or a pedestrian crossing. Suddenly I feel sick with fear. I start to sweat. I can't breathe properly. I'm terrified. Sometimes I manage to pull through it. Sometimes I can't and kindly passers-by help me. It's got to the point now when I'm scared of going out. What if I

> just froze in fear and collapsed in the middle of crossing a
> street or when I was driving my car?
>
> *Stephen, age 19*

All of us know what panic is. It is worry at its most spontaneous,
sudden and irrational. Fear at its most intense and overwhelming.
You are waiting for the train to arrive and as it draws into the
platform you have this overwhelming fear of falling in front of it.
You are walking home and hear footsteps behind you; your heart
beats loudly and sweat pours down your face. You turn a corner
and the person does too; suddenly you break into a run. You are
in an overcrowded lift; you feel that you have to get out now.

The symptoms of panic are similar to those of fear — only
intensified. You breathe faster, you get butterflies in your stomach
and there is a desperate urge to move or run away. Panic, when it
is justified, can make you fitter and more alert than you usually
are, enabling you to run to safety, attack or escape. However, when
panic seems to happen for no apparent reason it is like a space
rocket launching in your garden.

Panic attacks can be horrible. They produce intense physical
and emotional reactions, and you really do feel like you are on the
edge of the cliff, even though you may be sitting safely in front of
the TV or walking the dog.

Everyone feels panic once in a while, but if panic attacks are a
regular occurrence you may feel that you are going crazy; you are
not going crazy. You have an overly sensitive nervous system and
imagination that have become primed to overreact. The essence
of panic disorder is perceived danger, not real danger. On top of
that is fear of fear — fear of a panic attack occurring.

Not only is the panic itself debilitating, but the worry and
anxiety that accompany panic disorder are miserable too. You fear
what might happen next. The apprehension never fully subsides;
you live constantly on edge. Even if you have never had an
episode of panic you can fear bad outcomes all the time, and live
in a state of constant anxiety and worry every day. This is called
generalised anxiety disorder.

ADDICTED TO WORRY

Doctors are now suggesting worriers could be suffering from a psychiatric disorder and need professional help. Fretting about daily life has been officially classified by specialists as Generalised Anxiety Disorder (GAD) — a condition requiring therapy and sometimes medication.

Psychologists believe more than three percent of the population now worry to such an extent that they can be diagnosed as suffering from GAD. The phenomenon is believed to be second to depression as the most common psychiatric problem.

The World Health Organisation estimates that only half of those gripped by GAD are diagnosed, meaning vast numbers suffer in silence. Research suggest that GAD may affect women more than men, with those in their twenties, thirties and forties most vulnerable, but this can be misleading. Men tend to be among those who suffer in silence. In general men are more reluctant to seek help for their problems and as a result come to the attention of medical professionals less often than women. Common anxieties are about money, health, work responsibilities and chores; sufferers experience overwhelming, excessive worry, anxiety or tension almost daily. Other symptoms range from restlessness, unusual fatigue, difficulty concentrating, irritability, muscle tension and disturbed sleep.

According to anxiety expert Dr Allan Norris, a psychologist at the Birmingham Nuffield Hospital,

> GAD has been around a long time, but in the past people used to call it over-worry or fretting. In severe cases it can lead to people being unable to live a normal life. They may fear that they are about to crash the car if they drive, or simply find that they get caught up worrying and feeling anxious about life situations.

You may have generalised anxiety disorder and not even know that you have it. Some of us get so used to feeling anxious and worried all the time that we think everybody lives like that. But the truth is life isn't all worry and anxiety for everyone else.

> I just can't relax. I always have to have something to worry about. I don't want to worry all the time but I do. I never feel safe. I worry about driving, but if I walk I worry about being mugged. If I go by train I worry about being involved in an accident. Flying is a terrifying experience for me. I only do it as a last resort. I always feel as if everything is about to collapse all around me.
>
> *Mary, age 45*

Life for the person with generalised anxiety disorder, or GAD, is always on the edge. They know they are being illogical but they feel fear. The heart starts beating, the hair stands on end and the muscles tense. There may even be physical symptoms such as tapping of the fingers, restless twitching, irritability and insomnia.

It's hard to talk a person addicted to worry out of worry. It has become a way of life. It's not that you want to worry all the time; it's simply that you don't know any other way to be. You know you spoil your own fun and the fun of those around you with your constant worrying, but there doesn't seem to be any escape from them.

> I don't like the way I am. I hate it. I can't enjoy anything and it's hard to concentrate. My mind is always returning to my worry of the moment.
>
> *Laura, age 62*

We all worry, but what distinguishes the GAD sufferer is the intensity, duration and frequency of the worrying. The GAD sufferer worries more often, more intensely and over a longer period of time than others. Worry starts to control him or her in a damaging way. Sometimes the worry can destroy relationships, careers and even lives.

The exact cause of GAD is unknown, but it appears to run in

families — developing from both sad and happy situations, such as loss of work, bereavement, divorce, marriage or moving house. It's not been proved yet, but GAD may well have a biological basis. Some of us may be born with less effective shutting-off mechanisms than others. Some brains are less able to soothe themselves than others. It isn't your fault if you worry all the time. Don't blame yourself or feel guilty or weak. Simply accept that this is the way you are, and seek professional help to learn new ways to tackle anxiety when it strikes.

PHOBIAS

When anxiety is not generalised the diagnosis is not GAD but a phobia. For instance, you may be anxious about flying, making speeches or driving a car. Fears are common, and remember, some fears are healthy — we should all fear putting our hand in flames — but they become a problem when they are too intense and impair the quality of your life. Some phobias may not be a problem. For instance, if you have an intense fear of crocodiles you may never have to see them. But with some phobias it may be hard to function normally. Fear of enclosed spaces, or socialising, can be debilitating.

Phobias can be sorted into general categories:

- Phobias about specific objects or situations, such as wasps, vomit, blood and spiders. Whatever the source of fear a certain object or situation will trigger anxiety.
- Social phobia: a person may fear a situation when he or she will be exposed to evaluation such as public speaking or socialising.
- Agoraphobia: agoraphobia is a fear of leaving a place of safety and is often associated with panic attacks. The fear reflects a belief that something terrible might happen to the individual or to their property. Many agoraphobics become housebound as a result.

Phobias that cannot be avoided need to be faced so that coping skills and confidence can be developed. We all get tense and anxious at times, but if our worries and feelings of anxiety get so bad that common-sense ways of dealing with them don't work, it might be time to think about getting help. You can usually overcome everyday anxieties on your own; perhaps by using some of the methods described later in this book or with the help of friends and family. However, professional advice is advised if your life has become constricted by anxiety, panic or some kind of phobia.

ENJOYING WORRY

We all know someone who seems to be in love with worrying, my friend, Carolyn, for example.

> Carolyn is a lovely, charming woman, but she never seems to be relaxed. She worries all day and all night. She is confident with people who know her well but nervous with strangers. She worries about her health, her family and her house endlessly. I once asked her husband why she seemed so nervous all the time when there didn't seem to be anything to be nervous about. 'Carolyn loves to worry,' he replied.

Is it possible to love worry, even though worry causes such pain and distress? It would seem so. Some people, even when things are looking positive, seem drawn to possible negativity, failure and doom and only seem content when things are going wrong. I'll never forget Carolyn's discomfort when she won a considerable amount of money through the lottery. She couldn't cope with pleasant surprises and seemed almost relieved when a few months later a huge tax bill drowned most of her winnings.

Why is it that some of us do seem to get a kick out of worrying? Why is it that some of us find it hard to cope when good things happen?

Is it the sense of control? Anticipating negative outcomes can give us a head start, fooling us into thinking we're in control when bad things eventually happen. Is it because worry focuses the attention? Is it because worry is kind of exciting? It fills our brains with images that scare and torment, like a horror movie, or distract and overwhelm, like a fairground ride.

Worry is a type of mental stimulation, and it can become a habit. In the words of Samuel Johnson, 'Nothing focuses the mind better than the knowledge that you are to be hanged tomorrow.' Some of us can thrive under the pressure of worry.

> Right from school days onwards, when he crammed for his exams only the night before, Simon has thrived on the pressures of deadlines. 'If I don't feel that pressure, that gun at my head I can't get motivated.' Simon has achieved much success in his life in this way.

But the person who worries their way through life isn't as happy as they could be. He or she doesn't enjoy worry; they simply can't stop themselves doing it. Worry has become an unhappy way of engaging with life. If worry triggers depression, it has become chronic, unwanted and inescapable.

It is possible to worry about absolutely anything. Seasoned worriers may move on from current worries to past memories or future fantasies. Some may become superstitious, with worrying a sort of protection that bad things won't happen. Some may find worry stimulating, but at the end of the day it is terrible to be endlessly probing for danger, since danger is always around us. The danger may probably not occur, but the worrier doesn't know this, so the worrying and the anxiety this creates are torture.

Anxiety puts you on constant alert, limits your responses and creates emotional confusion. Worry paralyses you in this state of permanent tension. Rather like a hedgehog mesmerised by the headlights of an oncoming car, you can't move forward. Anxiety holds you back and life stands still.

In this chapter we have seen how worry, when it is out of proportion and out of place, lies at the heart of all anxiety and emotional vulnerability. If we don't find ways to manage the anxiety created by worry, stress levels will start to shoot up.

Repeated bouts of anxiety signal high levels of stress. In the next chapter we'll explore the relationship between worry and stress.

CHAPTER 9

A WORRIED LIFE

Maintaining cycles of worry and anxiety creates stress. Stress is linked to low self-esteem, relationship problems and problems at work. Stress can cause fatigue, insomnia, depression, weaken the immune system and make you vulnerable to disease. It may also bring on hypertension, a recognised factor in heart disease and some cancers. Stress can kill.

WHAT IS STRESS?

Stress is the physical and emotional response to the demands that are placed upon you. It can be a response to challenging circumstances in your life that you need to cope with, for instance a demanding schedule or a difficult relationship, but it can also be caused by too much worry.

Worry isn't the same as stress, but worry tends to create stress. Worry can trigger the stress response. This is a term used to describe the bodily, mental and behavioural changes that prepare you to cope with a perceived threat. If the worry is short-term these changes are helpful because they prepare you for physical action and focus your mind on the immediate problem. But if the tension created by worry isn't switched off, then the responses become chronic or excessive and will start to affect your physical and emotional health.

A cycle has been created that is hard to control. Worry creates stress. Stress creates more stress and more worry. This cycle is the common factor in all forms of worry, fear and anxiety.

WHY IT IS IMPORTANT TO REVERSE THE STRESS RESPONSE
If the stress response is sustained for too long by constant worry,

the body begins to think that the changes that have occurred are normal. The body has a number of mechanisms to maintain itself in a state of normality; this is called homeostasis. When homeostasis returns the body to the state of stress it will increase heart rate, blood pressure and hormone function in an unhelpful direction, even when there is no stress. You therefore experience all the bodily and emotional changes you don't want or need.

The bodily changes now become unpleasant. Muscular tension, so important for fight or flight, can develop into discomfort and pain. You may get headaches, back pain, stomachaches, weak legs and trembling. The raised blood pressure and increased heartbeat that prepare you for action may cause light-headedness, blurred vision and ringing in the ears. As breathing rate increases you may feel out of breath, dizzy or nauseous. Stomach upsets may occur, and sweating may become excessive and embarrassing.

The psychological reactions that help you focus may cause you to become too focused on what is worrying you, so that a problem becomes insurmountable and negative thinking sets in. Emotional changes that occur because of ongoing worry and anxiety are typically: irritability, fearfulness and demoralisation. When you feel like this it is much more difficult to cope with anxiety, and when your coping resources are low, stress is more likely to get on top of you.

The behaviour of people suffering from stress can change considerably. You may hate to be alone, or you may become withdrawn and indifferent. You may continually seek reassurance and become indecisive — a trip to the supermarket can require as much preparation as a family holiday. You may change your mind a lot, speaking fondly of someone one moment and finding him or her useless the next. You may become tearful, difficult and complaining and expect others to understand. You might start to fidget constantly or become extremely lethargic. You might try to seek comfort in food, alcohol, drugs or sex. There might be a change in sexual habits, and the previously mild-mannered might become verbally or physically aggressive.

If you were fairly relaxed stress may make you rigid and obsessive, for example, repeatedly checking locks and switches, or regularly cleaning things in the middle of the night even if they aren't dirty. Actions of this sort may be due to an effort to bring some order and certainty to the sense of confusion that you feel is surrounding you. You may not be aware of these changes, but others will be. You might want to ask anyone if they have noticed changes in your behaviour, but don't be cross with them if you don't like what you hear. Remember denying the truth can be a sign of stress.

POOR HEALTH

> Worry affects circulation, heart, glands, the whole nervous system and profoundly impacts on your health. I have never known a man who died from overwork, but many who died from doubt.
>
> *Dr Charles Mayo*

Earlier we saw how persistent anxiety and worry can trigger physical reactions associated with the stress response. If this is prolonged it will lead to poor health.

Sometimes poor health is the first indication that you are worried; worry can change the way you feel and look. This is reflected by the way we describe someone as having a 'worried look' or saying that we are 'worried sick'. Some people even think that your hair can turn grey with worry. All these associations presume that worry is associated with looking and feeling bad, and many experts believe there is a connection between worry and illness. Doctors often report that patients who worry about routine procedures or operations frequently take longer to recover.

It is believed that worry plays a major role in insomnia. Worry often keeps people awake at night. Losing sleep is unpleasant, and an irregular pattern of sleep may disrupt the balance of hormones that maintain health. Hormones are released at different times during the day, and some during sleep. Disturbed sleep can lead to hormone changes, which in turn can make certain illnesses more likely, anything from more colds to cancer.

Other common problems associated with worry include digestive troubles, headaches, raised blood pressure, worsening asthma, difficulty swallowing, sickness and diarrhoea. Stress can both cause and maintain these conditions. You might get diarrhoea and nausea in response to pressures at work, and this physical response may cause you additional worry, which will make you feel even sicker. Once again the vicious cycle perpetuates itself.

INCREASED RISK OF DISEASE

If the body is kept for too long in a stressful, heightened state created by worry the changes may begin to cause structural abnormalities. This is because consistent narrowing of the arteries and the resulting likelihood of the formation of clots within the arteries means that the blood flow through the essential organs becomes lessened. The adrenal glands may swell, the blood vessels become thickened and narrow and the stomach may become ulcerated. These structural changes add to the likelihood of diseases such as hypertension, heart attacks, strokes and stomach ulcers, as well as allergic reactions, skin rashes, infections and asthma.

High blood pressure can be made worse by the stress of constant worry, as can migraine and irritable bowel syndrome where you get alternating diarrhoea, constipation, abdominal distension and pain. Also linked to stress are peptic ulcers, diabetes, rheumatoid arthritis and intestinal inflammations such as heartburn and indigestion.

Without a doubt, the ability of the body to fight disease and infection is decreased when worry about problems in your life causes stress, particularly when it comes to the number of cells circulating and the ability to fight infections. Recent research has shown that you are much more likely to get infections when you feel anxious about something, which certainly fits in with my own experience as a teacher. My pupils always got more coughs, colds and flu when they were worried by exams and deadlines.

FATIGUE

Prolonged worry creates long-term stress and this can cause fatigue. You feel weak; your body aches; your face droops; you feel down. You feel washed out and worn out. You don't have the strength or energy to move and even simple tasks become difficult. You may become sedentary. Your productivity drops and your motivation suffers. For some, this persistent weariness can be so debilitating that they can't even get out of bed.

Fatigue can take a toll on your mind as well. Thinking becomes difficult and confused; decisions come slowly. Even your outlook on life becomes gloomy.

The result is that fatigue can lead to poor work performance, less interaction with family and friends, and less participation in activities you enjoy. Fatigue can also reduce sex drive.

LOSS OF LIBIDO

To have fulfilling, satisfying sex you need to feel healthy and relaxed in body and mind. When you are worn down by worry you are neither. Worry, anxiety and stress narrows your focus, reduces your energy and lowers your self-esteem to the extent that sex can't provide distraction and pleasure anymore. Loss of libido is common for both men and women when they are feeling stressed.

It's easy to shrug off low energy levels as just another sign that you are getting older or that you're coming down with something. But most of the time, it's neither. Fatigue can be due to the stress caused by constant worry. Low energy levels and loss of libido can be a signal from your body that you are worrying too much.

CHRONIC FATIGUE SYNDROME

Chronic Fatigue Syndrome (CFS) is fatigue at its most extreme. It is a debilitating disorder that leaves its sufferers weak, exhausted and barely able to function for months or even years. It may be caused by a variety of factors such as viruses, environmental irritants or too much stress acting on the immune system.

To be diagnosed with CFS you must have suffered persistent fatigue, which didn't exist previously, and which persists despite bed rest and cuts your daily activity in half, for at least six months. You must also have had most of the following unexplained symptoms for at least six months: sore throat, mild fever and chills, painful lymph nodes, muscle weakness, discomfort or pain, headaches, aches and pains that travel from joint to joint, loss of memory, difficulty concentrating, anxiety, depression or difficulty sleeping. If you suspect you may have CFS seek medical advice immediately.

PREMATURE AGEING

If you worry all the time you may end up looking older than your years. The stress created by constant worry speeds up the entire system and produces conditions that are commonly associated with growing old. Exhaustion may manifest as a total collapse of body function or a collapse or weakening of specific organs. Prolonged stress places a tremendous load on many organs, especially the heart, blood vessels, adrenal glands and immune system. Worry-induced stress can literally wear you out.

Ageing for the most part begins with worry. When you are worried you feel anxious and tired, and it's hard to think straight. Your ability to take care of yourself declines and you start to age faster. You don't pay enough attention to your diet and vitamin and mineral deficiencies creep in. You feel too despondent and tired to exercise. It is well-known that many of the problems that make you feel old before your time, such as weight gain, osteoporosis and arthritis, can be erased by regular exercise. You may neglect to take proper care of your skin and look older than you are by over exposure to the elements. You may feel so despondent that you turn to alcohol and cigarettes for distraction. Nothing ages you faster than nicotine and alcohol. Finally you may feel too distracted to keep your mind working, which can increase your risk of memory loss and muddled thinking.

Our bodies do modify as we get older, but if you take care of yourself you can be fit, active and alert well into old age. If, however, you neglect self–care, getting older won't be about health and contentment; it will be about aches and pains, irritability, fatigue and poor health. These things can rob you of your youth, but the real age marker is not physical; it's the mindset that allows you to worry, get stressed and neglect to take care of your body and mind.

RELATIONSHIP PROBLEMS

Worry can have a negative impact on your health and speeds up the ageing process, but it can also affect other aspects of your life, such as your relationships and work.

Worry can reverberate in relationships, resulting in heightened stress for all concerned. When you are worried you aren't as emotionally available to others; relationships will suffer.

> I didn't even notice how unhappy my husband was. It was like a bombshell when he told me he thought we should separate. I had been so worried about my job that I had neglected our marriage completely.
>
> *Anna, age 32*

Worry tends to be all consuming. When you are worried the people you care about often tend to feel neglected. It isn't intentional but it happens. Even if you are lucky and have family and friends who are supportive, worry is still a destructive force.

Worrying together can be a strong bond in a relationship, but if the worry becomes extreme or one-sided the balance of the relationship is upset. Few people realise the extent to which worry distorts relationships with partners, colleagues, family and friends. Worry can lead to a downward spiral between your anxiety and another's reaction to it so that you both end up unhappy.

If you suffer from anxiety, don't be misled into thinking that you are the only one with a problem; those that care about you will be affected too. Generally when one person is intensely worried or stressed, other parties get drawn into the process as well. When one party suffers from constant worry the other party may start to wear out too. It can be exhausting trying to anticipate a worrier's reactions. The people you care about can even end up getting stressed and anxious themselves.

According to certain American psychologists, anxiety is contagious. Like tired people who trigger yawning fits in others, anxiety is apparently like psychological flu; those who suffer from it spread it to others. Dr Thomas Joiner, editor of *The Interactional Nature of Depression* believes that colleagues, family and friends can all pass on the anxiety bug. It doesn't matter how positive a person you are, if you spend enough time with someone who is anxious you too are going to suffer anxiety.

Even with strangers or acquaintances — people who you are not emotionally involved with — anxiety rubs off and you pick up 'bad vibes'. In the workplace, for instance, if one member of the team is anxious it tends to bring down everyone's morale. Worry can be like a vicious circle — the more a person is worried the more they spread their mood to others. Take Amy, for instance, whose ex-husband, Mike, suffered from constant worry.

> I never knew what kind of mood he was going to be in. I felt like I was walking on a tightrope. I had to tread so carefully. He was so irritable and nervous all the time. I was constantly trying to support him and encourage him, but giving all the time and receiving nothing back eventually wore me down.

If you always appeared worried and anxious, friends and family may walk on eggshells trying not to cause any more problems. They may even retreat into themselves and inevitably start to blame themselves. If the situation continues for too long, those that care about you may reach the limits of their abilities to understand and be compassionate. They may start to feel frustrated and anxious themselves.

When anxiety arises in both parties the situation becomes serious. The relationship doesn't stand much of a chance unless ways are found to restore some kind of balance. If worry and anxiety aren't discussed, balanced out and dealt with they can poison even the most loving of relationships.

SELFISHNESS

When you are worried it can be hard to keep your interest in others and what is going on around you. Your world starts to shrink to your own needs and concerns. Your pain seems greater than anyone else's does. It's hard for you to sympathise with others. You start to resent the demands made upon you by others.

Selfish is a word that isn't often found in self-help books today. It's often replaced with dignified words like egoism, or expressions like over-inflated sense of self. As many people do suffer from low self-esteem there has rightly been an emphasis on taking care of yourself and your own needs, but like everything else you can take this too far. When you are so worried that your own needs start becoming the only thing that matters, you aren't empowering yourself anymore, you are becoming dangerously narcissistic. The end result can only be further unhappiness and loneliness.

WORK AND MONEY PROBLEMS

Worry can affect your performance at work too. Poor health associated with worry-induced stress may make you unable to work. Or you may find that worry affects your efficiency, focus and motivation at work.

> I was so worried about my impending divorce that I couldn't concentrate on my job. I decided to resign before I was fired for incompetence.
>
> *Justin, age 44*

Work can be a source of great satisfaction, but for many people today it is a source of frustration, and worry. Millions of us worry about our jobs. Why?

The unpredictabilities of the job market are one explanation. No one, not even the president of a corporation, can feel secure in his or her job anymore. Jobs for life belong to the past. The fast changing nature of the workplace is another. There isn't a sense of security and familiarity for many of us anymore. The misguided emphasis on youth and the devaluation of wisdom and experience means that once you hit forty the corporate ladder gets harder and harder to climb.

But perhaps more than anything the feeling of not being relevant has to be the biggest cause of worry. At the end of the day our biggest fear is the fear of not being needed anymore. We may convince ourselves that things would collapse without us and never take enough leave, always being available when work demands us and worrying constantly about our jobs, but the difficult truth is that in the world of work no one is expendable.

The fear of being surplus to requirements creates an incredible amount of worry and stress. We see that quality, dedication, experience and loyalty don't always get rewarded anymore and we worry about our future. We worry about who we can trust. We worry that we aren't good enough to survive. The net effect of all this worry is that huge amounts of potential energy get wasted. Instead of using our talents wisely we worry about work.

But isn't a certain amount of stress and worry a motivator? Wouldn't we get too complacent if everything were too safe?

Worry can improve our performance at work. There is such a thing as a performance anxiety curve, which illustrates that performance gets better up to a certain point. Many bosses work on this principle, believing that people only perform best when the stakes are high. They lead by instilling fear into their staff. This approach can work to an extent if the bosses are charging towards a goal, and stimulation or intensity is needed. But if the intensity becomes overwhelming for all but the very few, performance isn't enhanced, it is adversely affected. For most of us intense pressure and threat do not create helpful stimulation. They create harmful distraction.

Worry in the workplace is commonplace today. From worry

about losing your job, to not being good enough at your job, to a difficult boss, to difficult co-workers, to the fear of being left behind and not being relevant anymore; we all have reasons to feel worry about our jobs. And this worry can interfere with our ability to do our job well and our commitment and satisfaction with it.

PAIN UNDER PRESSURE

So far in this chapter we have seen how worry can create stress and lead to health, relationship and work problems. But why is it that some of us seem to cope better with pressure than others? Why does worry cause more stress for some people than others?

Clearly a tendency to worry is a key factor. Many experts believe that our emotions, personality and responses to pressure are genetically determined, but genes do not guarantee the development of a particular response; they just increase the chances of developing it. Many other factors need to be taken into account. Gaining an understanding of what has and is shaping your personality can be helpful. It can motivate you to change. We've touched on this before in Chapter 5, but now it's time for you to start thinking about some possible influences that may provide you with answers.

YOUR UPBRINGING

It might be a good idea to reflect on how the parenting you received continues to affect the way you cope with worry. The following illustrates some common experiences and may ring some bells with you:

My mother was always worrying.

My brother was always better than me at everything.

We were always doing things when I grew up. I can't remember my parents relaxing.

My father died full of regrets. I feel that I have to achieve for him.

I grew up in poverty. I'm terrified to be that poor again.

I was always taught that everybody else was more important than me.

I can't let my parents down. They did so much for me.

My parents didn't want me. I have never felt good enough.

I've always felt that I had to be perfect to make other people respect me.

Many of us grow up with a lifelong yearning to please our parents and to gain their love. This can make us incredibly driven, but it can also make us more vulnerable to worry and anxiety.

Your education may also have played a powerful role in how well you cope with worry. Perhaps the school you went to was competitive and you started to compare yourself with others at a young age. Perhaps there was a teacher who terrified you. Perhaps there was a teacher you desperately wanted to impress.

The past never really dies. It continues to live on in each of us. You may have less resistance to pressure because of harmful experiences or messages that have become ingrained in your way of being and doing. Later you'll learn that harmful messages don't have to continue to shape your attitudes and your behaviour in relation to pressure.

TRAUMATIC EXPERIENCES FROM YOUR PAST

Sometimes past events can be so traumatic that a condition called post-traumatic stress disorder or PTSD occurs.

After the train accident I started to think about it all the time. I would dream about it too. I expected to be in a state of shock but sometimes the memories were so vivid I seemed to relive it. I know this is a common experience after the kind of shock I had but the terrifying memories and dreams continued for weeks and weeks and started to affect my sleep and my ability to work.

Kenneth, age 30

PTSD is a stress reaction that follows unusually traumatic events such as accidents, rape, or witnessing violence or a disaster. The first studies of PTSD involved soldiers who had been engaged in military combat. The main features were usually accompanied by classic symptoms of worry and anxiety and recurrent, vivid memories of past horrors. In some cases this was associated with greater sensitivity to fright and unusual tearfulness, although emotional numbing could occur too.

Obviously trauma creates pressures. The amount you have experienced and the severity of it will affect your ability to manage pressure. But, however traumatic your past has been, it is possible to leave the stress behind. It takes time, but worries and fears can be managed. You don't constantly have to relive your fear. It is possible to move forward with your life.

YOUR CULTURE

Your cultural background can have a powerful effect.

I think being the only black girl in a mainly white school meant that I was under constant pressure to prove I was as good as everyone else.

I grew up in a very tight knit Chinese community. My father didn't even bother to learn English.

I was educated in a quiet country school. Then I went to a laid back middle-class university. It was a shock when I started my first job on my own in the city.

Cultural expectations of what we should believe, think and achieve are often ingrained at a time when we are at our most impressionable. Unconsciously they may shape our responses to pressure and to the extent that we worry.

YOUR SUPPORT NETWORK

Countless studies have proved that emotional ties with partners, family and friends have a healing potency. A support network seems to be a key factor in reducing worry, buffering stress and enhancing health and well being.

In his bestseller *The Healing Power of Intimacy*, Dean Ornish has demonstrated that loneliness can not only increase the risk of poor health and emotional problems, loneliness can kill.

> While the evidence on the relationship of psychosocial factors to illnesses is controversial, most scientific studies have demonstrated the extraordinarily powerful role of love and relationships determining health and illness.

Emotional support from others can help you cope with worry. It does seem that talking about problems, asking for advice and sharing them with others helps. A support network consists of family and friends who can give you emotional support, advice, encouragement, affection and friendship. When there is no social support the risk of worry, anxiety and stress increases tenfold.

YOUR GENDER

Do men and women react differently when they are worried or anxious? According to many experts they do.

> 'There seems to be a built-in gender difference,' writes Stephen Biddulph in *Raising Boys*. 'If girls are anxious in a group setting they tend to cower and be quiet, whereas boys respond by running about making a lot of noise. This has mistakenly been seen as boys dominating the space in

pre-schools and so on. However, it is actually an anxiety response.'

One theory is that men and women are raised to respond differently to the same stimuli. Worry causes very similar changes in the brain chemistry of men and women, but we react differently based on the way we have been brought up.

Generally speaking men are brought up to be more aggressive than women. Women tend to react rather than act, and to focus more on relationships with others as a source of happiness and self-esteem than men. Women are more likely to blame and punish themselves even for events over which they have no control. Men on the other hand tend to respond to frustration and disappointment by acting with violence and substance abuse rather than introspection and depression. In other words men are more likely to explode rather than implode when worry creates stress.

Others promote biological explanations for gender differences. Professor Shelley Taylor of the University of California, Los Angeles and senior author of the *Psychological Review* believes he has discovered a gender difference in the way the sexes respond to anxiety. According to Taylor's research:

> There is one fact we all know about stress — that it triggers the ancient fight or flight response, flooding the body with chemicals, such as adrenaline and cortisol, which help us respond to danger. But with a higher percentage of women now taking part in research projects it appears that the typical female response to stress is different. Instead of fighting or fleeing, women are more likely to 'tend or befriend' to become more nurturing or to seek support from others, hence the impulse to call a friend.

The key to this behavioural difference is the hormone oxytocin, which promotes relaxation and loving feelings. Both men and women produce oxytocin under stress, but women produce more of it and its effect is enhanced by oestrogen. It is believed by some experts that testosterone puts a brake on the effect of oxytocin making it harder for men to talk about their feelings and reach out to others when faced with stress. With a big helping hand from oxytocin women are less likely to fly off the handle or bury their feelings when confronted with stress. Men are more likely to respond with aggression or denial.

A MAN'S SPECIAL RISK

This is an area of huge controversy, but some experts believe that a man's capacity to feel is, to a greater degree than in a woman, physically divorced from his capacity to articulate. The emotional centres of a man's brain are located far more discreetly than in a woman and the two halves of the male brain are connected by a smaller group of fibres than in the female brain. Information flows less easily from the right side to the verbal, left side, so men tend to have difficulties expressing how they feel.

It may not be that men bottle things up but that their brains are not wired so easily for communication and feelings. Whether physical or social in origin, men feel less comfortable talking about their feelings or reaching out for support in times of crisis than women do. When worried, men are more inclined to solve problems by withdrawing from intimacy, or distract themselves with work or other activities. This can increase their risk of worry leading to stress.

The typical male response to painful and difficult emotions may contribute to the isolation depressed men often feel. He may be able to work things out in his head. He may be able to take the appropriate action. Sometimes, though, he can't cope on his own, and sometimes the action he takes isn't healing but dangerous. Men tend to turn violent towards others, women towards themselves.

Furthermore, the instinct to deny, divert or become aggressive under pressure simply enables anxieties to go undetected or unacknowledged for far longer than in women. And the longer feelings of despair are reinforced, the more likely they are to develop into a downward spiral that is increasingly difficult to resolve without treatment.

A WOMAN'S SPECIAL RISK

Certain risk factors may make women more prone to worry than men. Hormonal changes have been offered as an explanation, but although hormone imbalances may contribute to greater stress levels, there is no research showing that they cause worry.

It is argued that the psychosocial issues that surround biological events like the onset of menstruation, pregnancy, and menopause may be just as responsible for triggering depression as any surge or depletion in hormones. For instance, as menopause approaches, hormonal changes coincide with signs of ageing, loss of fertility and the spectre of death. The onset of puberty coincides with an increased awareness of body image and all the confusing signals and social changes.

Other social factors make women more vulnerable to worry. Although the status of women in society has risen in the last few decades, women still earn less than men for the same work, suffer more discrimination and harassment and the work they do still remains less valued. The work of women who stay at home to raise a family is particularly undervalued. Housewives and women who try to 'have it all', to be wives and mothers, as well as full-time employees outside the home, tend to suffer most from anxiety.

Another reason for shying away from the biological explanation are the justified fears of further discrimination against women. It implies that women are the weaker and more emotional sex. If biology is destiny how can women compete on an equal basis with men.

The science of gender differences is fascinating, but such studies are also hugely controversial and outside the scope of this book. Split brain studies and studies on the role of 'male' and 'female' hormones in other animals, including primates, yield inconclusive results in humans. This tends to surprise most people. Too often such studies are used as simple excuses for the status quo when in fact men and women may be more alike than we think. These theories also don't take into account 'neuro-plasticity,' the new research showing that chemicals in our brains change according to the everyday experiences we undergo.

At the end of the day it's impossible to generalise about how worry affects men and women. The neural connections in our brains that carry the blueprint for our responses continue forming through out our life. All of us have a unique experience of life and our pattern of response to worry is individual, regardless of what sex we are.

TIMES OF SPECIAL RISK

Why one person feels more pain under pressure is determined by many factors: your genes, upbringing, culture, gender, work, health, every part of your unique life may have a part to play. There are also times in your life when you are more likely to worry than others.

Life-changing events, such as the death of a loved one, divorce, illness, job loss, retirement, debt and marriage, are well-known causes of worry. Life is never completely worry free, whatever age you are and however satisfied and fulfilled you are.

CHILDHOOD

It's often assumed that worry is a very grown-up thing. But you can worry at any age; children also get worried. It's easy to forget how much anxiety is a part of growing up. Everything is new. Everything has to be learned for the first time. Everything is potentially a source of stress, embarrassment and failure. Everything is fraught with worry.

Worry is a normal part of childhood. We shouldn't try to take it away. Children need that sense of adventure and risk. They need to learn to get comfortable with a certain amount of danger and then pull back when the danger is too great. They need to learn how to manage worry. But there are times when children lose perspective and worry overwhelms them. It's important to recognise when the normal anxieties of childhood have crossed the line to excessive fear.

A parent should be concerned if:

- A child doesn't feel a sense of connection or love with his or her caregivers.
- If children don't feel that they are loved, they may create an inner world full of worries and fears, which can retard normal, healthy development.
- A child feels burdened down by the expectations of others. Sometimes parents can create worry for children by pushing them to succeed at the expense of childhood fun and spontaneity.
- A child has a diagnosable brain-based condition which can be medically treated, such as separation anxiety disorder, generalised anxiety disorder, obsessive compulsive disorder, or social phobia and shyness.

Children are prone to wild exaggerations of their emotions, and worry is no exception. What started as a normal everyday irritation can transform into a preoccupation with disaster and catastrophe that can induce a state of chronic stress, fear and panic which retards normal development. If a child is suffering from extreme worry and showing signs of stress as a result, a parent or caregiver should seek help immediately for that child.

Seeking help for children showing signs of anxiety at an early age can avert severe depressive episodes later. Severely depressed teenagers often displayed certain behavioural traits as children, such as aggressive, antisocial behaviour; research is proving that depressive illnesses often first show themselves in childhood or adolescence. If a child's parents are unresponsive or abusive in the first few years of life, some experts believe that the brain may undergo certain changes that make him or her susceptible to depression.

ADOLESCENCE

Adolescence can be a time of incredible excitement, but it can also be a time of worry, doubt, fear and stress. It is the period when children strive to separate from parents, establish their own identity, become comfortable with their sexuality, and think about what kind of life they want to lead. With so much going on emotionally and physically, it is small wonder that many teenagers suffer from chronic worry.

A common response to anxiety during adolescence is resistance to authority, and this can lead to moodiness, argumentativeness and violent behaviour. There may also be an increase in perfectionism. The drive to be the perfect son, daughter or student is one of the biggest risk factors for depression and suicide as well as eating disorders.

It can be hard to tell if a teenager is suffering from chronic worry or just being a typical teenager. This isn't made any easier by the fact that an adolescent with mood and behavioural problems is often the hardest of all to reach out to. But the worst thing you can do with teenagers who are worried and stressed is leave them alone and hope they will sort themselves out.

Look for problems at school, inability to bounce back after disappointments or any sudden change in mood that doesn't make sense. Remember that worry in teenagers is often cloaked in so called predictable teenage behaviour. Episodes of anger are typical, but persistent anger or disruptive behaviour is not. Complaints and behaviour taken to the extreme are warning signs. When teenagers frequently get involved in crime, sleep around, smash the car, get drunk or violent or abuse drugs, it could be a sign of excessive worry that could lead to depression. Don't ignore it.

ADULTHOOD

Life begins to take a more definite shape sometime in our twenties and thirties and the responsibilities of adulthood tend to increase the potential for worry. The thirties are a crucial decade of decision making about careers, relationships and having children, but making decisions about career and family life can create intolerable pressure.

When we hit thirty the pressure is really on us to make our mark in the world. Leading a rootless life and flitting from one job to another may have seemed exciting and carefree in our twenties, but in the thirties it starts to get jaded. Many thirty-somethings get the 'I should have by now,' dilemma.

On the other hand, you may feel that you are making your mark but feel worried about other aspects of your life. You may not be doing work that you believe in. You may not be working at all. The need to achieve seems to be universal amongst all adults. You may be unhappy about the state of the country and the world you live in, or you may long for spiritual strength and harmony. You may not feel comfortable or fulfilled with your sexuality. You may not have a partner and long for one. If you have a partner the relationship may not be fulfilling. Whether you are gay or straight, the issue of commitment to one particular person may loom large. You may feel anxious about the prospect of parenthood. If you have a child, parenthood can be one of the most rewarding experiences in a person's life, but it can also be one of the most demanding.

If you are approaching forty or in your forties you may feel that you have set your life course and there is little opportunity for change. This is not entirely your fault. Our youth-obsessed culture encourages us to feel that our value decreases with age. At forty a person crosses an age barrier that influences the way he or she is viewed at work, by his or her family and by society in general.

Your evaluation of your accomplishments, hopes and dreams in your forties and fifties will decide whether your life ahead is an exciting challenge or a demoralising drudge. You may be able to redefine yourself and negotiate the later part of your life with skill and ease, but sometimes the deep sense of crisis and failure can cause considerable worry and unhappiness.

RETIREMENT

After sixty, your health is more vulnerable, and palliatives that may have been tolerated by the body, such as alcohol, can't be tolerated so well anymore. Coping strategies that may have kept worry at bay, like work or sports, may no longer be relevant. The end of your working life could result in loss of status, loss of relationships with work colleagues, and the absence of the social network that had been provided by work.

Only recently has the anxiety caused by retirement been widely recognised as a serious concern, and there remains a great deal of ignorance about it among the general public as well as the medical profession. Part of the problem stems from a misunderstanding of the ageing process.

Most of us think of poor health, illness, slowing up, fatigue, low energy levels, fretting, irritability and mood disturbances as part of the ageing process. We often think it's natural to feel sad, anxious and worried as we approach the end of our lives, but this isn't the case at all. Old age isn't all about worry. Your personality may mellow but it does not change as you age. You can continue to develop new interests, meet new challenges and feel healthy.

Growing up isn't easy. The older we get and the more responsibilities we have to deal with, the more worries we seem to face. Hopefully as we get older we learn to cope better. We don't allow our worries to turn into catastrophes anymore. We learn to deal with worry in a positive way and by so doing we gain the maturity, wisdom and confidence to lead a fulfilling and happy life.

But, as mentioned earlier in this chapter, some of us just worry more than others. We may never fully understand why this is the case, but one thing is certain, if we are constantly worried and can't get a sense of perspective, worry brings us closer to the greatest danger of all: persistent unhappiness leading to depression.

CHAPTER 10

WORRYING YOURSELF TO DESPAIR

One of the fastest routes to unhappiness and depression is unproductive worry. Unhappiness can describe many different emotional states, from a simple case of the blues, when you can still function, to major depression, when you can only see hopelessness and despair.

THE BLUES

We all go through the blues — also known as dysphoric mood states — with some temporary symptoms of depression, but you can usually continue to function normally and recover without needing treatment.

Sadness is a natural reaction to worry about common problems, such as the loss of a loved one, failing an exam, financial setbacks, problems at work, depressing news or unresolved conflicts and disappointments. Sadness linked to a particular worry is an entirely normal and temporary phase.

Feeling sad and anxious for no particular reason is equally common. Sometimes you feel unbearably anxious, sad and alone with a bitter taste in your mouth. This experience, however, may be no more than a passing moment. In time the heaviness lifts through a change in attitude or practical action. Sometimes though the heaviness doesn't lift and persistent worry prolongs the state of unhappiness.

When you worry for too long life loses much of its magic. When low feelings that seem to have no obvious cause and can't be lifted by the sympathy and support of others make your life feel bleak and meaningless, the world starts to turn grey. You feel empty and hopeless. You feel tired and can't concentrate most of the time. Your relationships and work life start to suffer. Before long you aren't just feeling sad and worried anymore. When you feel cut-off and unreachable, and when you know there are good things in life but you can't feel them, worry has edged you towards burnout and/or depression.

WHEN YOU REACH YOUR LIMIT

When you feel physically and emotionally exhausted by worry, you may experience burnout. Burnout is a term used to describe a reaction to constant stress, which goes unnoticed until the sufferer realises they can't cope. It is the stress response taken one stage further. Burnout may occur as a reaction to taking on too much responsibility, not being able to say no, setting impossible targets, or it could be due to boredom or frustration. Either way you feel stretched beyond your ability to cope.

The symptoms of burnout can interfere with your sense of well being and performance. They include:

- diminished enthusiasm
- resistance to change
- feeling pointless
- getting quickly frustrated by minor irritations
- feeling tired or ill a lot of the time
- forgetting things and making mistakes
- ignoring what is important and spending too much time on trivia.

Burnout is not always a sign that you can't cope anymore or have lost your edge. It could simply be a sign that you need new goals and objectives in your life and/or help and support from others. If you can change your mental outlook and embrace change the feelings of despondency and exhaustion should pass.

Sometimes, though, it seems impossible to change the way you think. You may or may not be experiencing the symptoms of burnout, but when feelings of exhaustion, unhappiness and futility persist, and worry is excessive, then depression is likely.

You might not realise that your worrying has slipped into depression. Many of us think of worry as one of life's hardships that simply has to be toughed out. But chronic worry and unhappiness are never normal.

You may fail to recognise how exhausted and unhappy you are. You may just think you are being realistic. You don't trust anyone or anything. You keep alert by worrying about things before they happen. It's hard for you to relax. You think that people will betray you and that life is unfair and justice doesn't exist. You see suffering everywhere. You worry about everyone and everything day and night.

This is depression. Centuries ago depression was seen as a sign of weakness or moral failure; it wasn't talked about. But today depression has lost some of its taboo. We recognise that it is a treatable condition. We want to know more about it and this starts by knowing how to recognise it.

Recognising depression

Depression isn't always obvious, but there are signs you can recognise. If you are constantly worrying and anxious most of the time, have lost interest or pleasure in the everyday activities that you used to enjoy, and can answer yes to four or more questions on the checklist below, the chances are that you are depressed.

- Are you tired all the time?
- Have you lost interest in sex?
- Do you feel lonely and isolated?
- Are you overwhelmed by negative emotions?
- Has the nature of your relationships changed?
- Do you feel mysterious pains that seem to migrate around your body?
- Is it difficult for you to accomplish even simple tasks, such as washing, dressing and eating?
- Do you cry a lot?

- Do you feel confused and forgetful?
- Is it hard for you to make any kind of decision?
- Are your sleeping habits changing, either by getting out of bed or roaming around all night and day?
- Do you feel restless, panicky and anxious?
- Do you eat less than before? Have you lost weight without dieting (10 lb in a two-week period)?
- Have you suddenly gained weight, and are you eating far more than usual?

Are you:

- Regularly taking drugs or drinking to the point of losing control?
- Behaving badly, lying, stealing or cheating?
- Taking more and more time off from work or education?
- Harming yourself by cutting, burning or scratching?
- Having bouts of rage or violence?
- Having horrible memories of past events?
- Hallucinating sights, sounds and smells?
- Having periods of frantic energy followed by periods of little or no energy?
- Having panic attacks or surges of strong anxiety?
- Do you feel sad and pessimistic about yourself and the world?
- Do you feel hopeless, guilty and worthless?
- Do you find it hard to concentrate?
- Are you irritable most of the time — or alternatively, unusually placid, which may go so far as you physically slowing down in speech, action and thought?
- Do you show a preoccupation with death or suicide?

To summarise, if you notice the following five warning signs for more than two weeks you are suffering from depression:

- constant worrying
- emotional instability

- loss of sex drive or changes in sexual habits
- inability to make decisions
- lack of self-confidence.

It is important that you seek advice from a mental health professional. Suicide is a very real consequence of depression. If you ever reach the point when you feel you have become a burden and life is not worth living, immediately seek help from your doctor.

AM I DEPRESSED?

Depression manifests in many ways, and your experience of it won't be the same as anyone else's, but the following might help you recognise if you are displaying typical symptoms:

According to the New York Times' columnist Daniel Goleman in his book *Emotional Intelligence*, if repetitive thoughts about how sad you are feeling or how badly you are doing in life crowd your mind, depression is far more likely. Goleman believes that one of the 'main determinants' of whether or not a depressed mood will lift is the degree to which you worry or ruminate. Constant worrying is dangerous.

The clearest warning sign is a state of constant worry, also known as rumination, when negative, anxious thoughts about the past, present and future stubbornly predominate. You feel pessimistic about almost everything. You may start talking about a feeling of hopelessness and futility or life having no meaning. It may be hard to stop this flow of negative thinking.

It's likely that you lose interest in activities you used to enjoy. You feel anxious, sad, withdrawn, preoccupied or just despondent for longer than normal. Communication and intimacy is difficult, and when you do talk you use words like boredom, tedium, dreary, slow, fed up or pointless, to describe how you feel.

There may be problems thinking clearly and concentrating. You become forgetful and indecisive. You feel constantly on edge and are prone to fly off the handle for no apparent reason. In some cases you may lash out at others or blame them for your problems.

There may also be a feeling of absolute terror and dread out of all proportion to actual events.

> 'I feel like I am about to jump from an aeroplane and nobody has checked that I have a parachute' is how Simon, age 23, describes his anxiety. 'I'm frightened of just about everything.'

Eating habits may change when you are depressed. You may eat less or you may eat more.

> When Michael, age 39, lost his son in a car accident he found himself incapable of eating. He lost five and a half stone and was admitted to hospital when he was too weak to even get out of bed.

> Wendy, age 15, on the other hand, gained a massive six stone when her parents separated and she was put into care.

You may drink more alcohol than usual or start smoking. Your spending habits may change and your driving could become more reckless.

Other signals include habits like finger tapping, foot swinging or knee jigging or grinding of teeth in the night. You could start scratching itches that don't exist or smoothing hair that is already in place or just keep fidgeting. Facial gestures associated with stress include repeated swallowing, lip chewing, eye-blinking, lip-clicking or tic-like spasms. You may start to tune out what is going on around you. You hear but you don't listen. This may involve television tune in — when you switch on the television and stare at the screen without watching or listening to it.

You may lose your sex drive or have an insatiable need for sexual gratification. You may become obsessed with your health, weight or appearance, obsessive eating and exercising habits take over your life.

Getting a good night's sleep won't be easy for you. You may

wake in the early hours of the morning. You may be sleepy all day and wide awake all night. You may not even be able to sleep at all. Should you get to sleep, your sleep is restless and uneasy and there may be nightmares. On the other hand, you may sleep much longer than usual. Whatever the case, sleep won't give you relief from the constant fatigue and exhaustion you feel. 'I've got no energy' may become a constant refrain.

Your movements may slow right down, 'as if you are moving through a jar of treacle', is how one woman described herself. You may even notice that your breathing is heavy. Your posture will look dejected and you may shuffle rather than walk. You may find it impossible to go about your routine and even simple tasks like getting dressed defeat you. On the other hand you may be able to continue functioning with apparent normality.

ARE YOU UNHAPPY OR DEPRESSED?

In her seminal text *Depression: The Way Out of Your Prison*, Dorothy Rowe distinguishes between being depressed and being worried and unhappy. Unhappy people are able to seek comfort, comfort themselves and let that comfort come through to them to ease the pain. 'But in depression neither the sympathy and concern of others nor the gentle love of oneself is available.' Other people may be there, but their compassion can't pierce the wall of depression. 'Depression is a prison' where the depressed person is both the 'suffering inmate' and the 'cruel jailer'.

If a precipitating event has occurred, such as the loss of a loved one, a period of readjustment when symptoms of depression occur is normal. A diagnosis of depression won't be made until symptoms have persisted for longer than two months.

When you are unhappy because you are worried you feel out of sorts and dejected, but your low mood is a temporary state and it won't affect normal functioning. When you are depressed you have a mood disorder, or illness of the feelings, that is persistent, and destroys any chance of happiness.

HOW DOES DEPRESSION FEEL?

Many seriously depressed people say that, forced to choose between depression and a heart attack, they would chose the heart attack.

- Roger, age 65, felt that it was 'a living death, which robs everything of meaning or purpose. I felt numb'.
- Maria, age 46, who suffers from bouts of depression, compared it to 'a hammer hitting a bruise over and over again'.
- Patricia, age 37, described it as 'the gradual shutting out of all light'.
- Chris, age 20, told me that it was like 'an all-consuming dark swamp that took over my life'.
- For Perry, age 16, 'every day is a battle to survive'.

Spike Milligan told the psychiatrist Anthony Clare, 'It is like every fibre in your body is screaming for relief yet there is no relief.... The whole world is taken away, and all there is this black void, this terrible, terrible, empty, aching, black void.'

Dr John Horder, one-time president of the Royal College of General Practitioners, told the magazine *Medical News* that depression felt like a 'form of total paralysis of desire, hope, capacity to decide, to do, to think, or to feel — except pain and misery.'

F Scott Fitzgerald described depression as a 'nocturnal void where the self wages an intimate struggle against hopelessness and despair.'

William Styron declared in *Darkness Visible* that 'loss in all its manifestations is the touchstone of depression.... The loss of self-esteem is a celebrated symptom, and my own sense of self had all but disappeared, along with my self-reliance.'

A depressed person can't see anything in life other than futility, suffering, pain, anxiety, loss, destruction and misery. Emotionally, mentally and physically they feel drained, dysfunctional and defeated. This has gone way beyond worry and sadness. This is a living death.

CLINICAL DEPRESSION

Depression has many faces. Here very briefly are the various types of clinical depression. As you can see most are caused by or closely linked to excessive worry, but in some cases, such as secondary depression, other factors play an important part.

DYSTHYMIA

A more serious condition than the blues is low-grade melancholy, 'feeling down' for at least a year. The condition is known as dysthymia (literally meaning 'ill-humoured'), chronic depression, or neurotic depression, and it does not dramatically alter normal functioning.

Chronic mild depression tends to have milder symptoms than major depression, but it can be longer lasting. Whether or not dysthymia is a separate entity from major depression or simply a less intense form of the same disorder remains a subject of debate.

Although dysthymia usually develops before the age of twenty-five, most people are not diagnosed until they reach mid-life. Most sufferers with dysthymia claim that they've felt worried, low and depressed for so long they don't remember feeling any other way. 'Doubtless depression has hovered over me for years, waiting to swoop,' says William Styron, who wrote an autobiographical account of his own depression in *Darkness Visible*.

MAJOR DEPRESSION OR UNIPOLAR DEPRESSION

Major depression is the most widespread form of mental disorder, according to the National Institute of Mental Health. Major depression impairs a person's functioning. The situation can be life threatening; a person suffering from severe depression may think about taking their own life. Currently therapists identify three different forms of major depression: melancholic, atypical and psychotic.

Melancholic depression involves symptoms of deep anxiety, sadness and lethargy.

> Simon, age 18, suffers from melancholic depression. He wakes before dawn, and his mother can hear him silently crying until the alarm clock rings a few hours later. He has college to attend but rarely gets up. He has no appetite for food or for life and withdraws from social contact as much as possible.

A person with atypical depression may feel better when life gets more positive. He or she may enjoy food, sex and work. There won't be a loss of appetite or insomnia. On the contrary they may overeat and oversleep. The sufferer tends to be very sensitive to rejection and worries easily, but apart from that it is very hard to tell they are depressed. Frustration about the disparity between a gloomy inner state and the productivity of their life can precipitate a crisis.

Psychotic depression is the rarest form of major depression. Psychotic men and women completely lose touch with reality and experience delusions and hallucinations. They usually require immediate treatment and hospitalisation. Paranoia is a form of psychotic depression.

PARANOIA

Paranoia is one of the most painful states of worry. Few of us will probably ever experience it and thankfully so.

The paranoid person lives in a state of acute anxiety and constant fear. He perceives threats to his wellbeing all around him and trusts nobody and nothing. He is constantly vigilant and watchful and imagines all sorts of threats in the most insignificant of details. He lives in a terrifying, often worrying and violent world. Mistrust makes him lash out at anyone who tries to help him. This is worry at its most frightening.

To get some idea of what living with paranoia is like imagine how you would feel if you were alone in the middle of night in a graveyard. Even the innocent rustling of leaves would send shivers down your spine. But most of us when we feel intense fear and worry can take a deep breath and put things in perspective. Paranoia victims can't do this.

Paranoia can manifest in a spectrum from inability to distinguish fact from fiction, when a person is so sensitive they can't function efficiently and medical attention is essential, to a state of constant vigilance or a persistently suspicious nature. Sometimes a mild dose of paranoia can be put to good use. Those with a suspicious nature can make excellent lawyers, politicians and academics. They are always questioning and probing and never really trust what they see. But their existence is rarely a happy one. It's exhausting to be constantly on the alert and unable to trust.

All of us experience episodes when worry threatens to become paranoia. We've all thought that nobody liked us or that everybody was staring at us when nobody was. When distorted perceptions like these occur it is important that you don't ignore them but you listen to them to find out what they really mean; Part 3 will help you do this.

SECONDARY DEPRESSION

There are also depressions described as secondary because they result from other mental and physical problems. A high incidence of depression, for example, occurs with illnesses such as diabetes, cancer, heart disease and strokes, also disorders of the brain such as Alzheimer's, Parkinson's disease, epilepsy and multiple sclerosis. In the past doctors tended to think that it was natural that a person felt worried because of their condition. They did not depression as something that also needs to be treated. Fortunately, more doctors are recognising that depression needs to be treated as a separate condition because it is an illness that can impair recovery.

MANIC DEPRESSIVE DISORDER OR BIPOLAR AFFECTIVE DISORDER

Unlike unipolar depression, where the depressive mood doesn't lift, in bipolar affective disorder a 'down' mood is followed immediately by an 'up' mood, or after a spell of stability. At first the highs may seem mild; the person feels energetic, excited, talkative and euphoric. She may suddenly get very active. She moves fast, talks fast, barely eats and sleeps. She is self-confident, bordering on the arrogant. She begins new projects, acts impulsively or recklessly; she may become promiscuous. She is often impatient and may become irritable, agitated and even violent if someone tries to slow her down.

Manic episodes are invariably followed by deep depression. If untreated, the condition could spiral out of control so that mood changes become more and more frequent, even from hour to hour.

SEASONAL AFFECTIVE DISORDER (SAD)

SAD involves periods of depression on an annual basis during the same time each year; beginning most often between the months of October and November, in the northern hemisphere, as the days grow shorter and ending in March or April with the coming of spring. Symptoms include intense food cravings, especially for carbohydrates, lethargy, oversleeping, weight gain and general fatigue during the autumn and winter months. The National Institute of Mental Health estimates that about ten million Americans suffer from SAD, most of them in the northern part of the country where it stays darker longer.

CONDITIONS THAT COMMONLY CO-EXIST WITH DEPRESSION

If worry edges you towards depression, you are at risk of developing other mood disorder problems. More than forty-three per cent of people with major depressive disorders have histories of one or more other psychiatric disorders, according to the US department of Health and Human Services. The most common conditions that occur alongside depression are: alcohol and drug addiction, obsessive compulsive disorder, eating disorders, hypochondria, abusive behaviour and suicide.

ALCOHOL AND DRUG ADDICTION

Alcohol and drugs affect brain chemistry and mood. Like depression, addiction appears to have a genetic connection, with children of alcoholics more likely to develop an addiction. Also, like depression, addiction appears to involve a disruption of brain chemicals combined with psychological factors.

Many depressed people start drinking or taking drugs to self-medicate and to relieve the pain of excessive worry. The physical, social and psychological problems caused by substance abuse make a person feel hopeless, weak and sad. More alcohol, cocaine or other substances are needed to lift the mood. It is a morbid cycle of neediness and despair.

Alcoholism and drug addiction are complex disorders with complex causes and treatment options. Covering these problems in any depth goes beyond the range of this book. Suffice to say it is vital that if you are becoming addicted to drugs or alcohol you seek medical advice immediately.

COMPULSIVE BEHAVIOUR

Obsessive compulsive disorder may also co-exist with worry-induced depression. When obsessive thoughts and worry become severe a person may change their behaviour in order to cope. He or she engages in compulsive actions that don't make sense to anyone except himself. Common compulsive acts include continual checking or counting, hand washing, cleaning, counting or tidying.

The compulsion to exercise, perhaps triggered by the endorphins released during aerobic activity, can also occur. A person will spend hours running, swimming or engaging in other forms of aerobic exercise. If a session is missed there is anxiety. Sometimes the compulsive need to exercise can take over a person's life to the extent that work, relationships and even health suffers.

The compulsion to have sex with as many women or men as possible, and as often as possible, can also be associated with excessive worry. As is the compulsion to work, when a person reaches the point when he or she can't switch off anymore and engage in activities outside the workplace; and the compulsion to gamble or to use computers.

The correlation between constant worry, depression and various forms of compulsive behaviour is high. It is extremely important for concurrent addiction and depression to be treated. The combination can trigger deeper and longer depressions.

EATING DISORDERS

It is estimated that up to seventy-five per cent of eating disorder patients suffer from some sort of major depression. Most of these will be women, but eating disorders, such as anorexia, bulimia and obesity, seem to be increasing in incidence in men, according to a fifteen-year study conducted by Professors Harrison Pope and Katherine Phillips of Harvard and Brown Universities and clinical psychologist Roberto Olivardia.

Worry about health that is taken to the extreme is often the starting point. Bullying and taunts about appearance from the peer group may also be powerful triggers. Sometimes, though, it is simply a desire to conform to the media image of desirability.

Anorexia involves a distortion in body image and a morbid worry about fat that leads to self-starvation. Although hungry and abnormally focused on food, anorexics force themselves not to eat. No amount of logical reasoning will convince the sufferer to break the destructive pattern of reducing food intake to virtually none, weighing themselves repeatedly and fearing food. Bulimia, which involves eating vast quantities of food in short spaces of time and vomiting, is another dangerous disorder.

Like depression, eating disorders — including compulsive eating, obesity, and anorexia and bulimia — involve a disruption of brain chemistry as well as psychosocial stresses. Treatment usually involves a combination of medication and psychotherapy. It is important that any eating-related problems be discussed with doctors or therapists at the same time that depression is addressed.

HYPOCHONDRIA

Hypochondria is the term that describes distress in response to perceived health problems. It is often associated with extra sensitivity to bodily changes and preoccupation with the fear of catching a serious disease.

The worries of the hypochondriac are so strong that they tend to resist all reassurance, although the sufferer often seeks repeated reassurances. Hypochondriacs repeatedly check for signs of illness. We all have uncomfortable bodily symptoms at times. Therefore anyone who looks for them will find them and be alarmed by their discovery. In the great majority of cases the hypochondriac has no health problems but the stress caused by persistent worry about possible health problems can eventually create poor health and even disease.

ABUSIVE BEHAVIOUR

A depressed person may release their hurt by inflicting it upon others, especially those who care about them most. There may be verbal outbursts of anger or irritability or worse still violence. Violence is often a way to release pain and to feel better. It is like saying to someone else, 'Now you understand my pain'. This is one of the most terrible aspects of depression.

Others turn the violence inwards upon themselves. They may engage in self-mutilation, cutting the arm repeatedly with a knife, for instance. Jamie, aged nineteen, has been battling against self-mutilation for seven years. When asked why he cuts himself, he explains that it is 'like releasing all the bad and evil inside. I feel better, relieved, when I hurt myself and see the blood flowing.'

Finally depression may drive a person to the ultimate form of self-abuse — suicide.

SUICIDE

To take your own life is probably the single most extreme expression of worry and helplessness that any person can make.

Over the past few decades the suicide rate has been steadily increasing, especially among young men.

In the majority of cases depression can be successfully treated using a combination of anti-depressant drugs and psychological and social therapies. Despite this the World Health Organisation estimates that by the year 2020 depression will be the second largest cause of death and disability in the world. One of the main problems is that people who suffer from depression don't come forward for treatment and are left to fight their nightmares alone. Sometimes the anxiety and despair is so great that all sense of perspective is lost and suicide seems the only option.

It's still hard for people today to admit they are depressed. Such is the taboo surrounding depression. It's even harder to ask for help. But if you are feeling depressed it is vital that you do seek help, or at least unburden yourself to an anonymous telephone line. There are always options available to you, however disillusioned and despairing you may feel. Depression can be treated. Never lose sight of that.

WORRYING YOURSELF TO DESPAIR

In Part 2 we have seen how worry is the basis for all forms of unhappiness. It can lead to poor heath, low self-esteem, stress, depression and even death.

It is the root of all evil because it is a form of avoidance. Rather than confronting an issue, you worry about it. When you don't confront something it becomes a fear. You lose confidence in your ability to cope. You don't take action. You don't deal with problems; and when you don't deal with problems you don't move forward with your life. You get stuck in uncertainty, indecision, insecurity, helplessness, negativity, anxiety, stress, unhappiness and depression. You literally worry yourself to despair.

Too much worry is dangerous. But the intention of this book is not to terrify you the minute a worrying thought comes into your mind. The intention is simply to make you aware of how worry can gradually turn your life sour, how a nagging thought can drag you down into unhappiness. But worry can only make you unhappy if you let it. You have the choice.

This is so important I will repeat: *worry can make you unhappy only if you let it. You have the choice. You have the choice.*

No one can escape worry. It is a part of the human condition. We've seen how worry can turn into a deadly force if it is mismanaged. Now in Parts 3 and 4 it is time to explore how you can turn worry into a helpful force in your life, how you can learn to worry well.

Those who are able to deal with worry quickly and effectively generally have successful, happy lives. It sounds like positive thinking. It really is about positive doing — positive living. That skill can't make you instantly happy, but it can increase your chances of happiness.

PART 3
HOPE AND HELP FOR WORRIERS

That the birds of worry and care fly over your head, this
you cannot change.
But that they build nests in your hair, this you can
prevent.

Chinese proverb

CHAPTER 11

FIVE BASIC RULES

Those who do not know how to fight worry die young.
Dr Alexis Carrel

In Parts 1 and 2 of this book we established that worry is common and sometimes necessary, but it can develop into a problem. When cycles of negative thinking, fear, foreboding about the future and lack of confidence in yourself become established they create anxiety, stress, poor health and unhappiness. The longer you let worry last, the harder it becomes to escape. It's crucial that you learn to deal with it quickly and effectively.

But how do you respond to feelings of worry? How do you break the cycle of distress that worry causes?

A number of coping strategies can help you manage worry. They won't stop you worrying completely, but they will help you cope with the unpleasant thoughts and feelings associated with worry and help you deal with situations that worry makes difficult for you. Bear in mind, though, that coping strategies are skills that need to be learned. Some of them won't come naturally, and it will take time to apply them. Developing new skills is rather like learning to ride a bike or drive a car. It takes time and you need to practice until it comes naturally. Much also depends on the extent that you do worry.

If constant worry or nagging fear is holding you back, the advice given in this section will help you manage your worry and anxiety. The self-help approach is an excellent first step and may be all that you need to get back on track. You may, however, find that you need more support. If this is the case, contact your GP or a healthcare professional who can advise you where to go for help.

If you are suffering from GAD, depression, compulsive behaviour, or any condition that warrants medical attention, the self-help techniques may offer relief but they won't be enough to help you take control of the problem. If you have reached a point when worry makes it hard for you to function normally and is destroying your health be sure to see a doctor. Worrying too much can have dangerous consequences. It is vital that you seek help now.

A vast array of worry management techniques and coping skills are available. I have managed to scale the information down to five easy-to-follow steps for you to apply every time you feel anxious and worried.

- Step 1: Recognise you are worried
- Step 2: Understand what you worry about
- Step 3: Find out if you can do anything about what is worrying you
- Step 4: Think about what you can do
- Step 5: Do it!

STEP 1: RECOGNISE YOU ARE WORRIED

You need to be able to recognise worry so that you can deal with it effectively. Remember the more you worry, the unhappier you will get. It is important to act quickly.

Worry can hide in your feelings and in your body. You may not know you are worried. Review some of the worry signals mentioned in Chapter 6. Think about how you feel when you are worried. Do you feel tired, tense or unwell? Do you have problems paying attention? Do you keep thinking about the same worry over and over again? The next time you are worried, make a mental note of how worry makes you feel. Keep a record of the times when you are worried or anxious, and note your physical reactions, your thoughts, your feelings and what you do in response.

The next time you know you are worried, stop, recognise you are worried, and move to Step 2.

Five Basic Rules

STEP 2: UNDERSTAND WHAT YOU WORRY ABOUT
If you don't know what you are worried about, you can't do anything about it. The worry just stays there and gets bigger. Take a deep breath and think carefully about what exactly is worrying you. Write it down if you have to, and move to Step 3.

STEP 3: ASK YOURSELF IF THERE IS ANYTHING YOU CAN DO?
If the answer is 'no', accept that there is nothing you can do and worrying won't help. It will just waste your time and energy and make you feel worse. Let go of the worry. If there is something you can do, move on to Step 4.

STEP 4: THINK ABOUT WHAT YOU CAN DO
There are often things you can do when you worry to ease the situation. You may need to change your attitude, talk to someone, or get help and advice. As soon as you decide on the best course of action, go to Step 5.

STEP 5: DO IT!

> Do not fear going forward slowly
> Fear only to stand still
> Only in growth, reform and change, paradoxically enough, is true security to be found.
>
> *Chinese wisdom*

The best way to stop worrying is to do something about it. This gives you something positive to do with all that energy you are wasting on worry. It helps you feel that you and not worry are in control of your life. It helps you feel that you are strong, confident and ready to cope with anything.

Sounds easy, doesn't it? Until you actually have to apply the rules to your own worries. That's why the next few chapters will explore what you can do about worry in more detail. You'll

117

probably find that the biggest stumbling blocks are Steps 3, 4 and 5. How can you 'let go' of a worry? Worry is a form of fear, and when you fear something you lose a sense of perspective. Making decisions is incredibly hard when worry takes over. Hopefully, the worry management tips that follow will help you 'let go' of worry if you need to or make decisions and move forward with your life.

It's easy to feel overwhelmed when presented with advice, coping skills and techniques so I've kept the information brief, factual and to the point. Everyone worries in their own unique way, so I won't distract with lengthy case histories and examples. All too often these don't really apply to your situation or help you deal with your worry.

Throughout, my aim is to show that conquering worry isn't the impossibly difficult task you may think it is. The last thing you want to be doing is worrying about what to do when you worry! If at any time you start to feel confused or restless return to these basic rules to centre yourself. Remind yourself that at the end of the day it really is very simple to manage worry once you know how.

Chapter 12

WHAT TO DO WHEN WORRY STRIKES

Step 1: Are you worried?

It can sometimes be hard to know if you are worried or not. Chapter 6 showed you how to recognise the warning signs of worry. You might like to refer to it again. Unless you can recognise worry when it strikes, or becomes excessive, you can't really do anything about it.

Now that you know how to recognise worry it's time to change your attitude towards worry. As mentioned in Part 1, worry can be viewed as helpful. Unfortunately, because worry isn't a pleasant reaction and can lead to unhappiness, we tend to treat worry as a problem in itself. But worry is a symptom, not the cause of your problems. The real problem is the person, place, situation or thing that is bothering you in the first place. Worry is simply warning you that you need to take appropriate action to avoid getting hurt.

Think of worry as being to the mind what pain is to the body. If you touch something and it is very hot you drop it or put it down to avoid getting burned. The pain is warning you of potential danger. It's the same with worry. Worry has to be unpleasant and demanding, otherwise you wouldn't do anything about it. Worry alerts you to potentially dangerous situations by reminding you to think things through and solve problems early on.

Start to change the way you think about worry. Remind yourself that worry is letting you know that a problem needs to be faced. In this respect worry can be seen as a very useful response.

If you are not doing what you want with your life, you probably worry a lot. Believe it or not, that may actually be a good thing, something that you can use to your benefit; worry can be a powerful motivator. Whatever you worry about now may serve as the fuel in your quest for change. If your life isn't fulfilling and you aren't worrying, just mindlessly going through the motions then you haven't got the incentive to change. On the other hand if you feel anxious and doubtful then acknowledging that worry can force you to take action. Don't deny, or mask or mislabel worry; use worry to reach for change. Don't rationalise and feel sorry for yourself or decide that you can live with it. Admit you are worried and use that worry to propel yourself out of the situation you are in and get you to where you want to be. The worry that burdens you now can be turned to your advantage. It can be the motivation you need to change your life for the better.

Worry can be dangerous, destructive and damaging but it can also be helpful, useful and healing. It is something you shouldn't fear but take advantage of. The emphasis in this book so far has been to see worry as the enemy. Now it's time to start seeing it in a positive light so that you can move on to the next stage: sorting out what is worrying you.

STEP 2: WHAT ARE YOU WORRIED ABOUT?

Defining what is worrying you may not always be that easy. Worry is telling you that you have a problem, but it won't always tell you exactly what that problem is. Everyday problems can be straightforward or surprisingly complex.

You might find that writing things down helps, or talking things over with friends, family members you trust, or even a counsellor or therapist. Discussing things often helps you define a problem more clearly. Worrying alone often intensifies the worry. Simply talking through a concern you have can help you regain perspective. Remember worries often hide themselves in painful or negative emotions or unpredictable behaviour. You may have to deal with unresolved emotional issues from your past. Try to find out what is really upsetting you.

It might help to keep a mood diary. In order to manage worry you need to monitor it and become familiar with the feelings and behaviours it evokes in you. Paying attention to how you feel is the first step towards understanding why you are feeling a certain way.

WHEN YOU JUST DON'T KNOW WHAT YOU ARE WORRIED ABOUT

As you know, cycles of worry can blow your original fear out of all proportion. A slight pain convinces you that you are going to have a heart attack, stress levels rise, and the thoughts become more alarming, developing into a cycle of distress. Alarming thoughts tend to keep anxiety going, and anxiety tends to increase alarming thoughts. Cycles of distress with no apparent cause or justification become established. You simply don't know what you are worried about anymore.

Remember worries often hide themselves in painful or negative emotions or unpredictable behaviour. Try to find out what is really upsetting you. Sometimes unexplained worry in the present is connected with emotional pain or abuse in the past. You may need the help of a therapist to come to terms with this. Whether or not this is the case, there are ways you can help yourself break cycles of worry and anxiety and we'll explore those later.

STEP 3: ACCEPT THE THINGS YOU CANNOT CHANGE

When you are able to recognise that you are worried ask yourself 'Can I actually do anything about this worry?' If the answer is 'yes' then you can start problem solving and take action. Do whatever you can to make the worry go away. The next chapter will explore this in more detail.

If the answer is 'no' then you are worrying about something you can't do anything about. Worrying doesn't help and it just makes things worse. Worry makes you feel unhappy, stops you getting things done, stops you having fun and can even make you ill. Here are a few examples of things you can't do anything about:

- People you care about getting sick, dying or losing their jobs.
- You yourself dying.
- Natural disasters and accidents.
- Something you did in the past.
- Something that may happen in the future.

If you are worried about something you did in the past, like failing a job interview or going through a divorce, worrying won't help. We all make mistakes. We say and do things we shouldn't. We fail interviews. We hurt people without meaning to. You can't change what you did. The past is over. You can try to make things better, but if nothing can be done it is time to let go and move on. It isn't healthy to worry about what you can't change.

If you are worrying about the future you are wasting your time and energy. You are worrying about things that may never happen. Author Mark Twain once wrote, 'My life has been a series of terrible misfortunes, most of which have never happened.'

Some future events might need your attention but not your worry. You should be concerned about not getting sick, hurt or poor. It's good to plan to avoid these things; to take care of your health; be careful about your safety; apply yourself to get a good job, but worrying without taking any action only makes you feel hopeless.

You can take sensible steps to avoid these dangers, but sometimes they are out of control. Instead of worrying it's more helpful to spend your time and energy on things you can do something about. For instance, it doesn't make sense to spend all your time worrying about being hit by lightning when you could be using that time more productively. Do what you can to keep safe during thunder and lightning, but worrying about it won't stop it happening.

Remind yourself that you are worrying about things that may never happen or won't happen for a long time. Everybody fears dying, but why waste thirty or forty years of life worrying about it? Natural disasters happen, but not every day. Some people get shot, but it is rare.

You may also be wasting energy on worries that you imagine and have no basis in reality. For instance, you wave at an old friend across the street and they look the other way; you may worry that they don't like you anymore. But this may not be the case at all. They simply may not have seen you or have gone out without their glasses.

Choose what you worry about carefully. 'Life is too short to stuff a mushroom.' There just isn't time to worry about everything, so you might as well focus your energies on things you can do something about. Let go of worries that are beyond your control. If you can't try some of the techniques in this book and if they don't help ask your doctor for advice.

WORRY IS A CHOICE

You are the one who chooses what you do and don't worry about. If your worry is something you can't do anything about, it's up to you to let go. If you can't remind yourself that you are opening the door to feeling sad, tired or even sick.

It may seem unfair that one person is healthier, richer and another is poorer and less able bodied. Some people do seem cleverer, more talented and wealthier than others, but they aren't always happier. Happiness is doing the best that you can and enjoying life — no matter where you live, how rich you are, how popular you are or how intelligent you are.

The secret of happiness is letting go of worry that you can't do anything about, living every day to the fullest and enjoying what you do have. Happy people are not people who are rich and beautiful but people who have learned how to worry well.

ARE YOU READY?

You have recognised that you are worried about something. You think you know what the problem is, and you want to take action. But before you move on to Steps 4 and 5 it is important that you consider whether you are physically and emotionally ready.

If you are coming home after a busy day at work and the

children need feeding, bathing and bedtime stories, you are probably not going to think clearly. Recognise that at certain times you are not going to be at your best. Put off problem solving until you are feeling calmer. This will be difficult because worry doesn't like to be put to one side, but there are things you can do.

You can try to focus your attention away from the worry until you feel better able to cope, and you can try relaxing to promote mental and physical tranquillity.

DISTRACTION

'Crowd worry out of your mind by keeping busy' writes Dale Carnegie in *How to Stop Worrying and Start Living*.

It is possible to distract yourself from worrying thoughts and images. This will prevent your anxiety levels increasing. Anything that requires a lot of focused attention and interests you is a distraction. What distracts you may not distract someone else. You may find socialising distracting, whereas another may find the cinema a distraction. Distraction only becomes ineffective when the task isn't stimulating enough to hold your interest. Three of the most effective distraction techniques are keeping active, mental stimulation and paying attention.

Keeping active

One of the best ways to deal with worry is to change your physical state. If you keep active you are less likely to dwell on what is worrying you. Later we'll discuss in more detail the benefits of exercise for worriers, but for now just be aware that any activity that uses up adrenaline that makes you feel tense, like walking, jogging and cycling, is beneficial. It's even better if the activity also involves a lot of concentration.

Disengage from unnecessary worry the minute you feel it wrapping itself around you. You must do this deliberately. Get up, stretch, walk around, call a friend. Do not settle into a brooding mood.

How you keep active will depend on your situation. If you are worried about work, a game of tennis might help you unwind in the evening; if you are worried about an interview, a brisk walk up and down the corridor might help. If you are physically restricted, tidying your desk or tapping your fingers may release tension. Other distractions include dancing, tidying your room, reorganising your diary and so on.

Mental stimulation
Mental stimulation requires a bit more creativity than getting active. To distract yourself from worry you could try imagining a scene to take your mind away from worrying thoughts. You could imagine every detail in that scene. It may be a beach on a beautiful island or the peak of a mountain. You can practise mental arithmetic or studying people as they go about their daily errands. Other mental tasks include recalling a favourite tune in your head, redesigning a house, or recalling a happy day that you had recently.

Paying attention
Distract yourself from worry by really focusing on the task in hand. You could listen to the conversation of people around you, or study the details of someone's clothes, anything that interests you and absorbs your attention.

You might like to use distraction techniques when you feel worried and see how you feel. If it doesn't help it could be because the technique wasn't appropriate to the situation. Soothing music may not be suitable when you are stuck in a traffic jam, but singing along to up tempo music might be.

Distraction techniques can help, but they come with a warning. They don't work for everyone and they can be harmful if the distraction becomes avoidance. For example, if you were worried about being overweight and instead of facing your real worry you distracted yourself by shopping for expensive clothes, you never face your worry and it doesn't go away. It's often the case that those addicted to alcohol or drugs started using the odd drink or odd pill as a form of distraction until the distraction becomes a dangerous addiction.

RELAXATION

Being too stressed or wound up will affect your ability to solve problems. Put off problem solving until you feel calmer. You can do this by practising certain relaxation techniques.

Relaxation is the time when you recharge your batteries and focus on what makes you feel good. Unfortunately, many worriers tend to neglect setting aside time and space for themselves. Many find it impossible to relax at all.

When you worry, the muscles in your body tense and muscular tension creates unpleasant sensations such as headaches, tightness in the chest, difficulty breathing, churning in the stomach and difficulty swallowing. These sensations trigger more tension, and a vicious cycle is set up.

It is important to learn how to relax in response to bodily tension. You may be able to do this by watching a movie, reading a book, listening to music or playing an instrument, but if you can't relax, you need to learn how to take time out. One way to do this is to relax your whole body slowly, muscle by muscle. Start by dropping your shoulders, relaxing the muscles in your body and in your face — it's amazing how many of us frown without knowing it — breathing deeply and gently relaxing. There are many tapes on the market that can help you through the process. You could also try counting to ten before you react, or repeat some positive affirmation to yourself like 'I am in control'.

Techniques like meditation and yoga can also have astonishing results if you are stressed and tense. Try this simple routine: choose a focus word or phrase, for example, 'peace' or 'happy'. Sit quietly, and relax your body by tensing and then relaxing your muscles and breathing deeply. Say the focus word every time you exhale. If you lose concentration, simply return your thoughts to the word. Try this for just five minutes at first, and then gradually increase the amount of time. Do the routine at least once a day.

Don't expect relaxation to be easy. Relaxing for some of us is a skill that has to be practised. You may feel peculiar or uncomfortable at first if you are used to tension. Don't worry about this; just accept that it will take time before you feel comfortable. Make sure that you are breathing deeply and not practising when you are hungry, full or overtired. Make your environment conducive to relaxation. If you get a cramp, ease the tension by rubbing the painful area gently. If you fall asleep easily, you might want to avoid lying down.

Expect your realisation to be interrupted by worrying thoughts. The best way to deal with them is not to dwell on them. Just accept that they will drift into your mind from time to time, and then refocus on your relaxation.

If you don't feel the benefit straight away, don't give up or try too hard. Just let the sensation of relaxation happen. Correct breathing will help.

Correct breathing

Deep, slow breathing through the nose rather than the mouth, allowing your abdomen to move, can calm both body and mind and help you cope with stress. Simple yoga breathing exercises, for example, breathing in slowly through the nose while counting to five, holding your breath for a count of five, breathing out slowly through the nose for a count of five, waiting a count of five and repeating as often as you like, may also help. Concentrating on breathing and counting can be wonderfully calming for your mind, while the regular breathing will calm the body.

When you are stressed or worried you may hyperventilate or breathe rapidly. This rapid breathing is a natural response to stress or exertion. It uses the upper part of the lungs and results in too much oxygen intake.

Everyone hyperventilates when they are tense or are exercising. We breathe faster to give our muscles oxygen for increased activity to relieve the stress. Rapid breathing isn't a problem if it is short term, but it is if it becomes habitual. It results in too much oxygen being taking into the bloodstream upsetting the oxygen–carbon monoxide balance and causing unpleasant physical symptoms such as tingling hands or face, muscle cramps, dizziness, fatigue and aches and pains. These symptoms can be quite alarming, and they can trigger another cycle of stress.

It is easy to learn how to breathe correctly when you are anxious. Avoid breathing from your upper chest, and avoid gulping or gasping. When you first try to breathe correctly you might want to lie down to feel the difference between deep breathing and shallow breathing.

First exhale as much as you can. Then inhale gently and evenly through your nose, filling your lungs completely so that your abdominal muscles move outward. Then exhaling slowly and fully. Repeat this, trying to get a rhythm going. You might want to aim to take ten breaths a minute. If you are not getting enough air, return to breathing that is normal for you. Then try increasing the length of one breath, breathing out fully, then in fully, then out again. If that breath felt comfortable, try another one. To get a rhythm going it's important not to try hard but to co-operate as easily as you can with your breathing muscles.

It is important to practice correct breathing every time you feel worried or anxious. As you practise you will find that it gets easier to breathe deeply instead of rapidly.

Distraction and relaxation are techniques you can use to deal with worry. But they won't usually make worry go away. That isn't their function. Their purpose is to help give you an opportunity to think and plan more productively. If you are tense with worry this will affect your ability to solve problems. Relaxation and distraction help you put things in perspective. They help you feel better so that you are ready for the fourth step in worry management: deciding what to do.

CHAPTER 13

MAKING A DECISION

We noted in Part 1 that worriers tend to have problems with Steps 4 and 5 of worry management — making decisions and taking action. In this chapter we'll discuss how to devise a solution to your dilemma rather than panicking about it.

STEP 4: PROBLEM SOLVING

There are several stages in decision making and problem solving. First of all, find out what is worrying you and whether or not it is something you can do something about. Only try to solve the problems that you have a chance of solving.

Be as specific about your worries as you can. If you have lots of worries the best thing to do is to tackle them one at a time. Putting certain worries on hold will be difficult, because the whole purpose of worry is to capture your attention, but you can't deal with everything at once, and solving one worry at a time will make you feel less stressed.

The second stage is listing as many ways as you can of dealing with the worry. At this stage you need to give yourself as much choice as possible. The more choice you have, the more chance you have of selecting a way of coping that is right for you. This is also called brainstorming. List as many solutions as you can even if they seem far-fetched. Suspend your judgment and all the reasons why this or that isn't a good solution, and let those ideas come. When you've listed as many solutions as you can, even the trivial and outrageous ones, it's time to make a decision.

DECIDING WHAT TO DO

It might be helpful to list all the pros and cons associated with a solution. Making a list of all the good and bad consequences helps

129

you clarify issues and consequences associated with a particular decision. For example, if you can't make up your mind to apply for a job, the pros could be that you get the job, gain interview experience and so on. The cons could be that you don't get the job and your employer finds out.

When choosing between options, you need to ask yourself what do you really want to happen. Remember your real needs aren't always easy to recognise. You may want something, but you may also feel that others expect something of you. You may have taken ideas and values on board that don't really reflect who you are. It is important when you make a decision that it reflects what you want and not what others expect of you.

When you consider an option think if this is what you want to do. Or is it what your partner, your family or your friends want you to do. For instance, do you really want the job you are applying for? If you are always thinking in terms of should and ought, start thinking in terms of what you want or, better still, what is in everybody's best interests, including your own. Are you acting according to your own feelings or someone else's?

Once you become more attuned to your own feelings and what you want, life gets a lot easier. You start doing what you feel is right and not what others feel is right for you. You start considering choices you previously wouldn't have considered.

DON'T SET UNREALISTIC GOALS

Earlier I suggested that when you think of solutions to a problem that you list as many choices as you can, even ones that seem impossible or unrealistic. This was suggested to help you think up as many solutions as possible and to stop you thinking that there isn't an answer. However once you have thought of a number of coping strategies it is time to use your common sense. Don't try to solve a problem in a way that isn't suited to your abilities; we all have limitations. Problems often test our limitations.

If you set unrealistic goals you set yourself up for failure and unhappiness. Sometimes in a strange way failure is reassuring. It makes the world less unpredictable, and if you know you are going to fail you can use your incompetence or hopelessness as an excuse or a way of getting other people to solve a problem for you. So be careful. Don't try to solve a problem that needs skills you don't have or can't acquire. Ask for help if you need it.

If you keep approaching a problem in a way that has failed for you in the past, then try to change your approach and think about whether the solution you are choosing suits the demands of the coping strategy you have selected.

STEP 5: PUTTING A SOLUTION INTO PRACTICE

In very specific and concrete ways, decide what will be done, how it will be done, when it will be done, where it will be done, who is involved and what your back-up plan is if something goes wrong. For instance, you may decide that you do really want to change job and you are going to apply for it. You decide not to tell your employer unless you get the job. If possible, rehearse in role-play or imagination the chosen solution. Now you are ready to move to the final stage: putting your solution into action.

Make sure you are well prepared and try out your solution. Whether or not the solution is successful, review it and see what you can learn from the experience.

If your solution worked, congratulate yourself. You may, for example, be offered the job of your dreams. Perhaps you might like to treat yourself. If you aren't used to treating yourself, think about something you would like and indulge yourself. The important thing is to acknowledge your successes. Also make time to think about why your solution worked and what you can learn about your strengths and weaknesses from it.

If your solution didn't work, don't torture yourself with worry and anxiety. Try to understand why it didn't work. Say you didn't get offered the job you wanted; perhaps you just didn't have enough experience. Perhaps you didn't take something into account. Perhaps you weren't feeling strong that day; perhaps you misinterpreted something; or perhaps you didn't have a back-up plan or were not prepared enough.

Whatever conclusion you reach, remind yourself that you have not failed. Congratulate yourself for having the courage to try. Learn as much as you can from the experience and with the knowledge that you have gained select another solution and try again. The more solutions you try, the more you will learn and the better equipped you will be to deal with the situation.

It really isn't the end of the world if your coping strategy failed. You can always try another one or go back to the beginning and define the problem again. Don't be discouraged by setbacks. One setback doesn't mean you will always fail. It just means that you need to have a rethink. It's impossible to know what will happen in the future. Treat each attempt to solve a problem as if it is the first, however long it takes.

WHAT IF I MAKE THE WRONG DECISION?

Worriers are terrified of making mistakes; that's often the reason why you get stuck in worry. What if I do the wrong thing?

No one likes to make mistakes but it is impossible to go through life without making them. In fact the most successful people are often the ones who make the most mistakes. A large part of their success is that they don't view mistakes as failures but as learning experiences. Getting it wrong adds to their store of knowledge and is a step on the way to getting it right. They understand that you can't always know what is right and sometimes you just have to take a risk. If things don't work out they find out what went wrong, learn from the experience and try again.

If you are terrified of getting things wrong, make sure you read Joey Green's excellent, *The Road to Success is Paved with Failure*, highlighting hundreds of famous people who triumphed over inauspicious beginnings, crushing rejections, humiliating defeats and other speed bumps along life's highway. Next time you are paralysed by fear of doing the wrong thing, think carefully through all the issues and make the best decision that you can. If things don't work out as planned give yourself a pat on the back for having the courage to take action. Learn from your mistake and carefully consider what your next move will be. Above all remember that it's okay to get it wrong sometimes. Making mistakes doesn't mean you are a failure or that disaster will strike. It just means that you are experimenting with the options available to find the best solution.

Personal success is not about banishing worry, frustration and disappointment. A huge part of mastering personal success is learning how to cope with negative feelings and experiences. It is about experiencing the good and the bad. Mistakes, setbacks and disappointments are part of life and an important part of how we learn and grow. The main difference between those who succeed in life and those who don't is that they learn from their mistakes and know how to make the best of them.

So next time worry puts your life on hold and freezes you in fear and indecision don't let fear of making a mistake stop you from living, learning and growing.

WHAT IF I CAN'T MAKE A DECISION QUICKLY?

If your problem is immediate, the problem solving approach may work but you may find that you simply can't make a decision.

As discussed in Part 1, worry fills the time between realising there is a problem and doing something about it. The longer you postpone decisions, the more you worry. If you have a tendency to worry you will probably be very cautious and find it hard to make a decision about what to do, with the result that you do nothing.

Of course, hasty decisions are a bad idea, but the problem solving approach recommended above advises defining a problem carefully and considering all the pros and cons. This isn't being hasty. Unfortunately, though, some worriers are so intent on making sure that they are absolutely right that they are paralysed by indecision. You may find that you go over the same things repeatedly in an effort to be sure you are one hundred per cent right.

Unfortunately, it is impossible to predict the future. You cannot ever know if you are going to be right. All you can do is choose the best course of action to the best of your knowledge. All decisions have an element of risk in them, even ones that seem secure. You could get out of bed in the morning and strain your back. You could cross a road and get hit by a vehicle you didn't see.

Sometimes there isn't enough evidence to make it certain that a particular solution is the right one. If you are paralysed with indecision on a regular basis, it is time to start becoming accustomed to taking sensible risks. You can't tell for sure what will happen, but life experience and common sense will give you a pretty good idea. Start by making decisions about things that aren't too serious. For instance, there are two coats you like in a shop, but you only want one. Don't agonise for ages; just weigh up the pros and cons and make a decision. Even if in hindsight you make the wrong choice this isn't the end of the world. Does it really matter? You could always buy the other coat another time.

After you have practised with smaller decisions, move on to harder ones. Each time a decision needs to be made, remind yourself:

- Worry is a natural reaction to a possible problem.
- Decision making isn't always followed by catastrophe.
- The quicker you deal with the problem the less time you will spend worrying.
- You can't be one hundred per cent certain of anything.
- If you have thought about a problem, evaluated the pros and cons, and considered what is in everyone's best interests, including your own, you are not being hasty.

WILL MAKING DECISIONS STOP ME WORRYING?

> Once men are caught up in an event they cease to be afraid
> Only the unknown frightens men.
>
> *Antoine de Saint-Exupéry*

Doing is far less frightening than worrying about doing. When you worry you get stuck in indecision. Fear of making the wrong decision makes it impossible to act at all. The problem remains and the worry intensifies. Yet, when you start doing something about your problems you will find that you start to worry less about them. Your energy is tied up in action and not in worry.

Hopefully, in time decision making will become easier and the association with worry and tension will break down. Put another way, you will be replacing an unhelpful habit with a helpful one. Do remember though that to get to the point where worry followed by decision making becomes automatic that you need to practice, practice and practice. Treat even the most minor worry as an opportunity to engage in decision making.

In the past worry may have been associated with anxiety, sleepless nights and poor concentration. It is time now for you to break these associations. When you worry, think of it as a helpful signal telling you that something isn't quite right. Try to associate worry not with anxiety but with decision making.

But sometimes, however hard you try, you can't make a decision. Everyone makes mistakes. You might misunderstand what the problem is. You might choose the wrong coping strategy or try to solve a problem that can't be solved. When this happens it's easy to think that you are inadequate or have failed. Worry once again paralyses you in inaction and indecision. Negative thinking sets in.

If this applies to you, you need to try a different means of thought management. You need to challenge negative thoughts that make you want to give up or not even start at all.

CHAPTER 14

CHALLENGING NEGATIVE THOUGHTS

Men are disturbed not by things,
but by the view
which they take of them.

Epictetus

The mind is its own place,
and in itself can make
a Heav'n of Hell,
or a Hell of Heav'n.

John Milton, Paradise Lost

Our best friends
and our worst enemies
are our thoughts.
A thought can do us more good
than a doctor or a banker
or a faithful friend.
It can also do us more harm than a brick.

Dr. Frank Crane

If you have problems with Steps 3, 4 and 5 the chances are negative thinking is blocking your attempts to manage worry. In this chapter you'll learn ways to challenge negative thinking.

Although it's impossible to say what makes you feel a certain way, it is possible to suggest that your thoughts are closely related to your feelings. Try this little exercise. Think of a time in your life when you enjoyed yourself. It may have been a holiday, a trip to the park or the seaside. As you think about that time you may feel a little happier. Now think of a time when you were sad, like a funeral, and you will probably feel quite down. The way you think can change your mood for the better or worse. It can also affect the amount that you worry.

NEGATIVE THOUGHTS

We have already seen how worriers have a tendency to be more pessimistic. The glass is half empty and not half full. Worriers are often extremely negative about themselves and about the world. Many have low self-esteem and lack confidence in themselves.

It's hard to tell if negative thinking makes people worry or if worry makes people pessimistic. It's easy to see, though, how closely related the two are and how they set up a vicious cycle of despair. If you see only bad outcomes the future is depressing, and if you are feeling down then even minor irritations become major catastrophes.

If you think bad thoughts this is going to make you feel bad. When you only see disaster ahead thoughts like 'I'm useless' or 'I can't cope', start to become ingrained. Think negatively for long enough, and you may not even be aware that you are doing it anymore. You feel unhappy but don't realise the relationship between your thought processes and your mood.

Becoming aware of how your thoughts are affecting your feelings can be a big step forward. Once you start to recognise negative thought patterns you can start to replace them with other thoughts. Changing your thoughts can change your life and this is the basis of a kind of treatment called cognitive therapy.

Cognitive therapy is often used by people suffering from depression, but many of its techniques can be used with great success by people who worry too much. Research shows that cognitive therapy can help a person to take a less negative point of view and therefore be better able to make decisions and deal with problems.

You may argue that this just isn't realistic. You'd like to be more positive, but sometimes negative thoughts and outcomes are accurate. This may have a grain of truth in it. It's unrealistic to expect positive outcomes to everything; you set yourself up for disappointment.

Moreover psychologists and psychiatrists have shown that worriers are often biased towards anything that is negative. They also don't always get their facts right. Negative thinkers don't often question the accuracy of their thoughts. They tend to believe that what they think is the truth, but on many occasions it simply isn't. The next time you are negative about something, ask yourself if you are seeing all sides of the picture. Try to distinguish between a negative view that is realistic and a negative view that is misleading or doesn't take into account other possibilities.

Don't always believe everything you think. Question it. You don't always believe the things other people tell you, or what you read in the papers, so why accept everything your thoughts tell you? It's incredible how many inaccuracies are revealed when you start challenging negative thinking.

You don't have to replace negative thoughts with positive ones simply more appropriate ones. Positive thinking can be as unhelpful and as unrealistic as negative thinking. Always looking on the bright side when things are clearly falling apart around you won't do you any good at all.

Negative thoughts need to be replaced with more realistic ones, but fortunately realistic thoughts are much more optimistic than negative ones. Realistic thoughts take into account the negative, but they also take into account the positive. For example, saying to yourself, 'They didn't want me for the job, I'll never get another job', can be replaced by 'I could get the job but if I'm not right for it there are other jobs I can apply for'.

When negative thoughts start to appear evaluate them carefully. Don't treat them automatically as facts because you are thinking them. Most of the time they are inaccurate, misleading and unrealistic.

Every time you get a negative, worrying thought, try to

challenge it rationally and replace it with more realistic thoughts. The trick is to recognise when you have a worrying thought and to ask yourself, 'Am I being realistic?' If you aren't being realistic you need to replace it with something more constructive.

We've already seen how worry distresses us and gets us caught up in a cycle of anxiety, stress and more worry. Challenging negative thinking can interrupt this cycle of tension by lessening the impact of the worry.

When you feel worried, ask yourself what is going through your mind. It may be something like 'I'm worried I will look stupid,' or 'I'm worried that I may get ill'.

Now you need to look out for typical negative thought patterns, most of which are listed below, and start challenging them.

I'VE FAILED

If there is a person alive who never makes a mistake I don't think I would like to meet that person; they must be very boring indeed. Everyone makes mistakes. In fact, the most interesting, exceptional people are the ones who make the most. The only way to learn about your strengths and your weaknesses is to make mistakes. Making mistakes builds character.

Negative thinking can really handicap you when you are trying to achieve a new goal or solve a problem. Every mistake you make will be interpreted as a failure and proof of your inadequacy. Of course failures can be devastating, but they can also help you grow and learn about yourself. You can gain something from every experience, however disappointing. Seen in that light, there is no such thing as a failure.

Rather than labelling your mistakes as failures, try to view them as setbacks or learning experiences. This is less final than failure. Think in terms of temporary setbacks, which add to your store of knowledge, whenever you feel disappointed or let down. That way you will feel less inclined to give up and more willing to try again.

ALL OR NOTHING

I'm never going to get this right, so why should I bother?

Negative thinkers often see life in very black or white terms. Something is either totally good or totally bad. If something isn't perfect or done to the highest standards then it isn't worth doing. This kind of thinking sets you up for disappointment and heartache. It is impossible to do something perfectly, especially if you have only made a few attempts at it. There will always be room for improvement, however brilliant you are.

You may think, what's the point, if I'm never going to be one hundred per cent right or the best at what I do? The point is that there are a lot of advantages to learning new skills. There are great rewards through getting better at something; just because you aren't perfect at something doesn't mean that you can't do it well and get lots of satisfaction from it.

If you catch yourself thinking in all-or-nothing terms, try to challenge the negative thinking by seeing the advantages in your situation. Don't overlook degree or compromise. Tell yourself, 'I didn't get it quite right, but I am getting better all the time.'

THAT'S IT, I CAN'T DO IT

Negative thinkers often tend to think that if something has gone wrong once it will always go wrong.

- You have a bad day at work and you decide that you aren't good at your job.
- You have an argument with your partner and decide the relationship is in crisis.

Everywhere you turn there are examples of setbacks leading to success. Walt Disney, Steven Spielberg and J. K. Rowling are just a few examples of people whose ideas were initially rejected but who eventually achieved spectacular success. Sometimes when you are tuning into a radio station you get the wrong wavelength, but you keep fiddling with the tuner until you get the quality of reception that you want. Persistent effort pays off; just because you didn't get the radio station the first time didn't mean that you would never get it.

If you are prone to generalisation and sweeping conclusions whenever you have a setback, you need to start challenging your thought patterns.

- Just because you had a bad day at work doesn't mean you can't do your job.
- One argument does not mean that you need to head for the divorce courts.

Don't let yesterday's or today's disappointments stop you from succeeding tomorrow. Nobody knows what the future holds. Just because you had a setback doesn't mean things won't work out again later. If something minor goes wrong, this doesn't mean disaster will strike. Tell yourself, 'It didn't happen today but tomorrow is another day.'

IT'S MY FAULT

Humankind is always trying to explain why things happen. If things don't work out we want to find someone to blame. Worriers tend to blame themselves.

It's often the case when something like a natural disaster or a terrible accident occurs that a number of things contribute. It can be hard to point the finger of blame at just one thing. It's the same for our personal lives. When something goes wrong there are usually a number of reasons why it went wrong. Some of these things may have been out of our control.

If you have a tendency to blame yourself when things go wrong, closely examine the circumstances that led to the setback. Some of these may have had nothing to do with you.

If you feel you let yourself down at a job interview, try to think why. Maybe you weren't prepared enough, or maybe you had just been ill and were feeling tired. Is that your fault? Perhaps you just were not right for the job; that isn't your fault either. Perhaps you were right for the job, but need to work on certain skills or gain more experience. Use the interview as a learning experience, and improve your skill base.

Don't try to accept blame for things that are out of your control. Don't concentrate solely on your weaknesses, forgetting the positive aspects and signs of your strengths. When things go wrong, get out of the habit of saying it's your fault because you aren't good enough. Even if you do make mistakes, this doesn't make you worthless. Try to replace blaming thoughts with encouraging ones; 'This didn't work out, but how was I to know this or that would happen?' It is impossible for you to be in control of all the factors that create a situation.

FORTUNE TELLING!

Some things are likely to happen. The sun will rise in the morning and set in the evening. At night the moon and stars will come out. But there is no such thing as complete certainty. The world probably won't, but it could, end tomorrow!

When you worry and start to see only the negative you lose a sense of perspective. You also forget that you are only human. You can't see into the future. How do you know that things are going to go horribly wrong?

If you are prone to negative thinking it's likely that your predictions favour negative outcomes. You are also likely to treat these negative outcomes as facts. But nobody can tell what the future holds. It is unlikely that everything will turn out unpleasant all the time. Your predictions are unrealistic and biased.

If you keep searching the future for things you fear, start challenging that thinking now. How do you know? If you think you know what other people are thinking, question that assumption. You can never know what someone else is thinking. You can only guess.

It's more realistic to think that unpleasant things may or may not happen. It's more appropriate to conclude that someone is likely to think this but you are not a mind reader. Things may turn out wrong, but they may also turn out right. Start allowing yourself the possibility that things may go right. Get rid of over-the-top pessimism.

If you have a tendency to think the worst of yourself and other people, take a deep breath and think about the evidence for and against your forecast. It's probably biased towards the negative. Start replacing negative assumptions with more realistic ones; 'I keep thinking I'll never do well, but how can I tell what will happen in the future?'

WHO CARES!

This is perhaps the most difficult attitude to shift. You reach a point when you can't see any meaning anymore. You are tempted to give up. Sometimes despondency takes over and it can be hard to challenge worrying and troublesome thoughts. If you are unable to challenge them it may be time to seek advice from your doctor.

Life is full of disappointment and futility only if you think it is. Negative thinking can be very discouraging, and you will often feel like giving up. But if you can challenge negative thoughts as much as you can by looking for facts to disprove them, you will start to learn that negative thinking doesn't only make you feel unhappy, it is also misleading and inaccurate.

FINDING AN ALTERNATIVE WAY TO THINK

When you start becoming more familiar with your thinking biases, you can challenge them in the ways suggested above. The aim is to determine how real your worry is and to help you generate an alternative way to think.

Think about what is really upsetting you. Then focus on the reasons that can challenge your negative thinking. Remember worriers tend to misinterpret data in everyday life and lose perspective. Are you being realistic?

It might help to think about the worst thing that could happen. If you imagine that and prepare yourself mentally for the worst anything else won't seem quite so bad. Start improving on the worst scenario, and think of other more positive outcomes. Think about your strengths as well as how others can help you cope.

Once again it all sounds so simple, but in practice you may find it harder than you think. As stressed before, the key is practice. You are learning a new skill. You are learning to talk to yourself in a reassuring and supportive way.

You might find it hard to challenge worrying thoughts when you are in the anxiety-provoking situation yourself. If that's the case, keep a mood diary and when you feel less tense think about how you might have challenged your worry. In time you can progress to challenging your thoughts as they actually happen.

Remember you will have good and bad days. You may find it hard to challenge negative thinking on some days. If that's the case, don't worry about that too. Distract yourself and return to thinking of a more realistic response to your worries when you feel more relaxed.

Your irrational fears aren't used to being challenged. Keep practising, and in time it will become second nature to challenge them. You will start recognising when you are losing perspective and seeing only the negative and unnecessary worry will soon diminish.

One day negative thoughts won't seem so compelling anymore; they may even start to seem slightly ridiculous!

Chapter 15

TECHNIQUES THAT WORK

The previous chapters have outlined the basic steps of worry control. Step 1 focused on changing your attitude towards worry, and recognising that you are worried. Step 2 focused on defining what you are worried about. Step 3 focused on thinking about whether there is anything you can do about your worry. Steps 4 and 5 focused on decision making, taking action and challenging negative thinking by talking to yourself in a constructive way. In the next two chapters we are going to look at additional techniques that can help you manage worry.

IMPROVING SELF-ESTEEM

The dictionary defines confidence as a feeling of reliance or certainty, a sense of self-reliance. The word is derived from the Latin *confido* — to put faith or trust in someone. Confidence means we put faith and trust in ourselves. Worry eats away at your self-confidence. If you constantly think that you aren't good enough, sooner or later you will start to believe you aren't good enough.

People with low self-esteem often have problems communicating their needs, feelings and rights to others. They often don't feel that they can ask for what they want. It's hard for them to say no without feeling guilty. They don't recognise that it is okay to have opinions, make mistakes, make decisions, be successful, be unsuccessful, change their mind, be independent or need personal space. They worry a lot.

Improving self-esteem is an important skill that can help you conquer worry, fear and anxiety.

As we saw in Part 2 worry can destroy self-esteem. Thinking

negatively about yourself and your abilities can be a source of anxiety. Improving your self-esteem isn't easy. It may be a painful and difficult task especially if low self-esteem is caused by deep-seated emotional hurt. But when you have the confidence to achieve your full potential, the rewards are immense.

Apart from challenging negative thinking discussed in the last chapter there are three main areas that are particularly useful for people who want to improve self-esteem: assertiveness, emotional confidence and stress management.

BECOMING MORE ASSERTIVE

In learning to be more assertive you learn to communicate what you want or believe to others in a manner that is respectful of yourself and of them. This doesn't mean opting out of conflict and taking a passive approach, or being loud, aggressive and overpowering, or being manipulative, devious and undermining. It means seeing all sides of the situation and recognising your needs and the needs of the others. It means taking responsibility for your actions, keeping physically and mentally calm and being respectful to others.

The goal of assertiveness is to confront without undermining yourself or others. The assertive person needs to know what they want, to decide if what they want is fair to everyone concerned, and to ask for it clearly and calmly.

It is easier to be assertive if you are relaxed, calm and well prepared. Stress, anxiety and worry will undermine your ability to be assertive. It helps to be as encouraging and positive as you can when you are trying to get your point across. Objectivity is important for keeping calm and focused. Keep your request brief and don't get personal. Say how a person's behaviour or actions have affected you, not how that person has affected you. You also need to be able to handle criticism.

Criticism can come in many forms, but the basic intention is the same: to undermine you in some way. To deal with this you need to develop skills that help you stand your ground. One of these is not to take no for an answer. Repeat your message, however persistent or manipulative the other person gets, until they have heard what you say and agreed to negotiate with you. Another way is to acknowledge that there may be an element of truth in the criticism but follow that up with an assertion of your viewpoint; 'I understand what you are saying but I still feel ....' You may also decide to agree with the criticism depending on the nature of it or actively encourage it to find out whether your critic is being truthful or manipulative.

The goal of assertion is not to win or make someone agree with you, but to find a solution that suits everyone. This will involve a certain amount of compromise and negotiation. Negotiation gets easier if you really try to listen and understand what the other party is saying; avoid nerves by being prepared and keeping calm. Don't criticise the other party; keep to the point being discussed and be prepared to compromise, take risks or back down if you have to.

Like every other worry management technique mentioned in this book, assertiveness is a skill that improves with practice and training. Start with little things, like making sure the food you order in a restaurant is prepared the way you like it, and move on to more important things. You might find that a class helps you learn assertive skills more successfully. Look for assertiveness training classes in your area.

EMOTIONAL CONFIDENCE

Emotional confidence is a particularly important part of self-confidence. It is the ability to be fully in charge of your feelings and to express the full range of emotions without worrying that you will lose control. It is expressing your feelings appropriately and responding sensitively to the feelings of others. If you were emotionally confident you wouldn't say things like:

> I don't know what I feel.
> I don't know what came over me.
> I couldn't stop myself.
> I don't know what's happened to me.

If your feelings are not 'making' you act in ways that run counter to your values, self-esteem will improve and you will have a firmer sense of your own identity because you are more consistent in the way you react and behave. Because you are aware of the influence your feelings have on your reason, you will find it easier to make decisions. You will also have more chances for success and happiness because you can see the opportunities rather than the problems that come into your life.

Rock-solid emotional confidence is an impossible ideal but there are actions you can take to improve the way you handle your emotions. The first is by becoming more aware of your feelings and why you have them.

Many of us find it hard to understand or feel our emotions properly. It is not always easy to trust our emotions. Sometimes they seem so illogical, and we have been conditioned to delay or deny their expression. Yet the very nature of our emotions is to be illogical. Sometimes, for instance, you just need to cry. Worry can be a form of pent up tension and sadness. Instead of questioning and denying, we should simply allow ourselves to feel what our body and mind want us to feel; just let worry go in a torrent of tears.

You may find it painful to express your emotions, but feelings, including the so-called negative ones, such as anger, fear and sadness, will lead to improved mental and physical health. This is not to say that we should act on them all the time, but you should acknowledge that these emotions exist in order to alert you to an area of discomfort in your life. When emotions are not felt, they cause even greater stress. When they are bottled up they affect your whole body, especially the immune system, because you are not allowing yourself to feel what is true for you. Emotions are messages that come from your inner wisdom. If they are not worked through, the biochemical effect of suppressed emotions may cause physical and emotional problems.

Crying and laughing, feeling and expressing emotions, is the only real way we have to acknowledge that our life matters to us. Feeling our emotions shows us how important our life is to us and how important it should be to those around us. Sometimes these emotions will cause pain and distress, but difficult emotions also signal the need for some kind of change in our lives. They require us to act, to change the situation or mindset that is causing distress, to move on with our lives. Negative emotions are not bad emotions; they are necessary for us to grow and develop.

Reconnecting with your emotions won't be easy if you have been used to denying or suppressing them, but it is important that you do start to become more aware of what you are feeling. Once again a mood diary might help. Whenever you feel happy, sad, anxious, angry or simply confused, write it down.

Once you have become more aware of your feelings and allowed yourself to feel them, it's time to try and deal with them. Understanding why you are feeling a certain way may help, but also accept that sometimes you simply don't know why you feel the way you do.

If you find that your feelings start to get in the way of your doing what you want to do with your life, or being the kind of person you want to be, it is time to take positive action instead of continuing to remain helplessly dependent on your feelings.

Managing your emotions is a book in itself, so this section is by necessity brief. When you begin to notice that your emotions are hurting you or someone else, remind yourself that you are in charge of your feelings. Your feelings are not in control of you. Try the following simple strategies.

Accept

The first step in managing emotions is to accept what you are feeling and to take responsibility for it, even if that feeling is troublesome or embarrassing.

Choice

The next step is to choose how you respond to that emotion. In many cases you may wish to use a strategy to induce a state of calm within yourself. That way, when you act, you are acting out of your whole self rather than just out of the emotion.

Manage

Finally you need to manage the destructive habit that encourages your feelings to overwhelm and confuse you. Throughout the process remind yourself that managing your feelings can only enrich your experience of life. Feeling something is far preferable to feeling nothing at all.

But before we move on let's look at specific feelings that, when they are too intense, have the potential to be troublesome. Instead of getting depressed when you feel these emotions, here are some suggestions for taking positive action. You may be able to do this alone, with the support of family and friends, or you may need the guidance of a therapist.

CONFUSION

When you feel confused you don't know what you are feeling. You may find yourself reacting inappropriately in certain situations and not understanding why. For example, a traffic jam may make you feel wild with anger, or a sad film may plunge you into the depths of sadness. Here are a few suggestions to help you cope:

- Recognise that emotional confusion can be caused by inappropriate feelings from the past leaking into your present situation. For instance, if your first partner was unfaithful you may become extremely jealous of your current partner even if they are giving you no cause.
- Explore emotional pain from your past. Think about how your upbringing or past experiences may be affecting you.
- Understand that you may not see clearly in the present, if a feeling from an unhealed wound is echoed in the present. For example, if someone you trusted abused you, you may have problems trusting anyone again.
- Recognise that you may not be able to heal every emotional wound, but you can choose how much it will control your life.

Some hurts cut so deep they seem to permanently scar us. Yet it is possible to reach a stage where that hurt doesn't undermine your confidence anymore.

SADNESS AND DISAPPOINTMENT

When you feel sad or disappointed life does seem to turn a shade of grey. It's hard to get enthusiastic about things and find motivation. When sadness strikes the following strategies might help:

- Determine the cause if you can.
- Release some of the feelings; basically, have a good cry!
- Comfort yourself, and/or accept the support and comfort of others.
- Get a sense of perspective and try to salvage a positive aspect from the experience.
- If you can, find a constructive way to use the experience of your hurt to benefit yourself or others.
- If you can, forgive who or what was responsible for the hurt, even if it was you, and put the hurt firmly behind you.
- If the feelings of sadness become too overwhelming, seek medical advice.

GUILT

Guilt can be overwhelming at times. Life isn't about being who you are and doing what you want to do, it is about 'shoulds' and 'oughts'. When you feel guilty:

- Think about the values you have inherited from your past and which ones are likely to trigger episodes of guilt.
- Think about what your values are, not those of others.
- Keep your assertiveness skills going so that you can defend those values.
- Keep a sense of perspective.
- Be realistic about your own skills.

- Learn from your mistakes.
- If you hurt someone, make amends if you can.
- Get support from those that respect and value you, for who you are, not what you do.

SHAME

When you feel ashamed you feel bad about yourself and when you feel bad about yourself it is impossible to feel content. The following may help:

- Acknowledge emotional wounds from the past.
- Feed your self-esteem with self-nurturing or by helping others.
- Stop putting yourself down.
- Focus on your strengths, not your weaknesses.
- Accept support from others who respect and value you and accept you for the way you are.
- Be yourself.
- Think about what you want.

ANGER

Sometimes it is important to feel anger but when anger gets out of hand it can become dangerous and destructive. To avoid this:

- Deal promptly with minor threats so that tension doesn't build up.
- Think about what is worth getting angry about and what isn't.
- Understand what triggers episodes of anger, and make a plan to counteract that.
- Boost your self-esteem so that you aren't vulnerable to attack.
- Practice stress management techniques.
- Find an activity that releases pent-up tension, like sport or gardening.
- Find a way to channel your anger, like studying or starting a new hobby.

- Pay attention to your social support network.
- If you did lose your cool reflect on what went wrong and how you could behave differently next time.

FEAR

Fear is one of the most limiting emotions. It stops you doing what you want with your life. When fear threatens to become overwhelming:

- Practice correct breathing and stress management techniques.
- Talk to yourself in a constructive, positive way.
- Work through fear in small, manageable steps.
- Rehearse before going into stressful situations so that you are mentally prepared.
- Imagine yourself being calm, and bring that image to your mind.

JEALOUSY

Wanting other people to behave in a certain way can poison relationships. If you catch yourself feeling jealous the following might help:

- Don't constantly analyse your relationships; try to enjoy being in them.
- If you do get rejected, take time to heal and don't blame yourself.
- Keep your life outside your relationships full and satisfying to promote your self-esteem
- Keep making new friends.
- Learn to value the importance of personal space and solitude.

ENVY

Wanting things you cannot have can make you unhappy. The next time you feel envious:

- Think about the times you have been lucky and the breaks life has given you.
- Do your achievable goals merit the attention you give them. Do you really want them so badly? If you do, replace envy with realistic, achievable goals for yourself.
- If your goals are unachievable replace them with realistic ones.
- Always keep a sense of what you value and what your goals are.

APATHY

If you feel that nothing is worth making an effort for there are things you can do to get back on track:

- Keep mentally and physically active.
- Visit new places, meet new people and do new things.
- Don't accept everything you are told at face value.
- Try to eat healthily and get enough sleep.
- Sign up for some voluntary work.
- Learn new things.

FEELING NOTHING AT ALL

If you have reached the point when you don't feel anything at all anymore you could be suffering from depression. Depression is a medical condition that improves with treatment. Seek medical advice immediately.

LOVING TOO MUCH

When love becomes confused with need, relationships suffer and often don't survive. To avoid becoming too dependent on another person or group of people:

- Value the importance of personal space and solitude.
- Nurture yourself.
- Have more than one key relationship.
- Don't neglect everything else when you start a special relationship.

- Be on your guard if a person wants to change you.
- Be assertive in your relationships.
- Always remember what you want in a relationship.
- Don't put anyone on a pedestal.

Throughout the process of coming to terms with your emotions always try to seek out the positive potential in every emotion. Managing your emotions will give you the confidence to be the person you want to be and to live the life you want to live.

STRESS MANAGEMENT

Stress management is an important part of building and preserving self-esteem. We live in a fast-changing pressurised society, and few of us are strangers to stress. If you feel that your way of coping under pressure is inadequate I'd like to suggest the following:

1. Prepare a timetable of realistic goals that you want to achieve each day.
2. Keep a watchful eye on your posture and breathe correctly.
3. Regularly check that you are not tensing your muscles.
4. Take time out — short breaks from your routine — at regular intervals.
5. Eat healthy foods.
6. Get enough sleep.
7. Avoid stressful environments and situations if you can.
8. Cultivate a network of social support i.e. friends and family that make you feel good about yourself.
9. Engage in regular exercise.
10. Try some relaxation techniques e.g. a relaxing walk, sauna, massage or simply a hot bath with aromatherapy oils.

Most of the stress management tips mentioned above are also useful tools for worry control. We'll explore them in more detail in the next chapter.

CHAPTER 16

MORE TECHNIQUES THAT WORK

There are many ways you can help yourself cope with worry. Don't give up straight away if you don't see an immediate improvement, some of these skills take time and practice. Remember also that what works for one person may not work for you. You are unique. Use these additional techniques, alongside the five steps, to find ways to deal with worry that works for you.

TIME MANAGEMENT

Time management is straightforward, but you will need to make certain changes and to learn some new skills.

Not being prepared or organised can be a source of worry and stress. Learning to manage your time effectively may reduce many worry-related problems. Adding structure to your life can reduce time spent each day worrying about what you have forgotten, what you should be doing, and where things are. For example, if you are worried about being late plan your journey and allow yourself enough time. If you worry about losing your keys have one place that you put them.

Many worries are simply related to disorganisation. Try to plan ahead as much as you can; put your clothes out the night before; prepare that speech in time; write a shopping list before you go to the supermarket so you don't forget things you need. Writing a daily schedule will also help.

Before you reorganise yourself you need to look at your present routine and what your priorities and goals are.

Explore the way you work and what your strengths and weaknesses are. Look at your current routine and how you are using your time. How often do you procrastinate? You might want to write the details down in a diary. Once you become more familiar with the way you work, you can start looking at ways in which you can make the most of your working time. You need to consider how you can allocate time. This means you need to review important areas of your life, career, relationships and so on, and decide how to prioritise them. By doing this you will get your necessary tasks in perspective and can start allocating appropriate time to each.

In prioritising you need to be clear about what your responsibilities are as well as your preferences. Check that the tasks you are undertaking are actually your responsibility. Now you need to reflect on your goals to see how realistic they are, given your personality and your priorities. Don't undermine important areas of your life in order to achieve certain goals. Learn to compromise and rethink what is important to you regularly.

Organise your day. There will always be unplanned demands on your time, but try to create a definite plan for your day based on your priorities. Tackle the hardest jobs first when you have the most energy. Avoid putting things off until the last minute. You may find that you need to delegate some of your tasks. It's hard to do everything yourself. Delegation is fundamental to effective time management. It might mean giving up things you enjoy, but it is faster to limit yourself to the appropriate tasks. Remember that delegation doesn't just mean passing on boring tasks. For others to be productive around you they need guidance, challenge and stimulation too.

If you can't delegate because you don't trust others to do the job as well, consider how justifiable your objections are. If they are justifiable find someone you do trust. If they aren't justifiable you need to challenge your fears.

In order to manage your time effectively you need to devise a system that meets your needs but that is also flexible. If you think you haven't got time to sit down and think about your schedule remind yourself that time management is an investment that will pay off. You will feel calmer, better prepared, less worried and more in control of your life.

Finally don't be a perfectionist. Perfection is impossible to achieve. Do the best that you can and then move on to other tasks. If you have time you can always come back later and polish the work more.

SLEEP WELL

Worry more than anything interferes with sleep. Lying awake worrying is unpleasant and will leave you exhausted the next day. If you don't get enough sleep you are more likely to worry and feel irritable and anxious. Concentration will also be poor. Lack of quality sleep is one of the biggest causes of stress.

You probably know the importance of a good night's sleep, but you probably don't know that there is no such thing as the right number of hours to sleep. Some of us get by with six hours, others need ten. We also need less sleep the older we get.

Everyone wakes in the night; this is quite normal. Most of us don't even realise it. It only becomes a problem when we worry about it. Everyone also has times when they don't sleep that well and sleep patterns are disrupted. This only becomes a problem if the disturbance is long term. Sleep is also affected by many things: what we eat, how much we exercise, how much we have drunk, what medications we are taking and so on.

So don't panic if you are not sleeping the required eight hours every night. Everyone has different sleep needs. The best indicator of sleep needs is how you feel during the day. Are you alert, energetic and able to concentrate? If you feel exhausted, irritable and feel like you are about to doze off all the time, you are not getting enough sleep.

It is possible to get a good night's sleep without resorting to medication. Drugs are not always that helpful and may even become addictive in the long term. Here are a few suggestions to help you sleep better.

- Keep a diary. Record how much you sleep, what you ate, how active you were and how stressful your day was. You might be able to identify unhelpful patterns that interfere with your sleep.

- Relax before you go to bed. Take a warm bath or listen to soothing music.
- Avoid eating heavy meals two hours before you go to bed, but don't go to bed hungry. Perhaps a light meal in the evening would be best.
- Watch your stress levels during the day.
- Avoid caffeine (tea, coffee, chocolate and cola) late at night. A warm milky drink may help. Avoid alcohol, nicotine and spicy foods in the evening.
- Make sure your bedroom is comfortable and quiet. Use your bed for sleeping not for reading and watching television. Your bed routines need to be associated with sleep.
- Go to bed when you are sleepy. If you take more than twenty minutes to get to sleep get up and do something else until you feel sleepy. Do something that is simple and not too energetic, like light housework. Don't toss and turn worrying about why you can't sleep.
- Try to establish regular waking and sleeping times, even at the weekend. Long lie-ins don't really help until you have established a sleep routine.

Above all don't worry about not getting a good night's sleep. Remind yourself that everyone has the odd night of poor sleep from time to time. In fact, recent studies show that getting too much sleep can be as bad for you as getting too little. Hopefully if you follow these guidelines you should be able to establish a sleep routine. But if you still can't get a good night's sleep it is important that you see a doctor.

KEEP ACTIVE

The physical affects the mental, and one of the most effective ways to deal with worry is to change your physical state.

Regular exercise is a good antidote for worry. If you feel worried or anxious try going for a brisk walk, jogging or playing a game of tennis or other sport. It is almost guaranteed that you will feel less worried. When you exercise your body puts out chemicals, like endorphins, that can soothe a worried mind as well as mood enhancing neurotransmitters like serotonin. The hormones released during exercise affect your blood pressure, heart rate, body temperature and metabolism. After exercise most of us feel calmer and more alert.

Regular exercise will help reduce the amount that you worry. Exercise is also good in other ways. It will help manage your weight, improve your health and reduce the risk of heart attacks. It will also help you control aggressive emotions and help your mind to focus. It is an effective tool for treating depression. As far as possible, ensure that exercise is a part of your life. Pick an activity you enjoy, and try to engage in some kind of physical activity for at least thirty minutes every day. It doesn't have to be a strenuous aerobics class it can be as simple as walking home instead of getting the bus. The exercise should be moderate and not too intense. Too much exercise can strain your body and be as unhealthy as too little.

Instant exercise when you feel worried may also help. If you feel particularly anxious, a walk around the room may help calm you. Simply moving your body may also help. Intense worry can literally paralyse you; you feel stiff and tense. Motion may ease that feeling. Rocking, swaying motions, shrugging your shoulders or simply rolling your head may help.

You might want to try some gentle rocking when you feel anxious. The cerebellum, which governs receptive rocking motion, may send signals to help calm you down. Worrying does tend to subside when you engage in rhythmic motion. Perhaps that's why it can be so calming to watch the waves gently lapping back and forwards or to sit rocking in a rocking chair.

Even simple activities like filing your nails, brushing your hair or reading a book can change your brain's physical state. The next time you are worried brush your hair. This isn't as silly as it sounds. You are doing something structured and physical, and you are distracting yourself. It's just a tiny bit of movement but it might help.

Something else that might help is the simple physical touch of others. A hand on your shoulder, a pat on the cheek or a massage can help reduce worry. The excitement of sexual activity certainly alters your mood.

The act of sex itself can reduce worry. It can be a good form of exercise; it can also stimulate the pleasure centres of the brain, be a stress reliever and release human growth hormone. Orgasm, whether it is achieved with or without a partner, sets off a chain of positive neuro-chemical reactions that should leave you feeling rejuvenated.

Stay sensual and you will have what Dr Michael Perring (Spillane, Mary and Mckee, Victoria, *Ultra Age: Every Woman's Guide to Facing the Future* London, Macmillan, 1999) calls a 'moist look'. Sensual people don't tend to look worried or anxious; there is always that sparkle in their eye. You may have a partner to keep sensuality in your life, but if you prefer to stay single make sure that you are surrounded by good friends and treat yourself regularly to sensual pleasures, such as a massage or a bubble bath.

Dr Gail Ironson, a professor of psychology and psychiatry at the University of Miami in Coral Gables, showed in a study that massage is vital for a stronger immune system and for reduced stress levels. Massage relaxes your muscles and gives you a much-needed timeout when you can revel in a feeling of being cared for.

Dancing is also a good treatment. When you combine music with exercise you have two powerful remedies. Music is one of the oldest treatments for anxiety. All the arts can ease the worried mind but music is perhaps the most beneficial. It's hard to worry when you listen to music you enjoy.

As well as sleep, exercise, motion and music there are other ways you can influence your state of mind. Eating properly is one of them.

EATING TO BEAT WORRY

Most of us don't give our bodies the nutrition they need. If a machine isn't given proper fuel or maintenance how can it be expected to run efficiently? Similarly if you don't feed your body the full range of nutrients it needs, how can you expect to stay in a state of physical and mental health?

Diet can play a role in the treatment of worry and anxiety. Under stress our bodies produce chemicals which push up blood sugar levels. High blood sugar levels can make you feel anxious, tired and edgy. Certain food substances including alcohol, refined sugars and caffeine also elevate those levels. You may notice considerable improvements if you follow the guidelines below.

ELIMINATE OR RESTRICT THE INTAKE OF CAFFEINE

Chronic caffeine intake may cause worry and anxiety because it produces mental and physical stimulation. Caffeine in small doses can stimulate the brain and help you think more clearly and feel more alert. But the anti-fatigue effects of caffeine are usually short-lived. After the initial stimulation a period of increased fatigue results. A cycle can be established when a person drinks more caffeine to delay the onset of more fatigue.

If you worry a lot, caffeine should be avoided. Caffeine is found in tea, coffee, chocolate and colas and even a small amount appears in decaffeinated products. Caffeine is linked to symptoms of anxiety, nervousness, irritability and insomnia and people prone to worry tend to be especially sensitive to its effects. If a good cup of coffee is something you really enjoy this doesn't mean you have to stop drinking it all together, it just means you should cut down on the amount you drink. One or two coffees a day is fine, six or seven isn't.

Be aware that if you routinely drink coffee or tea, abrupt cessation will probably result in symptoms of caffeine withdrawal for a few days, and these include fatigue, headache and an increased craving for coffee.

ELIMINATE OR RESTRICT THE INTAKE OF ALCOHOL

Alcohol interferes with normal brain chemistry and sleep cycles. In small doses alcohol can be calming but more often it increases anxiety levels. If you suffer from worry and anxiety it is best to avoid alcohol entirely.

ELIMINATE REFINED CARBOHYDRATES FROM YOUR DIET

Refined carbohydrates, like sugar and white flour, contribute to problems in blood-sugar control especially hypoglycaemia — low blood sugar. When blood sugars are low the brain doesn't function well and you feel anxious, dizzy and confused. Headaches may also occur.

The association between hypoglycaemia and impaired mental function is well-known. Unfortunately people experiencing anxiety or depression are rarely tested for it. Simply eliminating refined carbohydrates from your diet may be all that is required to reduce the amount that you worry.

If you regularly crave sweets, are irritable if a meal is missed, get dizzy spells, headaches, have problems concentrating, often feel tired or shaky, and suffer from mood swings and periods of confusion, hypoglycaemia might be the cause.

If you think you may have blood-sugar problems consult with your doctor, reduce the amount of refined carbohydrates you eat and start giving more thought to the design of your diet.

FOOD AND MOOD

A good diet is one in which the food you eat contains the nutrients you need to promote physical, mental and emotional health. A bad diet can contribute to obesity, heart disease, cancer, digestive disorders, mood swings, irritability and insomnia — to name but a few problems.

If you are feeling worried you may neglect your body's needs; just when a balanced, wholesome diet is needed most. You may have no appetite at all, or you may crave unhealthy and fattening foods. As a result nutritional deficiencies or imbalances are likely, particularly a lack of B vitamins, folic acid, vitamin C and of the minerals calcium, copper, iron, magnesium and potassium. Malnourishment or weight problems clearly contribute to moods spiralling downwards.

More and more research is linking what we eat to how we feel. In her book *Food and Mood* dietician Elizabeth Somer explores how the food we eat can heighten depression. She believes that certain eating habits, like skipping meals or having erratic eating habits, aggravate negative moods. Somer advises five to six small meals and snacks spread through out the day.

Dr Judith Wurtman, a researcher at the Massachusetts Institute of Technology, believes that certain foods alter mood because they release insulin, which encourages the production of serotonin. Higher serotonin levels are thought to be linked with improved mood. Foods rich in tryptophan, such as eggs, cheese, milk, peas and soya beans and other carbohydrate — rich foods have an effect similar to that of some anti-depressant medication.

Don't be surprised if you start eating large amount of high-sugar foods when you feel worried. You are using food as a form of self-medication. The problem with this is that the effects tend to be short-term and if you eat too much of the wrong kind of carbohydrate you will gain weight and may become hypoglycaemic. Carbohydrate-rich foods, preferably wholegrain ones, rather than snacks high in simple sugars, like biscuits and crisps, should be your food of choice when you feel anxious or worried.

Somer advises that wholegrain breads and cereals or starchy vegetables like a potato or a sweet potato can make you feel less anxious. She suggests that cravings are not to be avoided, but responded to in moderation and with planned nutritious foods.

The relationship between the brain's chemistry and different nutrients is unclear, but nutritional guidelines from the Department of Health offer pointers on nutrition for worriers. Plenty of wholegrains, peas, lentils and other pulses, and regular amounts of lean meat, oily fish, shellfish and eggs will supply B vitamins, iron, potassium, magnesium, copper and zinc. A high intake of fresh fruit and vegetables such as asparagus, broccoli, cabbage, melon, oranges and berries will supply ample vitamin C. Dark green leafy vegetables will improve levels of calcium, magnesium and iron; dried fruits will provide potassium and iron, while dairy products (preferably low-fat) will boost levels of calcium. These recommendations can be kept in mind when considering the general guidelines for a good diet.

DESIGNING A HEALTHY DIET

In general your diet should contain a balanced mix of carbohydrates, proteins and fats. You should also be eating enough fibre, ensuring that you get an adequate intake of essential vitamins and minerals, and drinking lots of water. The guidelines given here are in accordance with the Healthy Exchange System originally developed by the American Diabetic Association and other groups for diabetics, but now used for the design of many therapeutic diets.

CARBOHYDRATE

The World Health Organisation (WHO) and the Healthy Exchange System recommend that between fifty to seventy per cent of a person's diet should be carbohydrate. The carbohydrate should come not from foods high in sugar, like cakes and sweets, but foods rich in complex carbohydrate. Complex carbohydrates are high in fibre, low in starch and sugar, rich in vitamins and minerals and help keep blood-sugar levels stable. Complex carbohydrate is found in bread, pasta, rice, potatoes, pulses, nuts and seeds, fruits, vegetables and salads. The best high quality carbohydrate is found in the following:

- Fruits: apples, oranges, grapefruit, strawberries, pears, peaches and plums.
- Vegetables: broccoli, asparagus, green beans, cauliflower and spinach.
- Grains: barley, rye, brown rice, wholemeal and pasta.

- Beans: black beans, white beans, chickpeas, kidney beans and lentils.

You should have five servings of fruit, vegetables or salad a day and four servings of carbohydrates, from other sources. A serving is one medium sized apple and one medium slice of bread.

PROTEIN
Protein should make up around fifteen per cent of your diet. Protein is found in meat, dairy produce, eggs, fish, poultry, pulses, nuts and seeds. You should try to have two servings a day of non-dairy products and one serving a day of a dairy product. A serving is two ounces of cheese or one egg.

FAT
Fats should make up around twenty-five per cent of your diet. Fats are found in most foods. Too much of the wrong sort of fat is bad for you. Avoid saturated fats from animal produce and fats that are solid at room temperature, such as lard and butter. Fats that are liquid at room temperature, such as vegetable oils, are far preferable, since they don't contain the chemicals that can clog arteries.

FIBRE
An adequate intake of dietary fibre is also important. WHO recommends around thirty grams of fibre a day. Foods high in fibre include fruits and vegetables, brown bread, rice, pasta, high-fibre cereals, potatoes and baked beans. A jacket potato contains around five to eight grams per serving.

Fibre swells the bulk of the food residue in the intestine and helps to soften it by increasing the amount of water retained. It is vital for the health of the digestive system; many ailments, such as irritable bowel, constipation and piles result if you don't get enough fibre. Western diets are often low in fibre, and those who eat a lot of processed and refined food are vulnerable. But there are easy ways to boost fibre:

- Have a bowl of high-fibre cereal for breakfast.
- Eat brown bread, pasta and rice.
- Snack on fruits and nuts rather than crisps and chocolate.

High-fibre foods are nutritious and can satisfy without being fattening. Some types of fibre — those found in vegetables, fruits and oats — can reduce blood cholesterol. Cholesterol is a variety of fat that has some health benefits, so it shouldn't be excluded from a diet, but too much cholesterol is linked to clogging of the arteries — especially those around the heart.

VITAMINS AND MINERALS

Vitamins and minerals are also vital for your health and sense of wellbeing. When there is a deficiency you may suffer from a range of health problems that undermine your wellbeing but are not normally treated by doctors. If you eat a wide variety of foods you should get all the nutrients you need. However, even fresh wholefoods can be less nutritious than you think. Nutrients can be leaked from our food in a variety of hidden ways, and chemicals are often added.

Foods most at risk of nutrient deficiency are pre-prepared or processed food, foods that have been frozen and canned. In addition alcohol, drugs, tobacco, stress and environmental pollution can deplete the body of essential nutrients. For all these reasons you might want to buy organic food, eat as much fresh wholemeal food as you can, and supplement your diet with extra vitamins and minerals. Vitamin B, C, magnesium and zinc are of particular importance for stress management.

Common vitamins
- Vitamin A: good for skin and eyes, it is found in liver, carrots and green vegetables.
- Vitamin B: good for the nervous system and energy production. B vitamins need to be replenished daily and their supply is reduced by refined foods, alcohol, sugar and coffee.

When it comes to supplements, B3, B5 and B6 are important for stress management. Vitamins B is found in tuna, beans, bread, breakfast cereal, dairy products and vegetables.

- Vitamin C: good for the immune system and iron absorption it is found in citrus fruits, vegetables, potatoes and green vegetables.
- Vitamin D: good for bones and teeth it is found in oily fish, salmon and dairy produce.
- Vitamin E: good for fat metabolism and the nervous system it is found in nuts, seeds and vegetable oils.

Common minerals
- Calcium: good for bones, teeth and blood clotting it is found in milk, cheese and broccoli.
- Chromium: good for sugar metabolism and blood pressure it is found in egg yolk, wheatgerm and chicken.
- Copper: good for healthy connective tissues it is found in most foods.
- Iron: good for blood, circulatory and immune systems it is found in liver, dried fruit, meat and green vegetables.
- Magnesium: good for muscles and the nervous system it is found in nuts, green leafy vegetables, chicken and cheese. Magnesium, along with calcium, can ease insomnia, high blood pressure and cramps.
- Potassium: good for nerve transmission and acid/alkaline balance in the body, it is found in raisons, potatoes, fruit and vegetables.
- Selenium: good for the heart and liver it is found in kidney, liver and red meat.
- Zinc: good for the reproductive system, hair and nails it is found in cheese, wholemeal bread, lean meat and eggs. Zinc is depleted by stress and is related to anxiety, loss of libido and stress.
- Vitamins A, C and E and selenium are anti-oxidants, which means they can help your body remove harmful toxins.

Warning — always consult a doctor or pharmacist if vitamin or mineral supplements are taken. Some, vitamin A, for instance, can be harmful if taken in large amounts.

WATER

The chances are you are not drinking enough water, an important part of your diet — it keeps you hydrated and helps flush toxins out of the body. Ideally you should be drinking at least six to eight glasses of water a day to maintain health.

SALT AND SUGAR INTAKE

Moderation in salt is also advised. Excessive intakes of salt can promote fluid retention and cause a rise in blood pressure, and an increased risk of stroke, heart disease and kidney failure. Much processed food contains salt. Crisps are high in salt and lots of us sprinkle salt on our food, which isn't necessary.

Refined white sugar is bad for your health. It rots your teeth, sends your blood-sugar levels up, affects your mood and makes you gain weight. Many of the foods we eat today are packed with hidden sugars and most of us consume far too much. If you have a sweet tooth you might want to try eating fruit rather than sweets, biscuits and cakes.

HOW MUCH SHOULD I BE EATING?

If you follow the basic serving guidelines given above you should be eating a diet that is high in nutrients and sensible in calories. Calorie counting as a means of determining the healthful nature of your diet rarely works, because when you focus on calories you often neglect the importance of getting all your nutrients. A diet high in essential nutrients is far more effective in combating anxiety and stress than a calorie controlled diet. You may also find that a nutritious diet helps you lose weight more effectively. So forget calorie counting and focus on nutrients.

WHEN YOU EAT

It seems that eating smaller, more frequent meals rather than larger, fewer ones is more beneficial for mental and physical health. Eating breakfast like a king, lunch like a prince and dinner like a pauper also improves alertness and a sense of wellbeing.

Breakfast is the most important meal of the day and ideally it should be the largest. Healthy breakfast choices include wholegrain cereals, muffins and breads along with fresh fruit and cereals. The complex carbohydrates give you the energy boost you need at the start of the day.

A light snack of fruit, vegetable, nuts or seeds around mid-morning will keep your energy levels high. Lunch is a good time to enjoy a nourishing bowl of soup or salad along with some wholegrain bread. This may be followed by another light snack around teatime.

Dinner should be the smallest meal of the day and preferably eaten within two hours of going to bed. Wholegrains and legumes can be eaten in salads, main dishes and soups. It really doesn't make sense to eat a large meal when you are not going to need much energy. Give your body the time to rest, cleanse and recharge itself for the next day.

CONTROL FOOD ALLERGIES

In addition to following the guidelines above, if you worry a lot you might need to consider the possibility of food allergies. As far back as 1930, Dr Albert Row noted that anxiety and fatigue were key features of certain food allergies.

A food allergy occurs when there is an adverse reaction to the ingestion of a food. Other terms often used to describe this effect include food intolerance, hypersensitivity and food reaction. Food allergies have been linked to many health problems, including anxiety, depression, fatigue, irritability and inability to concentrate.

Food allergies can be diagnosed by food challenge and laboratory methods. Laboratory testing, such as blood tests, can provide immediate identification of suspected allergies but are expensive. Food challenge requires no expense but requires a lot of motivation. Basically you act as the detective and search for the food culprit by going on a limited diet and eliminating commonly eaten foods to see if the symptoms disappear.

Once the food allergy is detected the best approach is to deal with it through avoidance. The most common food intolerances are to wheat, dairy produce, nuts, eggs, yeast, shellfish, citrus fruits and artificial colourings. Food allergies, especially to wheat gluten, have been linked to depression.

If you suffer from anxiety and worry you may find that supporting the biochemistry of your body by making certain changes to your diet really does help. In the next chapter we'll explore the role that supplements have.

DAYLIGHT

Not getting enough sunlight can make you feel more worried, gloomy and depressed. Sunlight is a source of nutrients; it is easy to become deficient if you stay in doors too much. A simple way to deal with this is to go outside and get fresh air as much as you can. Even if it is cold outside and the sun isn't out the light is good for you and will make you feel better. Don't take this to extremes, though. Too much sun can damage your skin. Once again moderation is key.

SUPPORT FROM OTHERS

Your ultimate goal is to learn how to talk to yourself constructively, but the reassurance and support of others is also beneficial. Researchers speculate that social ties might help us cope with stresses that lower our immunity. Immune cells have receptors that bind to stress hormones and when this occurs the immune cells don't work as well and we are likely to get ill and anxious.

Worrying by yourself often makes the worry worse, no matter what it is. When you worry alone you tend to have less perspective and objectivity, which another person could provide. It's often the case when you talk to someone about what is making you feel anxious that you regain perspective.

We all need to feel listened to and supported by others at

times, however independent we are. When we share our worries with others we aren't really looking for answers; what we are looking for is reassurance and a feeling that we belong. Reassurance is the feeling that things will be all right in the end. A supportive statement from someone else can reinforce the supportive messages we've been giving ourselves. Children need reassurance and support all the time, and adults also need it regularly.

It's often hard for worriers to let others know that they need reassurance and support, and sadly in today's world many of us aren't very good at asking for help or giving it to others. We don't want to look vulnerable, needy or insecure. We ask for support in indirect ways, or we can't handle the responsibility of giving someone else reassurance. But if you ask for reassurance in a simple, honest way from someone you know you can trust, this can be very soothing.

Knowing that you have the support of other people is the ultimate form of reassurance. You don't need to ask for it because you know that others are supportive of you no matter what.

Unfortunately, in states of intense worry you often feel isolated from the support of others, which makes the worry worse. But how do you go about regaining a sense of connection to others?

You could start by spending more time with your family and loved ones. The more connected you feel to the most important people in your life, the stronger you will feel. Schedule meals together, talk and play more. Don't neglect your friends either, or the ties you have with colleagues and neighbours. Take the time to spend time with your friends.

Learning about your social and historical background may encourage a sense of belonging; so can staying current with information and ideas that are topical. You will feel more connected to what is going on in the world around you; if you work in, or belong to an institution, nurture positive connections there.

You might find solace and emotional connection by turning to a higher source. Prayer or meditation can ease the worried mind.

Talking to God, or if you are not religious to some higher source where you feel connected to the world, to nature, to time and to space does seem to help. Research with brain scans shows that changes in the brain during meditation and prayer correlates with improved health.

Finding a faith community can be an important aspect of feeling connected. Researchers at Duke University Medical Center in Durham, North Carolina, recently found that people who attended religious services regularly had stronger immune systems. This might be due in part to the stress-reducing powers of social contact, but it is also possible that prayer itself can relax us. This is not to suggest that we should all go to church, but it seems that turning to another source or simply envisioning greater happiness for yourself, can make you feel more in control and less stressed.

A recent study conducted in Sweden showed that those who went out to cultural events like show or museums, or even sports events, tended to be healthier than those who stayed at home. Increased social contact and reduced stress were the key factors here.

In today's fragmented, fast-moving society it is hard to retain a sense of connection. Isolation and loneliness are modern epidemics. But it doesn't have to be that way. You don't have to feel lonely and isolated. Reaching out to those you know you can trust costs nothing and can be a source of great strength in times of worry and anxiety. Cultivating a network of social support could be the most healing thing you ever do for yourself.

With the changing shape of the family and the loss of traditional communities, loneliness, isolation and lack of intimacy are widespread causes of stress. Friendship, with people of both sexes, is important for good health and stress reduction. We need others to be happy, and we need many kinds of relationships to feel loved and supported.

It is important to remember though that although our lives find meaning through our relationships with others, how we feel about ourselves is just as significant. We need to feel loved and supported by others but we also need to be able to love and support ourselves.

According to author John Gray true contentment is only possible if we can meet all our love needs, both the love we give ourselves and the love we give others. In his book *How to Get What You Want and Want What You Have* (London, Vermillion, 1999), he outlines the ten essential love vitamins everyone needs in order to feel fulfilled.

> We need love and support from God, parents or carers, family, friends and having fun, peers and those with similar goals, ourselves, partners, and dependents. We also need to give back to the community, the world and to serve a higher source. 'A rich and satisfying life' is fuelled by these ten kinds of love and support.

Gray believes that when you don't feel happy or get what you want, it is because you are not getting your love needs met. 'Each of these different kinds of love and support is essential if we are to be whole.' Whether you agree or not, Gray's argument is insightful and uplifting. We would all certainly worry less if we loved and supported ourselves, and felt loved, supported and valued by others.

Reduce worry by building positive relationships with others. These relationships must not be ones that drain you, but ones that make you feel good about yourself. Hopefully, your self-esteem will be high enough so that you don't spend time with people who are only interested in themselves, or take you for granted. Also if you believe that friendship is all about your needs being fulfilled — you are not a friend. Friendship is about giving and receiving and is based on the capacity to accept, as well as to give love and respect. A good relationship with another person adds to your sense of zest and self-worth; if people sap your energy you are mixing with the wrong kind of people.

RELATIONSHIPS AS A SOURCE OF STRESS

It sometimes happens that the one person who is supposed to be the source of love, inspiration and joy is the one who causes you the most stress. Those who seem to have worry under control seem to be successful in dealing with people who no longer enhance their lives and in seeking out those that do. This applies not only to partners but also to friendships and work colleagues as well. Being in unhappy relationships of any kind causes unhappiness and poor health.

Dr Dean Ornish has shown in his books that happiness can strengthen the immune system and that unhappy people are likely to suffer poor health and age faster. We need to relate to each other to feel healthy in mind and body. But when relationships become difficult they can be a significant source of stress.

Relationships are all about give and take. But if you have tried compromise and communication with your partner, if your relationship is not making you happy, for your own health consider what changes you should make. This is especially the case if the relationship turns abusive in any way. If this is the case, seek help immediately.

IMPROVING COMMUNICATION

Learning to communicate more effectively may help reduce stress and conflict in your relationships. Here are a few pointers:

- Learn to listen. Allow other people to express their thoughts and feelings without constantly interrupting with your own. If you try to understand and be attentive to the needs of others you will find yourself better understood.
- Really listen to what others say. Don't think about what your response will be. Don't advise or criticise. Be reflective in your listening. Restate or reflect back what the other person has said to you to show that you have been listening.
- Communication is a two-way process and as well as listening to someone else you will also want him or her to listen to you. But wait until a person is ready to listen to you. If they are not

ready to listen they won't hear what you have to say. When they are receptive ask if they understand what you are communicating.

• Finally don't be afraid of silence in conversations. In times of silence you can collect your thoughts. A great deal can be said in times of silence: I'm listening. I understand. I'm there for you.

RELAXATION TECHNIQUES

As we have seen, relaxation techniques can help you manage worry. In addition to the techniques for relaxing bodily tension discussed earlier, here are some more ideas for relaxing.

Imagery, a relaxation technique similar to daydreaming, involves allowing images to drift through your mind. Relax and let images come to you. Listen to tapes that induce relaxation without the sounds of nature or verbal directions; that way you can let your inner images flow freely.

Such relaxation exercises done regularly can slow your breathing rate, calm your brain wave rhythms and lower your blood pressure. Yoga can also relax tense muscles, teach you better breathing, lower your blood pressure, decrease your heart rate and divert your mind from stress.

Soothing music can be beneficial, as can soaking in a hot bath, laughing more, interacting with others, cultivating outside interests and diversions from your usual routine. There are so many delightful ways to relax.

Many of us think of relaxation as time that we can't afford to lose. Rather than thinking of it as time lost, think of it as time gained. When you return to your routine you will feel refreshed and energised and have a better perspective on life.

ENJOY LIFE

One of the best ways to put aside harmful, toxic worry is simply to try and have more fun with your life. The positive emotions associated with laughter decrease stress hormones and increase the number of immune cells. Think about all the things you really enjoy doing, and then try to work as many as possible of them into your every day life.

Research is now proving that pleasure does the immune system good. The more fun you have, the more gracefully you will age and the healthier you will feel. When we are happy, positive hormone and enzyme levels are elevated and blood pressure is normal. Even smiling can send impulses along the pleasure pathways to make you feel good; besides, wrinkles from smiling are far more attractive than harsh frown lines.

Many studies have linked happiness to longevity and demonstrated that there are considerable health benefits in happiness and humour. From the interviews I conducted for this book it soon became apparent that positive thoughts reduce worry more than anything else. It is important not only to find pleasure in your daily routine but also to keep planning future pleasurable activities.

Looking back on the days when I worried excessively, I now see that part of my problem was that I didn't have a sense of humour. This is not to suggest that you treat life as one big joke, but simply that many of us take ourselves far too seriously.

Children laugh hundreds of times a day; as we get older we laugh less and less and sometimes not at all. If just the act of smiling can produce demonstratively lower stress levels, think what laughter can do. When you are worried your sense of humour is the first thing to go. Being serious and responsible are not one and the same thing. Laughter and play are cathartic; find time for them. Having fun and playing shouldn't stop just because you aren't a child anymore. Research shows that playing imaginative games can benefit concentration, co-ordination, attention span and general health and wellbeing. If you worry all the time, don't have enjoyment, laughter and fun in your life, then are you really living?

ENJOY THE WAY YOU LOOK

One of the biggest stumbling blocks many of us have when it comes to enjoying life is a poor body image. Feeling unattractive stops us living life to the full. Body image insecurity affects every aspect of our lives and is a major cause of fear, anxiety and depression.

A poor body image has a great impact on all areas of your life. According to Thomas Cash PHD of Old Dominion University, body image constitutes a huge twenty-five to thirty-three per cent of a person's sense of confidence. A poor body image can contribute to worry, low self-esteem and obsession about your physical flaws, all of which can age you faster. They use up energy that could better be used for creativity, productivity and to self-realisation according to Marcia Germaine Hutchinson, a Boston psychologist and author of *Transforming Body image; Learning to love the body you have* (1997). Body hatred can also damage your health and may even lead to stringent dieting and obsessive exercising which can contribute to the development of poor health or disorders such as compulsive eating, obesity, anorexia or bulimia.

Body hatred is unattractive at any age. So what do you do if you hate they way you look?

The chances are that if you begin taking care of your body with the right diet and regular exercise you will start to respect and like your body more. But this won't happen overnight. In the meantime you have to stop trying to change your appearance and start trying to change the way you feel about how you look. Changing the way you think about yourself won't be easy. Be patient with yourself and give yourself time. Take consolation from the fact that you are not alone and that you have to fight years of conditioning in the wrong direction. Here are a few tips that might help:

- Being thin does not improve your body image. I have spoken to many people who had lost fat or who were at or below their ideal weight who still disliked their bodies.
- Spend some time really looking at other people your age. Notice how very different their bodies are from one another. Think about people you consider beautiful. Often their features are not perfect.

- If you think you are overweight, get your body fat tested to see if you fall within the normal range. Twenty-two to twenty-five per cent means you are relatively slender and physically fit. If you are athletic twenty-eight to thirty per cent is okay.
- Get to know your body better. Have a look at yourself in front of a mirror. Counteract negative thoughts about your body with something positive. Instead of 'I look fat', focus on how beautiful your eyes are, how good your hair looks, how great you look in a certain colour.
- Have a good long think about why you want to look different. Why is it so important to you?
- Listen to your body. Commit to trusting that it knows what it wants. Be honest about what you are eating. Make sensible, healthy food choices. Eat when you are hungry. Stop when you are full. Exercise when you can to help boost body confidence.
- If how you look is really making you depressed, seek professional help. You need guidance about how to change negative thought patterns and a therapist might help. Call an eating disorder clinic at your hospital and ask for a referral. To keep you on track you might consider joining a support group that deals with food, weight and depression.
- Read some books on developing a healthy body image and self-esteem.
- Try to identify the real triggers for your body hatred. Every time you feel negative about your body think about what is going on at the time. Are you really angry with your partner? Has your boss upset you?
- Recognise that it is unnatural and unhealthy to look like the models on the catwalk. They are not real people but fantasies created by the media.
- Understand that thinness and youth do not equal attractiveness.
- Separate what you do from how you look.
- Focus on what you are good at. Put your energy into doing things you enjoy.

- A positive body image makes a person attractive regardless of build or weight. Gaining this kind of body confidence starts with treating your body with respect.
- Rethink your definition of attractiveness. Beauty is not about youth and slenderness but about feeling confident about yourself. The sooner you come to this realisation the happier you will be.

ENJOY YOUR WORK

Pleasure does not have to be separate from work. The ideal scenario would be that you found work that gave you a sense of vocation or pleasure; that you loved what you did for a living. There is nothing more ageing than watching the hours tick by at work, day in and day out. Being a workaholic is not the same as being someone who is enthusiastic about their work. The latter often find that their life is so invigorating that they rarely need vacations. The former are driven and obsessed who don't have time for anything meaningful.

Being happy in your work means enjoying it as part of a balanced life. Research shows that if you have a sense of control over what you are doing at work you will worry less and enjoy it more. This doesn't mean taking over the organisation. It means taking initiative and organising your routines as much as possible. If your job doesn't allow you this freedom, perhaps you should think about another working environment.

If you don't enjoy your work, do all you can to find an alternative. In the meantime it might help to pretend that you do enjoy it, however boring and mindless the task, and to do it to the very best of your ability. It may not be long before your enthusiasm is noticed and you are given the opportunity to do other work.

KEEP LEARNING

You may finish school or college, but the school of life is never finished. You need never stop learning and growing as a human being.

Don't stop learning new skills. It is often assumed that the older you get the less able you will be to adapt to changing circumstances. As your body starts to age, don't let your mind-set follow suit. You may get the odd wrinkle or two, but you don't have to be inflexible. The ability to adapt to change, is the distinguishing feature of people who don't let worries and insecurities take over their life. They think of life as one big adventure. They move with the times in not just work, but in all areas of their lives. They stay current, interested in the world around them. They don't live in the past; they aren't backward looking.

Your mindset, not your appearance or your age, is what can hold you back. So take advantage of every opportunity that is offered to you. Keep pace with what is current. Continue to learn. Keep up with the gossip. Find yourself a mentor to inspire you. Stay in the mainstream.

And if you don't work make sure that you love the life choices you have made; that you have friends, interests, hobbies, hopes and dreams. People who love what they are doing tend to look younger. If you don't really enjoy your life and have at the moment no avenue of escape because of financial or family commitments, for your own sake find an interest that really motivates you. The important thing is to make the most of every day of your life. And if work is a large part of your life you owe it to yourself to ensure that you use every day as an opportunity to learn, to grow, to be challenged and to enjoy.

STOP COMPARING YOURSELF WITH OTHERS

Comparing yourself with others is one sure route to anxiety and worry. It's natural, of course, because we all have expectations of what we should be and what we should have accomplished; many of us may feel that we have fallen short.

In this modern age of whizz kids it can be hard not to feel that you are lagging behind. But however beautiful, successful and talented your best friend is, he or she will have worries of his or her own too. And there will always be people who are better than you at some things; that's just a simple fact of life. Don't attend school reunions if they are going to worry you. Concentrate on your life, your skills, your talents and what makes you unique.

BE YOURSELF

Hopefully when you start trying to worry less and live more, maturity and self-confidence will gradually replace a vulnerable need for the approval of others. You discover that the important thing is whether or not you are being true to yourself. You don't always need friends, parents or partners to validate your every action and thought. You begin to enjoy your own company and trust your own opinions. You start being yourself. Expect to find this scary at first, but in time having the courage to be yourself and think your own thoughts is one of the most truly wonderful gifts that you can give yourself.

LET GO!

I'll finish this chapter with a skill that is both the hardest and the easiest thing to do: letting go.

You can do all you can to prepare yourself, you can try to make sense of your feelings, but there always comes a point when you simply have to let go, put your worries aside and take a risk. You may make a decision, take some kind of action or simply change your attitude. Is this the best thing to do? You may never know, but at least you are seeking a solution and moving forward with your life.

It is when you stop trying to find an answer to your problems and get stuck in worry and anxiety that life stands still. It's impossible to be in control of every detail in your life. Sometimes you just have to take a risk and let go. Life finds its meaning through facing your fears not by avoiding them. You can't always know if you are doing the right thing, but every time you search for an answer you add to your store of knowledge and life experience.

Worry will always be with us because absolute certainty in life doesn't exist. But whether we know it or not each time we confront our worry we are gradually letting go of the need for total control. We are learning to trust ourselves or a higher source. We are learning to hope. We are learning to have faith.

WHAT IF THE WORRYING STILL WON'T STOP?

You are worried. You are trying the techniques mentioned in the last few chapters and you still can't let go. What is going on?

First of all you may just need more time. It takes a lot of practice to get the hang of making decisions and talking positively to yourself; keep working at it. Remind yourself that the disasters you anticipate will probably never happen. Even if you can't solve a particular problem, remember that worry can turn molehills into mountains. The disaster may never happen, and if it does the consequences probably won't be as bad as you thought. This is not to belittle the importance of your problems, it is simply to urge you to be realistic and regain a sense of perspective. Are things really as bad as you think? It's often the case when people agonise over a dilemma that the consequences aren't as bad as they thought.

Secondly your problem may be unsolvable. There are some situations in life you cannot change. You can't do anything about them, but you can change your attitude to them. Use the suggestions given for challenging negative thoughts. However, sometimes worry may be part of a more serious problem.

This book is about common worry and not anxiety disorders, but when your problems and pain become too great and worry becomes too difficult to live with you may need a little extra help.

CHAPTER 17

WHEN YOU NEED A BIT OF EXTRA HELP

In this chapter we'll look at ways you can get extra help. Ideally any kind of medication, therapy or treatment should be used in conjunction with the self-help tips already mentioned.

MEDICATION AND THERAPY

Should worry become too intense you may need to be given antidepressant medication by your doctor. Medication won't heal the tendency to worry completely, but it can be an effective part of treatment. It can relieve symptoms enough to give you a ray of hope that recovery is possible. There are many safe medications that don't cure the problem but are an effective part of treatment.

The most common group of medications used to treat worry and anxiety are benzodiazepines. You have probably heard of Valium, but there are other types as well. Benzodiazepines reduce anxiety by altering brain chemistry to induce a calmer, more tranquil mood.

The benzodiazepines are best used as temporary medication to help get you on the right track. You can achieve a state of mind that is conducive to learning methods of dealing with worry that don't involve medication, such as relaxation, distraction, connecting with others, exercise, diet, breathing and sleep or counselling. As long as these medications aren't seen as the solution but potent allies on the road to recovery and their use is carefully monitored and administered under expert guidance, they can be extremely helpful.

If given correctly, a benzodiazepine can break the vicious cycle of worry in a relatively short period of time and open the way for other non-medicative methods to be mastered. There are many benzodiazepines for a doctor to choose from, but all share the ability to reduce anxiety.

There are other drugs besides the benzodiazepines a doctor could administer, and one that has been found to be helpful for worry and generalised anxiety disorder is buspirone (Bu Spar). It has fewer side effects than most benzodiazepines and is less sedating or potentially addictive.

Antidepressants can also play a role in the treatment of worry. There are several kinds of antidepressants:

- the tricyclic antidepressants, such as Tofranil
- the selective serotonin reuptake inhibitors or SSRIs such as Prozac
- the atypical antidepressant such as Wellbutrin
- the monoamine oxidase inhibitors or MAOIs such as Nardil.

The most well-known antidepressants today are the SSRIs like Prozac and Zoloft, which increase the amount of serotonin in the brain. SSRIs are very good for excessive worry. They can also help for panic disorder and compulsive behaviour. They can break the cycle for people who ruminate excessively, and they can be life changing. But it is crucial that the worrier doesn't stop with medication but goes on to master a non-medicative approach to worry.

The monoamine oxidase inhibitors, MAOIs, are gaining in popularity and are particularly helpful in the treatment of phobias and other states of fear like post-traumatic stress disorder. The reason they are not used too widely, however, may be because if you take them you have to comply with a restrictive diet and eliminate foods such as aged cheese and red wine. If you eat a forbidden food blood pressure shoots up and the risk of stroke increases.

Beta-blockers, such as Inderal, are also used to treat worry and anxiety. They are especially effective for symptoms of anxiety such as tremor, sweating or nervousness.

Stimulant medication like Ritalin can also diminish excessive worry, such as that associated with Attention Deficit Disorder.

All these medications have side effects, some of which are unpleasant. If antidepressant medication is an option you will be informed of all the potential risks and benefits by your doctor. Remember too that they can only administered by a doctor, who will ensure the correct dosage and closely monitor your progress. Sometimes you might need to experiment with various drugs to see which one is right for you. The mind is a mysterious thing, and it is impossible to predict with certainty which medication will be most beneficial for you. Don't give up if the first one doesn't work. The next one might. Let your doctor decide.

THERAPY

Psychotherapy broadly means 'talking cure', a client talking through their problems with a therapist; but it's actually a term used for a wide range and scale of therapies and practitioners. For centuries therapy, or talking about how we feel, was the only option available when worry became toxic. When done properly, by trained therapists, therapy can work as well as medication. The secret is finding the right kind of therapy for you. For most worriers cognitive-behavioural therapy seems to work best. Basically this involves learning to talk to yourself positively during episodes of worry.

Many lives are enriched and repaired by therapy, but an unskilled therapist can be far more damaging than no therapist at all. If you need therapy you may feel in a vulnerable position, so it's important that your vulnerability is not exposed and exploited. If you are considering therapy and wants to get something organised without first seeing a doctor, it's important that you are informed and educated about the different kinds of therapy available. Certification and licensing in various forms of therapy vary from region to region, so you need to exercise care in finding a therapist with adequate training.

PSYCHIATRY

This branch of medicine is concerned with the diagnosis and treatment of mental disorders. A psychiatrist is a medical doctor who has done further training in psychiatry. Treatment will involve a combination of drugs and therapy. It is important that you are aware that a psychiatrist is the only therapist who can prescribe drugs on prescription.

Psychiatry is suitable for people with a recognised clinical depression or other mental illness such as schizophrenia.

Not all psychiatrists have much experience in psychotherapy, but some do. In past decades psychiatric training emphasised the physical cause of depression and treatment with medication only. As a result the psychiatric community is increasingly divided between those who favour the biological explanation and those who favour more psychological causes and practice psychotherapy. Some work closely with a psychologist or therapist who is providing the psychotherapeutic portion of the treatment.

PSYCHOLOGY

This branch of medicine is concerned with human behaviour. It is illegal for someone without training or qualifications to be called a chartered or licensed psychologist. Psychology is suitable for people with psychological distress or mental problems, including anxiety, phobias, obsessive compulsive behaviours and addictive behaviour.

Many clinical psychologists work in private practice, but they are also found in health centres, hospitals and community centres. Counselling psychologists work with relationship problems and family issues. Educational psychologists deal with children with emotional or social problems and learning difficulties. Occupational psychologists help companies with training, motivation and matters such as stress and workplace bullying.

While searching for a psychologist look for the description 'chartered' or 'licensed psychologist'. The Psychological Society of Ireland can be contacted in Ireland. The British Psychological Society publishes a register of chartered psychologists and this is available at libraries or on their website. In the US contact the American Psychological Association to find out more about requirements for licensing, or call the state education department, division of professional licensing services, for the requirement of a particular state.

PSYCHOTHERAPY

Traditional psychotherapy, called psychoanalytic psychotherapy, is the original talking cure. A client sits facing the therapist and discusses life problems. Each session lasts for an hour, and the treatment can last for months or years. It is based on the principles of psychoanalysis, placing importance on a patient's early life experience and exploring their thoughts, feelings, dreams and memories. The psychotherapist's skill is to listen carefully and to suggest new ways of seeing patterns or thought behaviour.

Psychotherapy is suitable for people with depression, anxiety, relationship problems, eating disorders, obsessive behaviour and low self-esteem. The aim of a good psychotherapist is to be a guide and support for you to find your own solution.

When searching for a psychotherapist look for accreditation from The Irish Council of Psychotherapy in Ireland or either the British Confederation of Psychotherapists or the United Kingdom Federation of Psychotherapists in the UK. Training takes a minimum of three years. The confederation also publishes two free pamphlets called *Finding a Therapist* and *Psychoanalytic Therapy*. The UK Council of Psychotherapy can inform you about qualified psychotherapists.

In the US there are no rules or restrictions about who can call themselves a psychotherapist. If you are referred to someone who calls him or herself a psychotherapist be sure to ask questions about his or her psychological training to determine if he or she is suitable. In some states social workers are trained in psychotherapy. Check with your state authorities that the social worker is licensed and certified to be a psychotherapist.

It's impossible to describe all the various forms of psychotherapy in this book (for further information see resources section) but the form that has already been cited in this book as an effective tool for beating worry is cognitive-behavioural therapy developed by a University of Pennsylvania psychiatrist, Aaron T Beck.

COGNITIVE-BEHAVIOURAL THERAPY

Cognitive therapy focuses on practical techniques — changing thought processes and behaviour to solve specific problems. It does not try to alter your moods; rather it tries to find ways of altering how you look at things that are causing your moods. For example, you may live in fear of heart trouble and interpret perfectly natural aches and pains as meaning disease. A cognitist having identified such beliefs would show you how your thinking is wrong — showing you, for example, how your aches and pains can be due to poor posture or muscular strain.

Cognitive-behavioural therapists believe that thoughts affect feelings and vice versa. The therapist would use this approach to help you focus on self-defeating automatic thoughts such as 'I'm a failure' and the unconscious belief system behind them. Negative thoughts are analysed as you would analyse the hypothesis of a scientific experiment. They are taken apart and tested bit by bit. Beliefs are explored together, tested and finally changed.

For instance, if you think you are a failure, a therapist might ask, 'Are you a failure in every aspect of your life?' or 'Think of something you succeeded in doing last month.' The therapist helps you recognise for yourself that your thoughts may be illogical, distorted, one-sided and faulty. When you are able to recognise this you can then start challenging negative thinking so that your feelings about yourself improve.

The work you do outside of the therapy session will be as important as the time spent in the session. You'll be given assignments each week. These assignments can consist of listing negative thoughts that occur during the day, reading material about anxiety, reviewing the therapy sessions on tape, writing, role-playing and so on.

BRIEF THERAPY

Brief therapy refers to a combination of therapeutic techniques used over a short period of time. It often involves cognitive-behavioural techniques along with elements of analytical thinking or counselling. It is suitable for specific stress-related problems. The therapy is very goal oriented and practical. That doesn't mean, however, that there isn't opportunity to explore feelings or past experiences.

COUNSELLING

Counsellors often work in clinical or institutional settings along with other mental health professionals. There can be some confusion about the distinction between therapists and counsellors. Sometimes the difference involves qualification or training, but more often it refers to a different theoretical approach.

As a general rule counselling is shorter term and may be focused on particular issues that have arisen out of the past or present. It can enable a person to find solutions or insights into particular areas of his or her life. Counsellors can be seen as professionals who can help with emotional problems such as low self-esteem, loss, bereavement or addiction. During the course of the sessions a counsellor will help a person look at patterns of behaviour that are stopping him or her getting the most out of life. Sessions are just under an hour long and last for a period of time agreed between the client and counsellor.

FINDING THE RIGHT COUNSELLOR

Some doctors will give you a direct referral to a counsellor if this is advised. In the UK there may be one attached to the doctor's practice or you may be given a list of available counsellors in your area if you decide to refer yourself. Usually counsellors who are attached to doctor's practices will see clients in a room attached to the surgery. You will probably be offered about six sessions. Counsellors who are employed as part of a doctor's or GP practice will have had qualifications and references checked.

When You Need A Bit Of Extra Help

Finding the right counsellor may be a process of trial and error. Counsellors follow a range of theoretical backgrounds or models. You may find this confusing at times, but you shouldn't be put off by wondering where they are coming from. At the heart of the counselling process is helping the individual. A counsellor is there to help you look at how problems are presenting themselves and to help you find a way through the difficulties you are facing.

Should you wish to go into longer-term counselling after the first set of sessions, you can ask about continuing, and if you need to look elsewhere the British Association for Counselling has lists of counsellors in the local areas. There is also a reference directory on the internet of qualified and registered practitioners.

Above all, check that the counsellor or therapist you visit is properly trained and qualified. The British Association for Counselling can give further information and the address is at the back of the book.

In the US the term counsellor is used to describe a wide variety of different mental health professionals. They often work in clinics alongside other mental health professionals. Some counsellors hold a CAC, which means they are certified to counsel people on alcohol and drugs, but in most states, there are no uniform licences or certification required to call oneself a counsellor. Check that the counsellor has experience working with people who are mentally ill and a bachelor's or associate's degree in psychology, counselling or a related field.

COMPUTER REFERRALS

The computer on your desk may not be able to worry but one day it may be able to straighten you out. Already this is happening in a small way in the US. Dr Judy Proudfoot and a team at the Institute of Psychiatry have got together with Ultramind, a company specialising in healthcare to produce *Beating the Blues*.

Beating the Blues consists of 12 CD-ROMs and is designed to be operated under doctor's supervision, where it is currently being tested. Where there is a shortage of psychologists and cognitive-behavioural therapists the idea is that when a doctor diagnoses anxiety or depression the patient is referred to the computer instead of being given pills or put on a waiting list.

The program consists of eight sessions, one session a week, with activities and tasks to complete each week. It uses a combination of TV documentary type case studies and interactive therapeutic processes to encourage patients to think about their own situation. Most of the therapy techniques are cognitive-behavioural techniques, so it's about analysing and channelling how you think and looks at your behaviour and belief system to detect where your thinking system has become distorted. The aim is to encourage patients to apply these techniques to their own lives. It's not just for people who are worried, but also for people who are stressed and depressed.

Some people may prefer a computer screen to face-to-face contact because it is less personal and they see the therapist as judgmental. In the US this kind of program has been shown to be as effective as therapy. If there are problems a GP will intervene. So far the computers are only available in doctor's surgeries. In time this kind of program might be available at home.

Cybertherapy is already available on the internet, but the lack of regulation makes it an unreliable and potentially dangerous option.

WHAT DOES ALTERNATIVE MEDICINE HAVE TO OFFER?

Certain alternative remedies claim to be able to relieve the symptoms of anxiety and promote feelings of physical and emotional wellbeing. You might want to think about the following options.

NUTRITIONAL AND HERBAL SUPPORT

Nutritional and herbal support for the person experiencing signs and symptoms of toxic worry largely involve supporting the adrenal glands — two small glands that are located above each kidney. The adrenal glands play a critical role in the body's resistance to stress. If stress is too great the adrenal glands will become exhausted and not perform well, causing worry, anxiety, fatigue and depression.

Foremost in restoring or maintaining proper adrenal function is to ensure adequate potassium levels in the body — at least three to five grams a day. This is done by consuming food rich in potassium and low in sodium. A diet rich in fruit and vegetables should be able to do this. Food rich in potassium includes raisins, almonds, dates, carrots, mushrooms, garlic, dried figs and peanuts.

SHOULD I TAKE A SUPPLEMENT?

In an effort to increase the intake of essential nutrients many of us take vitamin and mineral supplements. Medical opinion is divided on the use of such supplements. Some say that diet alone should provide all the essential nutrition, while others say that it simply isn't possible to get adequate intake via food alone.

Bear in mind that most of us consume a diet that is inadequate in nutritional value. Various studies show that the chances of consuming a diet that meets the recommended daily intake of essential nutrients is unlikely, since most of us are too addicted to junk food. Better eating habits are the ideal, but for the majority nutritional supplementation is advised.

If you do decide to take a vitamin and mineral supplement make sure it provides the full range of vitamins and minerals. There are thirteen different vitamins and twenty-two different minerals, all are important for human function. Make sure that the vitamins and minerals are based on the RDA or recommended daily allowances prepared by the relevant national authority. Bear in mind though that the RDA are designed to prevent nutritional deficiencies and there is still much to be learned regarding optimum intake of nutrients.

Several nutrients are important for supporting adrenal function and reducing stress: vitamin C, vitamin B6, zinc, magnesium and pantothenic acid. All these nutrients play a key role in the health of the adrenal glands — levels of these nutrients plummet during times of stress.

It is well-known that during periods of anxiety and stress vitamin C needs increase. Extra vitamin C in the forms of supplements along with an increased intake of vitamin C rich food, such as fruit and vegetables, is recommended to keep the immune system strong during times of stress. Equally important is pantothenic acid (B vitamins). Deficiency in B vitamins causes fatigue, headache, insomnia, indigestion and nausea. You can find B vitamins in wholegrains, legumes, cauliflower, broccoli, salmon and tomatoes. It might be useful to take an additional one hundred milligrams of pantothenic acid a day. Adequate magnesium and zinc is also important. Magnesium, found in green leafy vegetables and fresh nuts, needs to be balanced with adequate calcium intake. Zinc, found in nuts and lean meat can be a useful boost.

HEALING OILS

The human body and mind can't function well without essential fatty acids. There is growing evidence that many people, especially women, suffer from a deficiency of omega-3 oils, a type of essential fatty acid. Deficiency in essential fatty acid is linked to dry skin and nerve disorders.

Regular meals of cold-water fish such as herring and mackerel and seafood provide enough omega-3, but you might need to take fish oil capsules. Your best source of high-quality flaxseed oil, a rich source of essential fatty acids, will be a health food store. It is best to take the oil in liquid rather than capsule form. Other popular vegetable oils, like olive, sunflower and corn, contain essential omega-6 oils. Green leafy vegetables are another good source.

PLANT-BASED MEDICINE

Various herbs support adrenal function, the most well-known are the ginsengs. Both Chinese Panax ginseng and Siberian ginseng can enhance the ability to cope with stresses, both physical and mental. Research shows that ginseng offers significant benefits to people suffering from anxiety and fatigue. Ginseng, particularly

Panax ginseng, can restore adrenal functioning for individuals under extreme stress.

Panax ginseng is generally regarded as more potent than Siberian ginseng. If you have been under chronic stress and constantly feel anxious Panax ginseng is advisable, but if you have been under mild to moderate stress Siberian ginseng might be your best choice.

There are many types and grades of ginseng extracts available; each individual's tolerance to ginseng is unique. It is advisable to consult with a qualified herbalist to get the dose that is right for you. Too much ginseng or the wrong kind of ginseng can produce unpleasant symptoms and increase anxiety levels.

In addition to ginseng the adrenal glands can also be supported by taking adrenal extracts, oral adrenal extracts made from beef.

ST JOHN'S WORT

St John's Wort or Hypericum perforatum is an herb that is widely used and prescribed in Europe for depression, although no longer available over-the-counter in Ireland. It is emerging as one of the most popular, effective and safest antidepressants — perhaps even more popular than conventional antidepressants. For example, in Germany it is the number one antidepressant prescribed by doctors, far outselling Prozac. Every year German doctors write three million prescriptions, as compared with 240,000 for Prozac. It could become an astonishing alternative to the drugs now used in the US and the UK to treat depression.

St John's Wort is a naturally occurring herb, not the result of pharmaceutical development. It does appear to help many people suffering from depression with minimal side effects. It can also help reduce the symptoms of anxiety and stress. Research on St John's Wort is still in its infancy, but recent studies show that it may affect the transmission of all the neurotransmitters serotonin, norepinephrine and dopamine, which are thought to create a feeling of well being.

The target dose in most antidepressant studies of mild to moderate depression is 900 milligrams of Hypericum a day, and the Kira TM brand is most often recommended. Side effects are rare but may include stomach upsets, fatigue and less commonly allergic reactions. It can also occasionally interact with other drugs, so you need to ask the pharmacist or your doctor for advice. It's perhaps best to start with a low dose and build up, but self-medication is a tricky business. Each person will react differently. Some enthusiasts are hailing St John's Wort as a wonder drug, but it is important not to put all your hopes in one treatment alone and to keep an open mind. Some people don't feel better after taking it.

Being properly informed is crucial. You will find information about the herb in books about the medicinal properties of herbs. Dr Norman Rosenthal's *St John's Wort: Your Natural Prozac* is an invaluable guide that will tell you everything you need to know about the herb, how it can help, how to take it, what the side effects are, and how to monitor your progress on it.

KAVA

Kava is a drink made from the Kava root and is used in the Pacific Islands for its calming effect and ability to promote sociability. Preparations of Kava root are now gaining popularity in Europe and the USA for their mildly sedative effect.

Kava drinkers relate a pleasant sense of tranquillity and sociability on consumption and a reduction in anxiety. If you take standardised Kava extracts at recommended levels there should be no side effects. High doses are unnecessary and should not be encouraged. Always follow the therapeutic dosage recommended, which is usually between 135 and 210 milligrams daily. In time you might feel more optimistic and have a relaxed mental outlook.

OTHER REMEDIES THAT MAY HELP

The therapies listed here all adhere to the principle of holism — the body, mind, spirit and emotions are interdependent parts of the whole person. If you feel anxious your therapist will want to build up a picture of your whole life and your unique constitution to make a diagnosis.

ALEXANDER TECHNIQUE

This is a system of re-education that is aimed at helping you regain natural balance, posture and ease of movement and to eliminate habits of slouching or slumping. You will be taught new ways of using your body and to think about new ways of keeping your spine free of tension. The Alexander technique can help with stress-related conditions, including fatigue and anxiety. The anxious tensing of muscles that often accompanies worry can contribute significantly to feelings of low self-esteem. It's harder to feel depressed when you stand tall and relaxed with your head high.

AROMATHERAPY

Aromatherapy involves the use of oils extracted from plants, herbs and trees, to promote physical and emotional wellbeing. It is often used in conjunction with massage. Oils can be rubbed into your skin or added to your bath. Oils most often recommended for anxiety are sandalwood, camomile, lavender, rose, clary sage, lavender and bergamot.

AUTOGENIC TRAINING

You might consider autogenic training — a gentle form of self-administered psychotherapy that teaches special mental exercises to help you relax mentally and physically and replace negative thoughts with positive ones.

AYURVEDA

Ayurveda is the name of the Indian science of life. It is a comprehensive health-care system and incorporates detoxification, diet, exercise, breathing meditation, massage and herbs. Herbs are used as part of remedies designed to correct different sorts of energy imbalances in the body. Anxiety is believed to be a symptom of such imbalances, and an important aim of the skilled practitioner is to eliminate them. Yoga can be a significant part of ayurveda.

BACH FLOWER REMEDIES

There are thirty-eight different flower remedies, all widely available in chemists and health stores. The remedies are good for health and balancing emotional, spiritual and psychological states such as uncertainty, indecision and despondency. Bach Rescue Remedy combines the benefits of several flowers and acts as a sort of quick boost if you are under stress. For sudden anxiety with no obvious cause, try mustard.

CHINESE MEDICINE

Acupuncture, together with t'ai chi and herbalism, form the basis of traditional Chinese medicine, a system of healthcare still widely practiced in Hong Kong, China and in some states in the US. Herbs are used to prevent ill health and to treat both mental and physical illness and to balance emotional upset. Ginseng is a well-known Chinese remedy used to stimulate energy. Tiger balm is used to relieve aches and pains.

A doctor of Chinese medicine will recommend the herbs that address the particular imbalances in the patient that are contributing to anxiety. Because the effects are gentle, improvement is seen after several weeks or several months of treatment.

Acupuncture involves using needles to stimulate points in the body called acupoints. Over thousands of years the Chinese have mapped the network of energy lines that permit the flow of vital energy through the body. In the Chinese system, worry causes or is caused by, blockages in these energy lines; acupunture relieves the blockage by stimulating select points. Those who have experienced acupuncture report feeling calmer and more clear-headed after treatment.

Acupressure is a form of massage built on the philosophy of acupuncture. In acupressure the acupoints are stimulated to alleviate depression. Pressure points associated with anxiety include a point four fingers' width from the inside of the ankle and a point two fingers' width from either side of the spine, just below the shoulder blades.

HERBALISM

Medicinal herbalism uses the curative properties of various parts of plants, such as flowers, trees, bark, nuts, seeds and herbs to maintain good health and treat disease. Herbs can be taken in a variety of forms — tinctures, teas, infusions, creams, ointments or capsules. St John's Wort is one such herb.

Warning — many natural remedies, such as herbal preparations, are available at chemists and health stores, but self-medication is not usually advised and you should always consult a qualified practitioner. Make sure also that you check with a doctor that the medications are safe and do not interact with any current medication.

HOMEOPATHY

The art of treating like with like, homeopathy relies on the belief that a substance that causes particular symptoms can also be used in minute doses to cure those same symptoms. Remedies are derived by diluting, in water and alcohol, sources taken from plants, minerals and animals. Homeopaths prefer to treat each case individually, but Natrum mur is often recommended when a person thinks constantly of past, sad events. Ignatia, Pulsatilla and sulphur may also help lift mood. A special homeopathic combination — L.72 Anti-Anxiety has been shown to be effective in treating anxiety.

HYPNOTHERAPY

Hypnotherapy can be a powerful aid for those fighting addictions to alcohol, cigarette or drugs, for those suffering traumas or phobias, and for those wanting to boost self-image. A hypnotherapist can induce a light trance in the client, which can bring to consciousness repressed emotions, which is particularly helpful if depression is the case. The client can become receptive to suggestions that can help him or her to accept or reject patterns of belief or behaviour; it is also helpful for depression. In unskilled hands hypnotherapy may be unwise, so make sure a therapist is chosen carefully.

MEDITATION

Meditation, or visualisation, is a contemplative technique that can calm and clear an overactive mind. During meditation brain waves change to a distinctive pattern linked with deep relaxation and mental alertness. Regular meditators can shift into this mode at will, allowing them to deal efficiently with stress.

It is one of life's ironies that those who would benefit most from meditation are invariably the ones who are most resistant to it. If you feel anxious meditation may not appeal to you, but studies show that meditation can reduce stress, anxiety and depression.

NUTRITIONAL THERAPY

Nutritional therapy uses diet and vitamin and mineral supplementation to balance the body and prevent illness. There are three basic diagnoses: food intolerances, nutritional deficiencies and toxic overload.

Nutritional deficiency is tested for by analysing samples of blood, sweat or hair. Mood disorders have been linked to low levels of serotonin. Serotonin is made from the amino acid tryptophan, and for the body to convert tryptophan into serotonin, vitamins B3, B6, and zinc are essential so levels need to be kept up. A diet high in complex carbohydrates is recommended. Naturopaths suggest eating turkey, nuts, milk and bananas as they contain tryptophan. Protein meals containing essential fatty acids, like salmon and white fish, are also good choices. Vitamin C is a powerful antioxidant that can relieve stress. Selenium is thought to elevate mood. Low zinc levels and deficiencies in B vitamins may also be linked with anxiety.

Toxic overload is diagnosed through an analysis of symptoms and diet, and fasting may be recommended to clear the system. A diet high in sugar and saturated fats, such as hamburgers and chips, can lead to fatigue and depression. Alcohol, caffeine, processed foods and smoking deplete the body of essential nutrients and increase the risk of anxiety.

SOOTHING THERAPIES

Soothing colours can be a good antidote to excessive worry by calming the activity of over-stimulated brain waves. Colour therapists often recommend blue to promote feelings of serenity and healing and orange to keep the spirits up when they are low.

Music can uplift and inspire. Whether it's Mozart, Beethoven, Mantovani, Bach or Abba, the Beatles, Diana Ross or Ricki Martin music can soothe a troubled mind. But music does more than uplift, inspire and soothe; regular rhythms and tonal structures can elicit suppressed feelings in need of expression and catharsis.

T'AI CHI AND YOGA

T'ai chi is a gentle art that employs meditation and calm, smooth dance movements to improve the health of mind, body and spirit. Breathing should be co-ordinated with movement. In order to make a significant difference to health, t'ai chi needs to be practiced regularly.

Like t'ai chi, yoga pays attention to breathing and incorporates meditation. Yoga poses keep the joints and muscles flexible, build strength and promote health through nourishing the internal organs with breathing and movement. Salutary effects on the immune system have also been attributed to it.

If you want any further information on any of these therapies, you should contact the Institute for Complementary Medicine (address in resources). It is an impartial organisation that acts on behalf of consumers of natural medicine, as well as promoting research into the safety and effectiveness of alternative therapies.

AN OPTIMISTIC NOTE

In this chapter we've considered the worst case scenario — worry that you can't deal with yourself — but I'd like to conclude this chapter on an optimistic note. Most worry you can do something about. In many cases it is only a matter of time before worry management skills improve and worry reduces. If you can't do anything about your problem, hopefully you can change the way you feel about it and worry less. And even if you think you need to seek professional advice this doesn't mean worry has won. Doctors, psychologists and counsellors will all be able to help you reduce levels of anxiety and worry.

It's rare for worry to totally destroy the quality of your life, but it is common for worry to make your life less enjoyable than it should be. Use the tips and advice mentioned in this book to analyse what is worrying you and find solutions that work for you. Keep practising and eventually you will be able to worry constructively. And when you start to worry well you may even find that although worry can be draining and difficult it can also be helpful and at times enjoyable.

WORRYING CAN BE FUN

'How can worrying be fun?' you may ask. If you learn to worry well. Let's explain.

In your experience you know that a certain amount of pressure can bring excitement. When you worry about something you show how it important it is to you. The greatest feelings of pleasure often come when something you have worried about resolves itself successfully.

There is a very thin line dividing excitement from anxiety, stress and pain. The basis of feelings of excitement and anxiety are emotional and physical. Both are based on the activity of our hormones and the excretion of adrenaline.

Some people such as stunt actors, racing drivers and circus artists, find feelings of tension exciting and actually seek them out to improve performance. Most of us are also guilty of seeking out tension from time to time, to make us feel more alive. Every time we choose to watch the scary movie, ride in the fast car, go on the big wheel, meet someone new and so on, we are choosing worry as a form of enjoyment. The tension makes us feel more alive.

If you can accept that you can seek tension it should be easier to start controlling it. Choosing when to seek tension is a way of beginning to manage it. Worry is a choice. It may not seem so at the time but you worry because you choose to. This is important. If you can stop blaming outside forces and take responsibility for your worrying, you can start to alter it; rather than dreading it, you can start enjoying it.

A certain amount of worry keeps you alert. It gives you that edge you need to think through the issues, make better decisions and pay attention to what is important. It points you in the direction of change when change is needed. It reminds you to think about what you really want to do with your life.

Your goal should never be not to worry at all, but to worry well. You can't and shouldn't try to banish worry completely. Worry can inspire you to take positive action and remind you to cherish what is important. It's only when you worry too much that problems arise. The secret is to worry less and to worry in a positive way.

In the unlikely possibility that you do find yourself without a care in the world, and are worried about having nothing to worry about, here are a few suggestions that will stoke up that tension and give you plenty to worry about.

- Have children.
- Spend more than you earn.
- Shop, commute and travel at peak times.
- Leave everything to the last minute.
- Buy a computer.
- Deal with bureaucracies.
- Move to a new house.
- Change job.
- Become a DIY expert.

- Visit your dentist regularly.
- Over commit yourself.
- Go on a diet.
- Be a fashion victim.
- Read women's magazines.
- Invite the relatives for Christmas.
- Choose the wrong partner.
- Make every second count.
- Research findings about the ozone layer and global warning.
- Watch the news.
- Read lots of self-help books!

PART 4
WORRY LESS AND LIVE MORE

Be the change you want to see in the world.

Mahatma Gandhi

CHAPTER 18

ADDRESSING SPECIFIC WORRIES

The information given in Part 3 will help you deal with worries of all kinds, but here are some additional reinforcements for specific worries. Use these suggestions in conjunction with the five steps of worry management. The 'Where To Find Help' section at the back of the book lists useful addresses and contacts too for you to find extra information, help and advice.

MINOR IRRITATIONS

You may find yourself worrying about things that are not very important, will not have far-reaching effects, are trivial and often petty and don't really matter that much. But these minor setbacks are annoying all the same.

You may be the kind of person who worries about the least little thing. The worry includes things you may have done in the past, are doing in the present or might do in the future. Some of the following might sound familiar.

> I wish I hadn't done that.
> I shouldn't have said that.
> Am I overweight?
> Am I taking too long?
> Will I get there on time?
> Will it rain?
> Will I get that job?
> What will they think of me?

Fretting about minor concerns isn't a major problem for most of us, but it can make us feel tense and irritable. It can also affect our concentration. Life would be much more enjoyable if we could let go of some of these worries.

When you notice that you are preoccupied with minor worries, you might want to do a reality check. In the general scheme of things, is this really so very important? If you feel that it is, then it is time to start working on your self-esteem.

When something becomes so important to you that it determines how good you feel about yourself, your self-confidence must be at a low ebb. You feel that without achieving this, doing that or looking a certain way you won't be happy. But it's dangerous when you start making your happiness dependent on external forces, because external forces are transient and unpredictable.

True happiness can come only when you start believing in and liking yourself. This doesn't mean that you stop wanting things. It means that you stop needing things to go a certain way to make you feel good. It's great when things go your way but if they don't this won't plunge you into the depths of despair. Your self-worth isn't based on what happens to you or who approves of you. It is based on feeling good about yourself.

As well as working on your self-esteem, when minor worries threaten to unsettle you it might also be helpful to think about how much you take for granted in life. On one particular morning when I was travelling home after failing a job interview and feeling sorry for myself and anxious about my future, I passed a man with stumps where his arms should be. He gave me the most wonderful smile and said 'It's a beautiful day isn't it'. I had been so self-absorbed that I hadn't even noticed that the sun was shining and it was a lovely day. I had so much to be grateful for.

Other helpful techniques include:

- Set aside a scheduled worry time of say fifteen to twenty

minutes when you do your fretting and then let your worries go.

- Remind yourself that worrying is normal. Rather than letting everyday worries overwhelm you, regard them as normal and let them go.
- Ask yourself if there is anything you can do about what you are worrying about; if there isn't, stop worrying. It's a waste of time and energy and won't achieve anything.
- If you can, try the relaxation and distraction techniques.
- Ask yourself if the worry is really worth bothering about; what the benefit of worrying about it is; and if there is anything else you could be doing with your time that would be more fun.
- And finally, lighten up a little and see the funny side of things. Inject some humour into the situation, and have a good laugh at yourself.

If you worry a lot about what other people think, remember that what they think is up to them and really has nothing to do with you. If that doesn't help, it might be good to bear in mind that although we often think other people are thinking about us, most of the time they really aren't. They are thinking about themselves!

THINGS YOU CAN CONTROL

Worriers often aren't clear about what they can and can't control in their lives. A lot of worry can be eliminated when you realise that what you do with your life, what you say and what you think are within your control. Here's a list of some of the things you can take control of:

- lifestyle
- health (to some extent)
- time management
- smoking
- eating
- alcohol
- relaxation

- spending
- exercise
- your behaviour towards others
- your job
- your achievements
- where you live.

Most of the worries associated with the above can be controlled. The trouble is lack of time, energy and self-doubt, along with apathy and procrastination often get in the way. If this is the case it is important to think about the thought patterns that may be hampering your efforts to bring these issues under control and replace them with more positive ones. For instance, if you think that you need to be working all the time to feel worthwhile, you need to realise that you can take time off to relax and still be a motivated person.

You also need to create some kind of action plan to create change in your life that can address and control specific worries. Decide what you want to achieve and why you think you can't. Then think about when and how you are going to put your plan into action. Finally, do it.

For example, if you constantly worry about your weight and can't diet, set yourself a realistic goal of weight loss that you want to achieve. Keep a food diary to record the times that you eat. Think about what has stopped you losing weight in the past. Find ways to eliminate these factors. For instance, if you eat chocolate when you feel emotional, stock the fridge with healthy food choices or decide to go for a brisk walk instead. Keep a record of your progress, and continue to monitor yourself until you have achieved your goal.

It sounds easy on paper, you and I know that this often isn't the case, but it is possible to replace old behaviours with new behaviours so that they become habits. Never lose sight of the fact that you can relieve worry about things that are within your control. But what about those things you can't control?

Addressing Specific Worries

WHEN THINGS ARE OUT OF YOUR HANDS

When you can't do anything about a particular worry this can be disturbing, even frightening. Worries of this kind include anxiety about:

- the health and well being of those you care about, especially your children
- relationships
- rejection and disappointment
- illness
- family issues e.g. divorce
- war
- crime
- violence
- accidents
- how others behave.

Worry about things that you can't control can be overwhelmingly burdensome. It can be hard to be happy at all when you are always thinking about issues like world poverty, the possibility of having an accident, losing someone you care about and so on. Should these worries become obsessive, they can seriously affect the quality of your life. The following suggestions might help:

- Get involved in some positive or rewarding goal that requires mental and physical effort, like music, dance, writing or voluntary work.
- Cultivate lots of interests and relationships.
- Find time to relax and reduce stress.
- Remember that life should be about pleasure and fun as well as achievements and work.
- Remember that worrying about things you cannot change is a waste of time. It won't achieve anything; all it does it make you unhappy and less productive.

- Setting aside worry about things you can't do anything about isn't uncompassionate; it is realistic.

SERIOUS CONCERNS

Worry can be a nuisance when it is about trivial things, but sometimes the situation is so serious and desperate that worry can totally consume you. Some situations involve loneliness, grief, pain and deep despair.

- The loss of a loved one.
- The ending of a relationship.
- Terminal illness in yourself or a loved one.
- Having a disability.
- Being the victim of crime.
- Being abused in some way.
- Someone you care about abusing themselves.

While you may not be able to do anything about the situation, how you deal with the worry the situation brings, can make a difference. Worry management skills can help you stay focused and consider what is best for all concerned.

Obviously dealing with this kind of worry is much harder than dealing with worries about minor situations. In these kinds of situations you need to have all your mental, emotional and physical capabilities in peak condition. If your mind is clouded by worry it can be hard to concentrate and think clearly. Relieving worry in these situations is essential. Never before has an action plan been so important.

- Start by asking yourself if there is anything you or someone else can do to improve the situation. You might need to ask others for help, call a help line, check out community services in your area, talk to a counsellor and so on.
- Take good care of your health so that you can cope with the higher level of stress.

- Keep as much order, routine and structure in your life as you can so that you feel in control. Go to bed and get up at the same time, have regular meals and stick to familiar routines.
- Get as much support as you can from family and friends. Make sure you keep in touch with people who make you feel good about yourself. Avoid people who are difficult to handle.
- Don't neglect to do things that you enjoy. Read a book, bake a cake, plant flowers in the garden, listen to music, enjoy yourself.
- Try to incorporate as much exercise as you can into your life. Exercise is a great way to lift your mood and distract you from unproductive worry.

Finally remember that however difficult and painful things seem to be for you right now, you won't feel like this forever. Everything changes, including worry. Remember that this is true, and wait for the moment when your despair begins to shift. The darkest night is just before the dawn. Never give up. Never lose hope. Believe in yourself and know that you can and will feel more hopeful again.

WORRYING ABOUT WHAT MAY BE

Imagining possible problems in the future is something many worriers do. Even when things are going well you may worry that the tide will turn and everything will fall apart around you. Typical worries include:

- life choices and goals
- ageing
- health
- losing a job
- death of a loved one
- loss of money
- possibility of accidents or poor health in loved ones
- approval of others.

If this is you, remind yourself over and over again that worrying about the future is a futile activity. It achieves or resolves nothing. These worries stop you enjoying life and often have no basis in reality. It is time to make changes.

When worries about the future crop up, take note of them, remind yourself that they have no basis in reality and then let them go. If there is anything you can do to prevent a possible future disaster do it; if there isn't, worry is a complete waste of your time. Instead of trying to address your worry you might benefit more from distraction.

Keep busy with other things that will distract you. Focus on the present, breathe correctly and try to relax. Find ways to keep your worry in check.

WORRY ABOUT THE WORLD

Worries about the state of our world may affect us, but most of the time we are able to put them aside and focus on the detail of our lives. If you are one of the few people who do worry intensely about global issues such as:

- poverty
- overpopulation
- war
- environmental degradation
- nuclear disaster
- social justice
- future quality of life
- violence
- human suffering and oppression
- the brutality of people towards other people.

The following ways of addressing worry may be helpful. Educate yourself so that you really do know what is going on and can make decisions about any action that you might want to take. You might want to contribute financially to a cause you worry about.

You might want to write letters, make phone calls to let your concerns be known to the individuals who can take action on your behalf. For instance, if you are concerned about how your country is dealing with unrest in other parts of the world write to your TD, MP, Prime Minister or President.

If it is appropriate you may be able to take action. A friend of mine feels passionately about the environment and involves herself regularly in pollution-reduction schemes. You might want to volunteer with an organisation that works on issues of global concern. You could become a spokesperson about an issue once you know about it. You could talk on radio, TV or write to newspapers. You could even run for election if you feel so inspired. This gives you a platform to speak out and do something about the issues you feel passionate about. Above all, remember that you can make a difference. In the words of Mahatma Gandhi, 'Be the change you want to see in the world.'

WORRIES ABOUT VIOLENCE, CRIME AND PERSONAL SAFETY
In a world where violence is widespread, crime can be rampant and accidents happen, such worry is to be expected. Most of us worry about being mugged, attacked or robbed.

The way to reduce such worries is to take precautions. Here are some actions you can take if you want to relieve worry about being the victim of violent attack.

- Avoid high-risk places and go in the company of others.
- Take self-defence classes.
- Carry a whistle and a mobile phone at all times.
- Walk in a self-confident manner.
- Always lock your car doors.
- Have your key in your hand ready to unlock your door when you get home.
- At home get a reliable security system of locks for doors and windows and perhaps an alarm.
- Have emergency contact numbers posted by the phone.

To avoid unnecessary accidents at home follow simple common-sense precautions such as keeping the walking areas and stairs clear, or having electrical systems checked and upgraded. The same applies for automobile safety. Wear your seat belt at all times, and never drink and drive. Find simple, practical ways you can minimise worry about risks to your personal safety.

MONEY WORRIES

Worry about money is often at the top of the list of specific worries. All of us worry about money at some time or another, regardless of the level of our income.

You can of course make a deliberate choice not to worry about money. This is an effective way to deal with financial concerns as long as you don't lose sight of how much you are earning and how much you are spending. Probably, though, you will find this approach impossible. Your money worries may be minor or major, but the following strategies might help:

- Set financial goals for a certain time period.
- Decide what you need to do to achieve those goals e.g. reduce spending, increase income or work more hours.
- Put your plan into action.
- If you can afford it, hire a financial planner to do your worrying for you.

A budget may be all that you need. This means setting up a system for allocating how much money you spend in each expense category, based on what you have spent in the past, with ongoing expenses and income. Determine your anticipated income, figure out your expenses categories, e.g. rent, tax, shopping, bills and so on, determine how much you can spend in each category. Ongoing budgeting on a yearly, monthly or weekly basis can keep you informed of your spending habits and relieve a lot of worry.

If you do need to reduce expenses it's amazing how easy that can be if you review your current expenses. Once you start thinking about your spending habits it becomes easier to change them and cut out unnecessary expenses. Living more simply and frugally may help you reduce expenses.

If you worry about being destitute, do some research to find out what benefits you would be entitled to. Keep a file of this information for easy access. Think about if there is anyone you could ask for support during a difficult time, and maintain strong connections with friends and family. Setting up a savings account may also bring peace of mind.

Setting up a savings plan and putting money aside for emergencies may help ease anxiety about money. Many of us think about saving money but don't get round to it, but if you are serious about reducing money worry, putting even a little money aside each week can give you a feeling of security.

WORRY AT WORK

Yoy may be in a job that you don't enjoy or that doesn't pay enough; or you may be worried that you aren't good enough at your job. Yet you feel that you can't leave your job. You may worry that you won't get another job; or that you aren't being paid enough.

One of the most common causes of worry is a difficult boss or colleagues. You may be putting up with a lot for the sake of that essential paycheque.

You can combat work-related worry by really thinking about what you want to do with your career. You might find that further education or study controls your worries and points you in the right direction.

If you are tied to a job you don't like because you don't think you are good enough to do anything else, ask yourself one question, how do you know? How accurate is your self-assessment? Self-appraisal is hard to do, but it is important that you do it. List your strengths and weaknesses. You may surprise yourself.

If the problem is dealing with difficult co-workers, don't get sucked into a feuding war. Assertiveness skills will certainly help here and may be all that is required for the other person to back off. If he or she doesn't, speak to someone in authority in confidence about your concerns. If need be, consult a lawyer. Remember too that in some way you might be contributing to the problem. Are you at times also being difficult?

One of the most powerful answers to work-related worry may well be increased togetherness and co-operation with others. Talk to the people you work with, involve them and don't get so wrapped up in your own work that you fail to recognise their needs.

HEALTH WORRIES

Health can be a constant concern for some people. In extreme cases bodily symptoms can become the major focus in life — family, work and happiness are neglected. The concern tends to intensify with age. This excessive focus on illness can destroy the quality of life, but there are a lot of things you can do. Today we know that we don't always have to get all the answers from our doctors. We know that the state of our health and wellbeing often depends on us.

First of all, we can educate ourselves about any illness that we might feel concerned about. We can learn about the pros and cons of taking certain medications and understand that there may be alternative treatments that are less invasive and often as effective.

Regular check ups with your doctor, immunisations, and screening tests for common diseases are also in your best interest. If you are worried about AIDS, use a condom or other barrier type protection when having sex, avoid the use of intravenous needles used by others, avoid contact with body fluids of others and get an HIV test through a healthcare provider.

Make sure that the treatment you get from healthcare professionals is of the highest quality. If you feel that your doctor isn't listening to you, change your doctor.

If you are diagnosed with a condition that can't be changed or in which the outcome is uncertain, worry just eats away at precious time. You can do all you can to make adjustments appropriate to your situation, but after that you have to let go or make a change in your attitude in order to stop worry making your life less comfortable than it should. Positive statements to counteract negative ones can be crucial.

The best strategy for minimising worry associated with health is taking care of your health in a sensible but not obsessive way. Remember that obsessive preoccupation with health is detrimental to peace of mind. Here are some changes you can make that will ease health-related worry:

- stop smoking
- reduce alcohol intake
- take more exercise
- eat healthily.

Smoking can make you ill. Just in case you need reminding, smoking causes cancer not just of the lung but of the nose, throat, mouth, larynx, oesophagus, stomach, bladder and probably colon. There are also associations with other cancers such as breast and pancreas. It also contributes to heart disease, vascular disease leading to circulation problems and stroke. It can harm an unborn child. It damages the lungs leading to bronchitis and respiratory problems. It can cause premature menopause. From a cosmetic point of view it leads to a hoarse voice, thinning and wasting of the bones, loss of teeth, dry skin and hair and wrinkles. It may also contribute to loss of libido. And it all that wasn't enough to put you off, it's dirty, discolours you skin and teeth, makes you smell of tobacco and your breath stink like an ashtray.

Given all this, why on earth would anybody smoke? If you choose to smoke you have to be prepared to accept the consequences. If you want to get out of harm's way you can choose to stop.

Giving up is easy for a few people and incredibly difficult for many others. Addiction to nicotine is not the main problem; nicotine passes out of your system in a matter of days; it is addiction to the habits you associated with smoking. Smoking is often a way to relax. It gives nervous people something to do with their hands when they feel uneasy. There are lots of programs and books to help you give up smoking; but perhaps the best way is to simply stop. Smoke your last cigarette and say that's it. When the cravings come, distract yourself and find other things to do. Remind yourself of the benefits of not smoking — more energy and improved health. In time the cravings will disappear and you will wonder why on earth you ever did something so wasteful and harmful to yourself.

Excessive alcohol consumption is also linked to poor health. If you drink more than one or two glasses of alcohol a day you are not doing yourself any favours. Diabetes, heart and liver problems are all linked to alcohol consumption. Alcohol isn't inherently evil. It is your ability to control and limit consumption and recognise the side effects that determines the damage to your health. Again, it's your choice.

Try to get some exercise each day. Human beings aren't meant to be sedentary. Don't neglect the use of that marvellous body you have been given. Earlier we outlined what a tonic regular exercise can be for the person who worries too much, how calming and strengthening it can be and how it can clear a mind clouded by worry. If you can't find time to squeeze in regular exercise, incorporate it when you can. Use the stairs instead of the lift; walk instead of using the car.

If you are concerned about your health, breaking poor eating habits will result in an improved sense of health and wellbeing. Reduce your intake of animal products, which are associated with the risk of heart disease, colon cancer and perhaps breast cancer. You can obtain much of the protein you get from animal products from other sources such as grains, legumes and fish. Increase your intake of fruits and vegetables. The latest dietary recommendations from the American Diabetic Association and the Food and Drug administration is up to five servings of vegetables a day and four servings of fruit a day.

Much has been learned about nutritional needs and health. You may need to rethink your attitude towards food. The essential elements of a healthy diet are in general: increase your nutrient intake by eating more vegetables and fruit; eat less meat and more grains; avoid sweets, refined and fatty foods; try to eat fish at least twice a week; avoid foods high in chemicals and preservatives; and cut down on caffeine and alcohol.

Most of us can do a better job in choosing what we eat. Healthy eating can alter your health and sense of wellbeing. It's your choice.

If you get anxious about your health, learn to approach symptoms of illness in a common-sense way. You may not always need to rush of to the doctor at the slightest ache and pain. Remember colds are common and usually last about a week. If the symptoms are debilitating and if your temperature lasts for more than twenty-four hours it is time to call a doctor. If you get the odd bout of indigestion, check what kind of food you ate, but if indigestion is continuous or there is something unusual in your bodily functions call your doctor. However, if the problem doesn't seem to immediately threaten life it makes sense to give it a little time to see if it will resolve on its own. In either case it's your choice.

Remember too that if you have a stressful life or are worried about something you may feel unwell. It doesn't matter how well you eat or how much you exercise if you can't find some joy and meaning in your life. Focus your mind on what really matters, and find a way to wake up grateful for every day. If you haven't got your health you haven't got anything. It's when you are grateful for what you have that you have everything.

RELATIONSHIP WORRIES

Relationship worries can involve many issues. You may be single, married, in a relationship, or worry could be related to your family and friends.

This isn't a book about relationships so it's impossible to explore this subject in detail. We've seen how worry can be a destructive, contagious element in relationships. It can turn minor problems into major problems, and the anxiety of one person can affect another.

If you are single much depends on the attitude that you have towards your status. You can see it as liberating and a wonderful opportunity to develop your own interests, or you can see it as limiting, painful and lonely.

If you are single, how do you feel about it? Do you think that being in a relationship would affect your worry? There are things you can do to ease your loneliness and meet new friends and potential partners. You could do voluntary work, start a hobby, contact a dating service, and network with friends. But it is important to remember that a relationship is not the answer to feelings of low self-esteem and loneliness. Binding your self-worth to other people is a recipe for disaster. It makes you dependent and them resentful.

At the end of the day the only person who can make you feel a lasting sense of fulfilment and satisfaction is you. Once you feel good about yourself you will find that relating positively to others becomes much easier. You can choose to find a partner to enrich your life, or you may decide that you are just fine without one.

If you are a single parent, this brings its own set of worries, but again there are creative solutions. You can network and gather support from others in similar situations. You can also let go of what others think and focus on doing the best you can to raise the children that you love. If you don't know whether you should stay in a relationship for the sake of your children, get involved in counselling and make the happiness and wellbeing of your children your first priority.

Being in a relationship carries with it a set of worries. You may worry about the health of your partner; you may argue a lot with your partner; you may want more or less commitment from your partner; you may be jealous of your partner; you may fear losing your partner; you may feel resentment towards your partner. Whatever the case, don't ever think that a solution can't be found.

If your relationship is important, you will be willing to put a lot of time and energy into it to keep it strong and healthy. You might want to read books on relationships, attend workshops or counselling. Some of the following strategies might help:

- Regular, open communication.
- Do things together.
- Enjoy silence.
- Focus on what you love about each other.
- Give each other plenty of space to be who you are.
- Practice unconditional acceptance and love, but don't ever let someone else try to make you say or do things that you don't feel comfortable with.

If you are in an abusive relationship these strategies may not be appropriate. Seek advice immediately from your doctor or a crisis centre.

Relationships with family members can bring their own set of complex worries. Children can be a great source of joy, but they can also be a great source of worry. You may worry about their health, safety, behaviour and their development. If you have such worries get support from family and friends, make sure your children are well cared for, and take appropriate health and safety measures. Reassure yourself that you are doing the best that you can, but accept that there will come a time when you simply have to let go and trust that your loving care has given your children enough resources and common sense to take care of themselves. If your anxiety is making you overprotective and your children aren't ever allowed to find out for themselves how difficult life can be, you are doing more harm than good.

You could also feel anxious about your family. Who will take care of your parents? Are your family disappointed with you? Wondering why you have lost contact? Worrying that you have too much contact? There are possible solutions to all these worries. If you are concerned about caring for your parents, plan in advance with them and realistically assess your ability to take care of them. If you feel that you are letting your family down, learn to accept yourself more. If you are afraid that you won't have your family's support in times of hardship, have regular communication and be there for them. If you don't get on with family members, realistically assess the situation, go to counselling if you have to, and don't let it stop you doing what you want with your life.

Finally, friends and acquaintances can contribute greatly to the richness, enjoyment and security in your life. Because we can choose our friends but we can't choose our family, people tend to worry less about friendships, but the importance of friendships for our health and wellbeing suggest that worries do arise and can affect us strongly.

You may worry about not having friends, whether or not people like you and what other people think of you. But there is a simple answer to such worries. If you want to have friends be a good friend yourself.

When you meet someone you feel that you could have a positive connection with, be interested in them, don't criticise but respect their opinions, be there for them and make them feel important. Don't impose yourself on others, and avoid being dependent, needy, negative, argumentative, critical or demanding. Enjoy their company but have a clear sense of who you are. Don't let boundaries blur. Don't behave in a way you think you ought to behave; be yourself, be a friend, and you will have friends.

And if you can learn to accept yourself you will always be the kind of person people will want to spend time with because you are confident, easy to talk to and a pleasure to be with.

Next we'll explore how worries about the kind of person you think you are can often make the difference between a life that is exciting and a life that is frightening.

Personal worries

Let's explore briefly those personal issues that can define us as individuals and often bring with them particular worries.

Criticism from others can be a cause of pain and worry. We all want to be liked and praised, criticism hurts. Much of course depends on the spirit in which the criticism was given. If it was intended to help you correct and improve, then see criticism as an opportunity to learn and grow, but if the criticism was unjust how do you cope with that?

You might want to bear in mind that unjust or unfair criticism is usually given to make the critic feel important. It often means that you are worthy of attention and the critic feels jealous or threatened. So the next time you are worried by unjust criticism, take it as a compliment.

Expectation placed on you because of your gender, or judgements made about you can be a cause for worry. Your gender may force you to confront roles you are not content with or make you worry more about issues that concern the other sex less.

This is a generalisation and there are many exceptions but women often feel trapped in the role of caretaker. There may be worries related to sexual harassment, low-paid jobs, limited career opportunities, unequal treatment, self-esteem, social expectations of how to look and behave. Men tend to have worries related to lack of intimacy, emotional repression, social expectation, self-esteem and providing financial support.

Creative solutions can be found for gender-related worries. Most of them involve confronting and letting go of stereotypes you or others may have, being clear about how you are and what you want and setting reasonable goals for yourself. The same applies to worries about sex or sexual orientation, worries related to religious, cultural and ethnic background and worries related to physical appearance.

If any of the personal issues above cause you worry or concern, above all you need to work on self-acceptance. Put simply, that is liking yourself and having confidence in yourself no matter who you are, what you look like, where you come from, where you are going and what others say about you.

If you don't think you are good enough, attractive enough, popular enough or talented enough ask yourself one question. How do you know? Are you being realistic? There are things you are good at, there are aspects of your personality to admire, you do have interests, you do have unique gifts, and there is something attractive about you. Nobody is ever wholly good or bad. It's time to stop focusing entirely on the negative and to allow the positive into the picture as well.

Worriers tend to suffer from low self-esteem. If this book has encouraged you to do anything, I hope it will be to feel more positive about who you are and where you are going. It might help to remember that never before and never again will there be someone like you. You are something totally unique in the world. There is no one else like you. You can only be who you are.

Confidence in yourself comes from the thoughts that you have about yourself. Everything begins with your thoughts. You are what your thoughts make you. Or in the words of Marcus Aurelius in his Meditations, 'Our life is what our thoughts make it.'

If you can think about yourself in a positive way, if you can find the courage to be yourself and to celebrate your uniqueness, then worry won't be able to overpower you or make you unhappy anymore.

You'll feel strong, confident and ready to take on anything that life throws at you.

CHAPTER 19

A WEEKLY WORRY
MANAGEMENT SCHEDULE

Many of the tips given here and in the final chapter will already have been mentioned in the book. But because of the temptation to worry needlessly they can't be repeated and emphasised enough.

The tips are all designed to help you worry less and enjoy your life more. Use them often enough and you shouldn't need to seek medical advice. However if symptoms persist you should see a doctor. Obviously worry management skills need to be practised on a daily basis, but the following weekly schedule might bring focus.

SUNDAY
Sunday is the day of the sun — the healer and bringer of light. It is a day to work for self-healing.

- Use this day to work on issues of low self-esteem.
- Practise self-acceptance.
- Focus on your strengths and not your weaknesses.
- Remind yourself that you don't need to be perfect. You just need to be yourself.

Use this day to think about how you can take better care of yourself. Make changes in your life that will affect not just your physical but your mental well being.

There are many ways you can do this, and they are all simple, free and natural. Eat healthily, exercise regularly, get the right amount of sleep, improve your posture, breathe deeply, schedule time for relaxation. All of these changes will help you worry less and feel better.

Do something that makes you feel good today. Distract yourself from unpleasant thoughts by doing something positive. Take a deep breath, look out of the window, smell a rose, sing a song, read a book, the list is endless. Life is about so much more than worrying. There is so much yet for you do to, feel, learn and experience. You haven't got time to worry. Let go of it.

MONDAY

Monday is the day of the moon — the world of feelings and intuition. It is the day to try to make sense of what your feelings are telling you.

Use this day to listen to your feelings. Write them down if this helps. It is okay to feel — anything. Worrying isn't a bad emotion. Try to think of it as helpful. Think of your worrying in terms of the basic questions you are asking yourself. Why do I feel vulnerable, and in what ways do I feel helpless? How can I change things to make me feel better? Try to see if there is a pattern to your worrying. Does it fit into a particular diagnosis, or is it more general?

If it fits in with one of the diagnostic patterns discussed in the book learn as much as you can about it and consult with a doctor. If you aren't sure if your worry fits a diagnosable pattern ask your doctor all the same. Make sure that you feel totally comfortable with your choice of healthcare. If you are one of the millions of people who worry but don't fit into a particular diagnosable category try to look at your worry in relation to the suggestions in this book.

You may be able to help yourself or you may choose to get support from a counsellor or therapist. Whatever you decide, looking at the pattern of your worry is in itself therapeutic, because you can begin to make sense of why you are worrying. You can begin to organise and categorise it, which is the beginning of managing it. If you can see worry coming, for instance, you can be better prepared and deliberately plan worry antidotes for times of anxiety.

A Weekly Worry Management Schedule

TUESDAY

Tuesday is the day of Mars — the warrior. It is the day to talk to yourself with courage, strength and determination.

Learn to talk to yourself constructively. Balance old patterns of automatic negative thinking whenever you can with positive ones. View problems and change not as obstacles but as challenges.

If you are working on worry management skills, strengthen your determination and resolve. You may find this tough because you are coming face-to-face with your own weakness, anger and unresolved emotions from the past. Demonstrate your resolve by not giving up. If you endure a setback try another approach.

As well as being firm in your convictions learn from your mistakes. You need both strength and humility to achieve your goals. Nobody said it would be easy to control worry. But like any challenge that is life enhancing, the rewards are great.

WEDNESDAY

Wednesday is the day of Mercury — the messenger of the gods. It is the day to reach out to others.

Focus today on making connections with others. Gather support from friends, family, partners and colleagues. Talk about how you feel to people you can trust. Ask for their help, reassurance, advice and support.

The resources section lists useful addresses and contacts for you to get information, help and advice. Worrying alone intensifies the anxiety; one of the oldest and still the most effective ways to deal with worry is to find a sympathetic ear. Explain your concerns to other people; ask for help and advice if you need it. It won't be long before you regain perspective.

THURSDAY

Thursday is the day of Jupiter — whose power is that of expansion and growth. Use this day to take action whenever worry sweeps over you.

Do something about worry when it strikes. First look at the situation you are worrying about and try to understand it. Then make an appropriate plan of action. Finally, implement the plan.

Your goal is to take action to remedy a problem. The action may be to ask for help, to do a budget, to work on your attitude, to talk to a doctor, to think about something else and so on. These may seem like simple steps, but taking action will make you feel less helpless and trapped.

FRIDAY

Friday is the day of Venus — whose power is love and harmony. Use this day to focus on love, harmony and partnership.

Concentrate today on partnerships of all kinds, both personal and at work or the community. Cherish the very special people in your life, remembering that to win the love, friendship and respect of others you must give love, friendship and respect yourself. And finally, don't forget to cherish yourself and your life too. Think of all the things you have to be grateful for.

SATURDAY

Saturday is the day of Saturn — the planet of wisdom and insight. Today is the day to learn and let go.

Use this day to consolidate all that has been gained; reflect on advances made, learn from setbacks and revise your plans for the future in light of what you have learned about yourself.

Today is the day to lay a firm foundation for the week to come and to ensure that you keep out the unwanted distraction worry causes. Today is also the day to reward yourself for any progress made, acknowledge what you have to be grateful for, and take responsibility for your feelings.

Today is the day to remind yourself that although you can't always choose what happens, you can always choose how you react to it. You don't have to succumb to worry. You can simply let go of it.

CHAPTER 20

ONE HUNDRED TIPS FOR MANAGING WORRY

Happiness is not about being perfect, successful, rich or beautiful. It's not about living forever. The secret to happiness is to be yourself, to use your common sense, and to avoid unnecessary worry, which prevents you from enjoying your life. You'll be surprised how much the common-sense advice of the review tips given below will help.

1. Think of worry as something that is helpful and natural.
2. Understand that worry can bring about difficult feelings, such as fear, anger, panic and confusion.
3. Base your worry on the facts rather than terrifying possibilities.
4. Most of the terrible things you worry about won't happen.
5. Remember you are not alone. Everyone worries.
6. It's normal to worry some of the time. It's not healthy to worry all the time.
7. Worrying about things is more frightening than doing something about them.
8. Happiness lies in channelling worry in a positive direction.
9. If you can't do anything about your worry, learn to give it up.
10. Worrying complicates things, and can make you feel ill and tired.
11. Worrying disrupts your concentration, creates indecision and causes physical, mental and emotional strain.
12. Worrying wastes time.
13. Ask for support and guidance when worry gets out of hand.

14. Know your limits.
15. Take deep breaths every time you worry.
16. Remember it's okay to make mistakes. Sometimes the only way to learn is through your mistakes.
17. It's okay to feel — even if those feelings make you feel scared and vulnerable.
18. Take care of yourself first.
19. Eat more carbohydrates and foods rich in tryptophan, such as eggs, cheese, milk, peas and soya beans.
20. Eat right.
21. Get enough rest.
22. Get enough fresh air and daylight.
23. Exercise a little every day if you can.
24. Learn to relax your muscles.
25. Stay sensual.
26. Control worry, don't let it control you.
27. Worrying doesn't achieve anything.
28. A worrier only sees problems. A doer sees challenges and opportunities.
29. Recognise that the problem-free life doesn't exist.
30. Life finds its meaning in meeting and solving problems.
31. Think of worry as helpful. It can alert you to potential danger.
32. Take responsibility for your feelings.
33. Be yourself.
34. Don't think you have to be perfect.
35. Tackle one problem at a time.
36. Not trying is a form of failing.
37. Winning isn't the answer; being happy with yourself is.
38. Mastering worry and fear is the beginning of wisdom.
39. Have a network of people who can give you reassurance and a sense of belonging.
40. Learn from your setbacks.
41. Listen to your conscience. If you do wrong it will give you a hard time.

42. Manage your time. Prioritise your tasks. Get organised.
43. Stop being a prophet of doom. The glass is also half full.
44. Don't make mountains out of molehills. Practise under-reacting.
45. Spend a day not watching TV or reading bad news in the newspapers.
46. Avoid caffeine, cigarettes, alcohol and drugs.
47. Remember all that you have to be grateful for.
48. Replace words like 'should', 'ought', 'must' with 'often', 'sometimes', 'either' and 'or'.
49. Be more flexible in your approach to life.
50. Give without worrying what you will get in return.
51. Don't take yourself so seriously.
52. Have more fun with your life.
53. Listen to music that inspires you.
54. Have patience. Learning and growing takes time.
55. The power of touch can be a great healer.
56. Try some massage.
57. Try some yoga.
58. Take a holiday.
59. Get a sense of perspective.
60. There is always more than one side to every story.
61. Talk to yourself in a calm, reassuring way.
62. The minute you recognise wasteful worry, do something about it.
63. Distract yourself by doing something positive when worry threatens to strike.
64. Remember that life is constant change. Nothing is permanent, not even worry.
65. See the larger picture, and don't let the devil bog you down in detail.
66. Reward yourself for your achievements.
67. Feel the fear and do it anyway.
68. Know that for every negative thought there is a positive to match it.

69. Expect to succeed and be happy.
70. Discover your strengths and weaknesses.
71. Set realistic goals and work towards them.
72. Understand that worrying stops you enjoying life.
73. Share your worries with people you can trust.
74. Children are copycats. If you worry they will copy.
75. Worry can be contagious.
76. Confront your worries instead of suffering them.
77. Think of creative solutions to your worries.
78. Worry is not your enemy. Accept it, deal with it, and make it your friend.
79. Complain if you are worried; don't bottle things up.
80. Keep your mind open.
81. Take calculated risks.
83. What others think about you is none of your business.
84. When you like and trust yourself, worry disappears.
85. You have a right to be happy.
86. Misery loves company. Seek out people who make you feel good about yourself.
87. Don't underestimate yourself.
88. Never give up.
89. Do something you enjoy every day.
90. Stressful events will pass. Worrying just complicates the situation.
91. Confidence in your ability to handle problems is more effective than worrying.
92. Believe that you will feel happy again.
93. Analyse the problem and take corrective action.
94. Don't exaggerate; tell the truth.
95. Ask for advice if you need it.
96. Count your blessings.
97. Do the best you can.
98. Have faith.
99. Smile more often.
100. Worry is a choice you make.

To control worry and attain the highest level of satisfaction, you need to do what you want to do with your life. Worry is the root of all evil because it stops you doing what you want to do with your life. Constant worry makes you feel trapped and helpless. But worry doesn't have to make you feel helpless.

Everyone worries but it is how you choose to worry that determines how happy and successful your life will be. Worry should drive you into action, not into depression. It should inspire positive change, not fear and indecision. The worry management skills in this book won't stop you worrying but they will help you worry in a positive, exciting way.

As you learn to cope with worry you will realise how important it is and you won't want to live without it. If you want to lead a worry-free life without setbacks, and uncomfortable feelings you may as well start looking for a coffin. Being alive means worry.

Life isn't perfect and it wasn't meant to be. You hold the key to your future. Always remember you have the choice. Worry isn't your enemy. What you do with it is up to you. Worry constantly and feel restless and unhappy. Turn worry in to a positive force and start creating the kind of life you want to live. It's as simple as that.

Worry doesn't have to be the root of all evil; it can be the root of all good. It offers you the gift of understanding yourself better and improving the quality of your life. Remember that the next time and every time you worry!

Chapter 21

WHERE TO GET HELP

You may wonder where you should go to seek advice and help and what kind of help is available. Worrying alone often makes things feel worse than they need to be. One of the most helpful things you can do when you are burdened down with worry is seek help and support from family, partners, colleagues and friends. If you feel you need more help the following suggestions may help clarify things for you.

THE HEALTH CENTRE OR DOCTOR'S SURGERY

If something you have read in this book has struck a chord and you'd like to talk it through further, your first port of call should be your doctor. He or she may be able to help you or suggest a referral to a more appropriate specialist. It's important to point out that worry and anxiety can be caused by a number of medical conditions. That's why it's important that a doctor checks for possible underlying medical problems.

A doctor will want you to explain how you feel in detail, whether any triggers might explain your mood. A mental health assessment will also be made. You may be asked if there is a family history of depression or if you are on any current medication. All this is important in confirming the diagnosis, deciding the type and urgency of treatment and whether or not you need to be referred to a mental health professional.

Your doctor is your link to a wide variety of support services. Through your doctor you may be able to get counselling on the NHS if you live in the UK, practical help such as meals on wheels, or other support services. You can find doctors listed in the phone book or call direct inquiries or NHS Direct. In an emergency call

999 in the UK or Ireland, 911 or your local police in the US, or go to a hospital's casualty department or emergency room.

CITIZEN INFORMATION CENTRES (THE CITIZEN'S ADVICE BUREAU (UK))

Citizen Information Centres are for practical and not medical problems. This is where you can get free, impartial and confidential information or advice about subjects ranging from divorce to employment, law, discrimination, debt and so on. You can find your nearest Citizen Information Centre by checking in your phone book.

HUMAN RESOURCES OR PERSONNEL OFFICER

If you have work-related worry or if worry is affecting your job, the human resources department or personnel office may be a resource. Ask for confidentiality if you think that acknowledging problems will affect your job prospects. The personnel officer should be able to help with friction at work or, if the problem is outside work, to suggest the next step to take. If you don't have a personnel officer or are out of work, the citizen's advice bureau, local libraries or information centres may be able to advise.

TURNING TO A HIGHER SOURCE

You may not be religious, but many people turn to spirituality for comfort in times of trouble. Talking through the possibilities with members of a person's faith may help. They may also be able to give practical, day-to-day assistance. The phone directory or local newspaper has details of local places of worship.

TELEPHONE HELPLINES

If you want support instantly, a telephone helpline is a good option. This sort of support is often linked to a particular crisis, illness or issue, and many of the helplines are run by charities or major national organisations.

Not all helplines are satisfactory, so be careful. Make sure they aren't charging for the call and that the calls are confidential. The phone helpers should also be fully trained in offering the correct kind of emotional support and in suggesting further treatment. Your local library should have a Telephone Helpers Directory which lists those with trained and qualified staff in your state or country. In the UK find out if the helpline is a member of the Telephone Helplines Association — an organisation that encourages good practice. You can find the Telephone Helplines Association on http://www.helplines.org.uk. The resources section lists useful helpline numbers.

One of the most well-known helplines in Ireland and the UK is the Samaritans (see Resources). The Samaritans are not just for moments of utter despair; the Samaritans are also there for anyone who needs to talk about how they are feeling in a safe and confidential manner. In fact, the Samaritans prefer it if you contact them before worry threatens to overwhelm you. Nothing is too trivial to the Samaritans. Other crisis lines in your state or country, like 'Contact' in Dallas, Texas, in the US (972-233-2233), have trained staff and operate along similar guidelines.

If you have never called a helpline you may wonder what to expect. The answer is that when you call a person will say hello and ask how he or she can help. That person will then listen to what you have to say. They won't judge, criticise, or give advice, and the conversation is in complete confidence. The listener will simply allow you to explore your feelings.

SUPPORT GROUPS

Support groups meet regularly, often locally and often in halls or houses. They are formed around the experience of anxiety or addiction and offer every member of the group a chance to share their experience. Talking to others can be reassuring and comforting. Support is given and support is received and there is less sense of isolation.

Lists of support groups can be found at doctor's practices or health centres. Many of the organisations listed in the resources section of this book also run support groups, and you might want to phone them for details. Your library, health centre or hospital may also have a list of self-help support groups in your areas.

SELF-HELP INFORMATION GATHERING

Books, magazines, TV programs, video, the internet and leaflets are a terrific source of information. Many of the organisations listed in the resources section provide information or recommend books. Usually this is free although sometimes a SAE and a small fee are required. Your library should have a list of Voluntary Agencies in your state or country.

In the US a number of excellent information centres, research institutes and consumer advocacy groups are dedicated to understanding and treating depression. Some, but by no means all, are listed in the resources section.

In the UK the National Association for Mental Health (MIND) offers nationwide support for anyone worried about their own or another's mental health.

Selected books are listed in the resources section, but you can get lots of good information under the medical, health, self-help, psychology, popular psychology sections in your local bookshop or library. You could also try books in print to track down subjects that interest you.

The internet is a vast maze of information, some of it incredibly good, some of it downright inaccurate and written by non-experts. Don't rely on it as an accurate source of information at all times. The resources section lists internet sites provided by various support organisations that you can trust.

RESOURCES

A lot of information can be gathered from organisations, phone helplines, websites and support groups, which aim to educate the public about disorders associated with worry. Here are some of the best known and respected. Where no phone number is supplied send a SAE for information.

REPUBLIC OF IRELAND — TELEPHONE HELPLINES
The Samaritans is a registered charity based in the Republic of Ireland and the UK that provides confidential emotional support to any person who is suicidal or despairing. The Samaritans also aim to increase public awareness of issues surrounding anxiety and depression.

The Samaritans
112 Marlborough St
Dublin 1
01 872 7700
Helpline CallSave 1850
609090

Victim Support
Haliday House
32 Arran Quay
Dublin 7
01 878 0870
National Helpline
1800 66 17 71

Abuse
Childline
Freephone 1800 66 66 66

Women's Aid
Freephone Helpline
1800 34 19 00

Rape Crisis Centre
70 Lr Leeson Street
Dublin 2
01 661 4911
Freephone 1800 77 88 88

Men's Aid
01 237 5402
LoCall 1890 39 09 99

Addictions

Alcoholics Anonymous
Office 109
SCR
Dublin 8
01 453 8998

Narcotics Anonymous
4 Eustace St
Dublin 2
01 830 0944

Merchants Quay Project
Merchants Quay
Dublin 2
01 679 0044

Rutland Centre Ltd
Knocklyon Rd
Dublin 16
01 494 6358

Carers

Carers Association
St Mary's Community Centre
Richmond Hill
Dublin 6
01 497 6108
Freephone 1800 24 07 24

Depression and mental illness

Aware
17 Phibsborough Road
Dublin 7
01 676 6166

Mental Health Association of
  Ireland
6 Adelaide St
Dun Laoghaire
Co. Dublin
01 284 1166

Schizophrenia Ireland
38 Blessington St
Dublin 7
01 860 1620

Gay issues

Gay Switchboard Dublin
Carmichael House
North King St
Dublin 7
01 872 1055

Homelessness

Focus Ireland
14A Eustace St
Dublin 2
01 671 2555

Simon Community
St Andrews House
28 Exchequer St
Dublin 2
01 671 1606

Health
AIDs Alliance Dublin
53 Parnell Square West
Dublin 1
01 873 3799

Irish Cancer Society
5 Northumberland Road
Dublin 4
01 668 1855
Freephone 1800 20 07 00

Irish Heart Foundation
Mediscan
4 Clyde Road
Dublin 4
01 668 5001

Relationship and family problems
Accord Marriage Counselling
  Service
39 Harcourt St
Dublin 2
01 478 0866

Age Action Ireland
30/31 Lr Camden St
Dublin 2
01 475 6989

Marriage and Relationship
  Counselling Service
24 Grafton Street
Dublin 2
01 679 9341

PARENTLINE
Carmichael House
Nth Brunswick St
Dublin 7
01 873 3500

Bereavement Counselling
  Service
St Anne's Church
Dawson St
Dublin 2
01 676 7727

Men's Networking Resource
  Centre of Ireland
1 Sillogue Rd
Dublin 11
01 862 2194

Therapy/Counselling
Irish Association for
  Counselling and Therapy
8 Cumberland St
Dun Laoghaire
Co. Dublin
01 230 0061

Irish Council for
  Psychotherapy
73 Dunns Road
Shankill
Co. Dublin
01 272 2105

UK — TELEPHONE
HELPLINES
The Samaritans
General Office
10, The Grove
Slough
SL1 1QP
01753 532713
08457 909090 or 0345 909090
(24 hr helpline)

If you want to contact the
Samaritans by post or Email
write to
Chris
The Samaritans
PO Box 90 90
Slough
SL1 1UU
jo@samaritans.org or
Samaritans Aanon.twwells.com
Textphone number for hard of
hearing 08457 909192

Careline
(counselling on all issues)
Cardinal Heenan Centre
326-8 High Road

Ilford
Essex
1G1 1QP
0208 514 5444
0208 514 1177

Youth Access
(counselling for young people
  and children)
1a Taylor's Yard
67 Alderbrook Road
London
SW12 8AD
0208 772 9900

Abuse
Childline,
Free post 1111
London
N1 OBR
0800 1111

Rape Crisis Centre
PO Box 69
London
WC1X 9NJ
0207 837 1600

Survivors
(support for men who have
  been raped)
PO Box 2470
London
SW9 9ZP
0207 833 3737

Resources

Victim support
0845 303 0900

Women's Aid: for women in
violent relationships
0345 023468

Institute of Drug Dependency
Waterbridge House
32–36 London St
London
EC1 OEE
0207 928 1211

Addictions
Alcoholics Anonymous
PO Box 1
Stonebow House
Stonebow
York
YO1 2NJ
01904 644026 (for local
helpline numbers)

Al-Anon Family Groups
61 Great Dover Street
London
SE1 4YF
0207 403 0888

Narcotics Anonymous
UK Service Office
PO Box 1980
London
N19 3LS
0207 730 0009

National Drugs Helpline
0800 776600

Assertiveness training
The Industrial Society runs
courses in assertiveness.
Tel 0870 400 1000
Also many adult education
centres run assertiveness
training classes, ask at your
public library.

Anxiety and phobia
There are many support
groups including:

No Panic
93 Brands Farm Way
Randlay
Telford
01952 590545

Phobics Society
4 Cheltenham Road
Chorlton-cum-Hardy
Manchester
M21 1QN
0161 881 1937

Stress Watch
(workshops and information)
PO Box 4
London
W1A 4AR

Triumph Over Phobia
TOP U.K.
PO Box 1831
Bath
BA1 3YX

Carers
Carers National Association
20-25 Glasshouse Yard,
London
EC1 4JS
0345 573369

Counsel and Care
(support for the elderly and
  their carers)
Twyman House
16 Bonny Street
London
NW1 9PG
0845 300 7585

Patients Association
(details of organisations and
  support groups for different
  illnesses and disabilities)
0208 423 8999

Young Minds
(for parents and carers worried
  about a young person's
  mental health)
102-108 Clerkenwell Road
London
EC1M 5SA
0345 626376

RADAR
(for those with a disability and
  their carers)
Unit 12, City Forum
250 City Road
London
EC1V 8AF
0207 250 3222

Debt
Citizens Advice Bureaux
For local address see your
phone book under C or
yellow pages under
Counselling and Advice

National Debtline
Birmingham Settlement
318 Summer Lane
Birmingham
B18 3RL
0121 359 8501

Family Welfare Association
501–505 Kingsland Road
London
E8 4AU
0207 254 6251

Depression and mental illness
Your GP or doctor

NHS Direct
0845 4647

Depression Alliance
35 Westminster Bridge Road
London
SE1 7JB
0207 207 3293
http://www.depressionalliance
.org

Depressives Anonymous
36 Chestnut Avenue
Beverly
North Humberside
HU17 9QU
01482 887634

Manic Depressives Fellowship
8-10 High Street
Kingston–upon–Thames
Surrey
KT 1 1EY
0208 974 6550

Postnatal depression helpline
Meet –A –Mum
0208 768 0123

MIND (National Association for Mental Health)
The headquarters are London based but there are regional offices and local associations — see your telephone directory for local associations. Now over 50 years old, MIND is the leading mental health charity in the UK. It aims at working towards a better life for everyone experiencing mental distress.

Support if you are worried about your own mental health and that of someone else.

Granta House
15-19 Broadway
London
E15 4BQ
0208 519 2122

MIND information line
0345 660163
08457 660163 outside greater London
0208 522 1728 London
http://www.mind.org.uk

SANE
2nd Floor
199–205 Old Marylebone
Road
London
NW1 5QP
Tel 0345 678000
http://beta.mkn.co.uk/help/e
xtra/charity/sane/index

Seasonal Affective Disorder
Association
PO Box 989
London
SW7 2PZ
01903 814942

Eating Disorders Association
First Floor
Wensum House
103 Prince of Wales Road
Norwich
Norfolk
NR1 1DW
01603 621414

Gay issues
London Lesbian and Gay
Switchboard
PO Box 7324
London
N1 9QS
0207 837 7324
http://www.llgs.org.uk/info.
htm

Homelessness
Shelter
0207 253 0202
London Helpline 0800
446441
Local Shelter Housing Advice
line listed in the Yellow pages
under I for Information
Services

Health
NHS Direct
Tel: 0845 46 47
Health Education Authority
(general advice on healthy
  living, diet and exercise)
Trevelyan House
30 Peter Street
London
SW1P 2HW
0207 222 5300

British Heart Foundation
14 Fitzhardinge Street
London
W1H 4DH
0207 935 0185

AIDS helpline
0800 56712

Cancer Link
0800 132905

British Pregnancy Advisory service
Tel 01564 793225

Post-Abortion counselling Service
0207 221 9631

Relationship and family problems
Conciliation services
These provide support for separating and divorcing couples so they can sort out arguments for their children and property.
Family Mediation Scotland — tel 0131 220 1610
Family Mediation Association — tel 020 7881 9400
National Family Mediation — tel 020 7383 5993

CRUSE Bereavement Care
Cruse House
126 Sheen Road
Richmond
Surrey
TW9 1UR
0208 940 4818

Age concern
Astral House
1268, London Road
London

SW16 4ER
0800 731 4931
http://www.ace.org.uk

Help the Aged
0800 650 650065

Anti-bullying Campaign
185 Tower Bridge Road
London SE1 2UF
0207 378 1446

Family Crisis Line
c/o Ashwood House
Ashwood road
Woking, Surrey
GU22 7JW
01483 722533

Exploring Parenthood
(support for parents)
20a Treadgold Street
London
W11 4BP
0207 221 6681

Parentline
Endway House
The Endway
Hadleigh
Essex
SS7 2AN
01702 559900

Relate has a network of around 130 centres nationwide which provide couple counselling for those with problems in relationships, psychosexual therapy and relationship and family education.

Relate
(National Marriage Guidance
  Council)
Herbert Gray College
Little Church Street
Rugby
Warickshire
CV21 3AP
01788 573241
http://www.relate.org.uk

British Association for Sexual
  and Relationship Therapy
PO Box 13686
London
SW20 9ZH

Institute of Psychosexual
  Medicine
11, Chandos Street
Cavendish Square
London
W1M 9DE
0207 580 0631

Single Concern Group
  Support group

(for lonely and socially isolated
  men and women)
PO Box 4
High Street
Goring-on-Thames
Oxon
RG8 9DN
01491 873195

Single again
Freephone 0800 731 1180

Families need fathers —
support for men living apart
from their children
0207 613 5060

More-to-life
(support group for people
  without children)
114 Lichfield Street
Walsall
WS1 ISZ
070 500 37905
www.moretolife.co.uk

Therapy/Counselling
The British Psychological
  Association
St Andrew's House,
48, Princess Road East
Leicester
LE1 7DR
Tel 0116 254 9568
http://www.bps.org.uk

British Association of
  Behavioural and Cognitive
  Psychotherapists
BABCP
PO Box 9
Accrington
BB5 2GD

The British Association of
  Psychotherapists
37 Mapesbury Road
London
NW2 4HJ
0208 830 5173
http://www.bcp.org.uk

Psychotherapy Register
67 Upper Berkeley Street
London
W1H 7QX
0207 724 9083

UK Council for
  Psychotherapy
Regents College
Inner Circle
Regent's Park
London
NW1 4NS
0207 436 3002

The British Association for
  Counselling
1 Regent's Place
Rugby

Warickshire
CV21 2BJ
01788 550899

Alternative Therapies

Institute of Complementary
  Medicine
PO Box 194
London
SE16 IQZ
0207 237 5165

Council for Complementary
  and Alternative Medicine
179 Gloucester Place
London
NW1 6DX
0208 735 0632

British Federation of Massage
Practitioners — for details of a
qualified masseuse or masseur
in your area.
01772 881063

Massage therapy Institute of
Great Britain — will supply
names of practitioners who
trained with the Institute.
020 8208 1607

Transcendental Meditation
Freepost
London
SW1P 4YY
08705 143733

Resources

Relaxation Tapes available from
Lifeskills
Westleigh
Broomfield
Bridgewater
Somerset
TA5 2EH
Freephone 0800 980 1774

British Wheel of Yoga
1, Hamilton Place
Boston Road
Sleaford
NG34 7ES
01529 306851

US
1-888-8 ANXIETY
(1-888-8-269438)
Operated by the National Institute of Mental Health this line provides extensive information on all worry related disorders and well as listing resources near where you live. The service is free and open 24 hours.

Freedom from Fear
308 Seaview Ave.,
Staten island
NY 10305
(718)-351-1717

National Anxiety Foundation
3135 Custer Drive
Lexington
KY 405 4001
(606)-272-7166

National Alliance for the Mentally Ill (NAMI)
2101 Wilson Blvd
Suite 302
Arlington
VA 22201
(703) 524 7600

Depression Awareness, Recognition and Treatment (DART)
National Institute of Mental Health
5600 Fishers Lane
Rockville
MD 20857
(800) 421 4211

National Foundation for Depressive Illness (NAFDI)
P.O Box 2257
New York 10116
(800) 248 4344

National Depressive and Manic Depressive Association (NDMDA)
730 North Franklin Street
Suite 501

Chicago
IL 60610
(800) 826 3632

National Mental Health
  Consumer's Self-help
  Information Clearinghouse
211 Chestnut Street, Suite
1000
Philadelphia, PA 19107
(215) 751–1810
(800) 553–4539

Depression and Related
  Affective Disorders
  Association (DRADA)
Meyer 4–181
600 North Wolfe Street
Baltimore
MD 21205
(301) 955 4647

American Psychological
  Association
750 1st Street, N.E
Washington
DC 20002
(202) 336 5500

American Psychiatric
  Association
1400 K Street
N.W.,
Washington
DC 20005
(202) 682 6066

Behavioral Psychotherapy
  Center
23 Old Mamaroneck Road
White Plains
New York 0605
(914) 761 4080

White Plains Hospital Center
  Anxiety and Phobia Clinic
Davis Ave., at Post Road
White Plains
New York 10601
(914) 681 0600

National Organization for
  Seasonal Affective Disorder
  (NOSAD)
P.O. Box 40133
Washington,
D.C 20016

Administration on Ageing
330 Independence Avenue SW
Washington, D.C.
(202) 619–0724

American Anorexia/Bulimia
  Association
293 Central Park west, Suite
1R
New York
NY 10024
(212) 501 8351

AIDS hotline
(800) 342–AIDS

Anxiety Disorders Association
  of America
6000 Executive Boulevard,
Suite 513
Rockville
MD 20852
(301) 231 9350

National Clearinghouse for
  Alcohol and Drug
  Information
P.O. Box 2345
Rockville
MD 20847-2345
(301) 468 2600
(800) 729 6686

Al-Anon Family Group
Headquarters
(212) 302-7240

Alcoholics Anonymous World
  Services
(212) 870-3400

National Association on
  Alcoholism and Drug
  Dependence
12 West 21 Street
New York
NY 10010
(800) NCA-CALL

Phobics Anonymous
P.O. Box 1180
Palm springs
CA 92263
(619) -322-2673

SUGGESTED READING

Bloomfield, Harold and McWilliams, Peter, *How to Heal Depression*, London: Thorsons, Harper Collins 1995.

Carlson, Richard, *Don't Sweat the Small Stuff ... and it's all Small Stuff* , London: Hodder and Stoughton 1997.

Carnegie, Dale, *How to Stop Worrying and Start Living*, London: Vermillion 1999.

Chevalier, A.J., *What if: Daily Thoughts for those who Worry too much*, Florida: Health Communications 1995.

Copeland, Mary Ellen, *The Worry Control Workbook*, Oakland, CA: New Harbinger 1998.

Covey, Stephen, *The 7 Habits of Highly Effective People: Powerful Lessons in Personal Change*, New York: Simon and Schuster 1990.

Downing-Orr, Kristina, *What to Do if You're Burned Out and Blue*, London: Thorsons 2000.

Dyer, Wayne *Pulling Your Own Strings*, New York: Avon Books 1979.

Gilbert, Paul, *Overcoming Depression: A Self-help Guide using Cognitive Behavioural Techniques*, London: Robinson 1997.

Goleman, Daniel, *Emotional Intelligence*, New York: Bantam Books 1995.

Gray, John, *How to Get What you Want and Want What you Have*, London: Vermillion 1999.

Green, Joey, *The Road to Success is Paved with Failure*, New York: Little Brown 2001.

Hallowell, Edward M., *Worry: Hope and Help for a Common Condition*, New York: Ballantine 1997.

Hallowell, Edward, *When you Worry About the Child You Love*, New York: Simon and Schuster 1996.

Jeffers, Susan, *Feel the Fear and Do It Anyway: How to Turn your Fear and Indecision into Confidence and Action*, London: Arrow 1991.

Suggested Reading

Kennerley, Helen, *Over Coming Anxiety: A Self-Help Guide to using Cognitive Behavioural Techniques*, London: Robinson 1997.

Lindenfield, Gael, *Self-Esteem: simple steps to develop self-worth and heal emotional wounds*, London: Thorsons 2000.

Lindenfield, Gael and Vandenburg, Malcolm, *Positive Under Pressure: How to be calm and effective when the heat is on*, London: Thorsons 2000.

Loehr, James, *Stress for Success*, New York: Random House 1997.

INDEX

Index

Index

Index

Index

Index

Index